Manipulators

OF LIFE

They were gentle, friendly little creatures and their merry eyes sparkled with intelligence. Clothed in short slick fur, they reminded the Earthlings of children masquerading as bunny rabbits.

They were masters of manipulation, skilled in sleight-of-hand tricks which delighted their human guests.

But when they began their other experiments, like that thing in the incubator that was once Marion Schmidt—the hand with too many fingers, the hoofs instead of toes . . . horror dawned on the visiting Earthmen and the Garden of Eden became a planet of madness.

Methuselah's
CHILDREN

Robert A. Heinlein

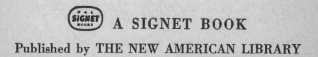 A SIGNET BOOK

Published by THE NEW AMERICAN LIBRARY

To Edward E. Smith, Ph.D.

SIGNET TRADEMARK REG. U.S. PAT. OFF. AND FOREIGN COUNTRIES
REGISTERED TRADEMARK—MARCA REGISTRADA
HECHO EN CHICAGO, U.S.A.

SIGNET BOOKS are published by
The New American Library of World Literature, Inc.
501 Madison Avenue, New York, New York 10022

PRINTED IN THE UNITED STATES OF AMERICA

1 "Mary Sperling, you're a fool not to marry him!" Mary Sperling added up her losses and wrote a check before answering, "There's too much difference in age." She passed over her credit voucher. "I shouldn't gamble with you—sometimes I think you're a sensitive."

"Nonsense! You're just trying to change the subject. You must be nearly thirty . . . and you won't be pretty forever."

Mary smiled wryly. "Don't I know it!"

"Bork Vanning can't be much over forty and he's a plus-citizen. You should jump at the chance."

"You jump at it. I must run now. Service, Ven."

"Service," Ven answered, then frowned at the door as it contracted after Mary Sperling. She itched to know why Mary would not marry a prime catch like the Honorable Bork Vanning and was almost as curious as to why and where Mary was going, but the custom of privacy stopped her.

Mary had no intention of letting anyone know where she was going. Outside her friend's apartment she dropped down a bounce tube to the basement, claimed her car from the robopark, guided it up the ramp and set the controls for North Shore. The car waited for a break in the traffic, then dived into the high-speed stream and hurried north. Mary settled back for a nap.

When its setting was about to run out, the car beeped for instructions; Mary woke up and glanced out. Lake Michigan was a darker band of darkness on her right. She signaled traffic control to let her enter the local traffic lane; it sorted out her car and placed her there, then let her resume manual control. She fumbled in the glove compartment.

The license number which traffic control automatically photographed as she left the controlways was not the number the car had been wearing.

She followed a side road uncontrolled for several miles, turned into a narrow dirt road which led down to the shore, and stopped. There she waited, lights out, and listened. South of her the lights of Chicago glowed; a few hundred yards inland the controlways whined, but here there was nothing but the little timid noises of night creatures. She reached into the glove compartment, snapped a switch; the instrument panel glowed, uncovering other dials behind it. She studied these while making adjustments. Satisfied that no radar watched her and that nothing was moving near her, she snapped off the instruments, sealed the window by her and started up again.

What appeared to be a standard Camden speedster rose quietly up, moved out over the lake, skimming it—dropped into the water and sank. Mary waited until she was a quarter mile off shore in fifty feet of water, then called a station. "Answer," said a voice.

" 'Life is short———' "

" '—but the years are long.' "

" 'Not,' " Mary responded, " 'while the evil days come not.' "

"I sometimes wonder," the voice answered conversationally. "Okay, Mary. I've checked you."

"Tommy?"

"No—Cecil Hedrick. Are your controls cast loose?"

"Yes. Take over."

Seventeen minutes later the car surfaced in a pool which occupied much of an artificial cave. When the car was beached, Mary got out, said hello to the guards and went on through a tunnel into a large underground room where fifty or sixty men and women were seated. She chatted until a clock announced midnight, then she mounted a rostrum and faced them.

"I am," she stated, "one hundred and eighty-three years old. Is there anyone here who is older?"

No one spoke. After a decent wait she went on, "Then in accordance with our customs I declare this meeting opened. Will you choose a moderator?"

Someone said, "Go ahead, Mary." When no one else spoke up, she said, "Very well." She seemed indifferent to the honor and the group seemed to share her casual attitude—an air of never any hurry, of freedom from the tension of modern life.

"We are met as usual," she announced, "to discuss our welfare and that of our sisters and brothers. Does any Family representative have a message from his family? Or does anyone care to speak for himself?"

A man caught her eye and spoke up. "Ira Weatheral, speaking for the Johnson Family. We've met nearly two months early. The trustees must have a reason. Let's hear it."

She nodded and turned to a prim little man in the first row. "Justin . . . if you will, please."

The prim little man stood up and bowed stiffly. Skinny legs stuck out below his badly-cut kilt. He looked and acted like an elderly, dusty civil servant, but his black hair and the firm, healthy tone of his skin said that he was a man in his prime. "Justin Foote," he said precisely, "reporting for the trustees. It has been eleven years since the Families decided on the experiment of letting the public know that there were, living among them, persons who possessed a probable life

6

expectancy far in excess of that anticipated by the average man, as well as other persons who had proved the scientific truth of such expectation by having lived more than twice the normal life span of human beings."

Although he spoke without notes he sounded as if he were reading aloud a prepared report. What he was saying they all knew but no one hurried him; his audience had none of the febrile impatience so common elsewhere. "In deciding," he droned on, "to reverse the previous long-standing policy of silence and concealment as to the peculiar aspect in which we differ from the balance of the human race, the Families were moved by several considerations. The reason for the original adoption of the policy of concealment should be noted:

"The first offspring resulting from unions assisted by the Howard Foundation were born in 1875. They aroused no comment, for they were in no way remarkable. The Foundation was an openly-chartered non-profit corporation——"

On March 17, 1874, Ira Johnson, medical student, sat in the law offices of Deems, Wingate, Alden, & Deems and listened to an unusual proposition. At last he interrupted the senior partner. "Just a moment! Do I understand that you are trying to *hire* me to marry one of these women?"

The lawyer looked shocked. "Please, Mr. Johnson. Not at all."

"Well, it certainly sounded like it."

"No, no, such a contract would be void, against public policy. We are simply informing you, as administrators of a trust, that should it come about that you *do* marry one of the young ladies on this list it would then be our pleasant duty to endow each child of such a union according to the scale here set forth. But there would be no contract with us involved, nor is there any 'proposition' being made to you— and we certainly do not urge any course of action on you. We are simply informing you of certain facts."

Ira Johnson scowled and shuffled his feet. "What's it all about? Why?"

"That is the business of the Foundation. One might put it that we approve of your grandparents."

"Have you discussed me with them?" Johnson said sharply. He felt no affection for his grandparents. A tight-fisted foursome—if any one of them had had the grace to die at a reasonable age he would not now be worried about money enough to finish medical school.

"We have talked with them, yes. But not about you."

The lawyer shut off further discussion and young Johnson accepted gracelessly a list of young women, all strangers, with the intention of tearing it up the moment he was outside the

7

office. Instead, that night he wrote seven drafts before he found the right words in which to start cooling off the relation between himself and his girl back home. He was glad that he had never actually popped the question to her—it would have been deucedly awkward.

When he did marry (from the list) it seemed a curious but not too remarkable coincidence that his wife as well as himself had four living, healthy, active grandparents.

"—an openly chartered non-profit corporation," Foote continued, "and its avowed purpose of encouraging births among persons of sound American stock was consonant with the customs of that century. By the simple expedient of being close-mouthed about the true purpose of the Foundation no unusual methods of concealment were necessary until late in that period during the World Wars sometimes loosely termed 'The Crazy Years——' "

Selected headlines April to June 1969:

BABY BILL BREAKS BANK
2-year toddler youngest winner $1,000,000 TV jackpot
White House phones congrats

COURT ORDERS STATEHOUSE SOLD
Colorado Supreme Bench Rules State Old Age Pension
Has First Lien All State Property

N.Y. YOUTH MEET DEMANDS UPPER LIMIT
ON FRANCHISE

"U.S. BIRTH RATE 'TOP SECRET' "—DEFENSE SEC

CAROLINA CONGRESSMAN COPS BEAUTY CROWN
"Available for draft for President" she announces while
starting tour to show her qualifications

IOWA RAISES VOTING AGE TO FORTY-ONE
Rioting on Des Moines Campus

EARTH-EATING FAD MOVES WEST: CHICAGO PAR-
SON EATS CLAY SANDWICH IN PULPIT
"Back to simple things," he advises flock.

LOS ANGELES HI-SCHOOL MOB DEFIES SCHOOL
BOARD
"Higher Pay, Shorter Hours, no Homework—We Demand
Our Right to Elect Teachers, Coaches."

SUICIDE RATE UP NINTH SUCCESSIVE YEAR
AEC Denies Fall-Out to Blame

" '—The Crazy Years.' The trustees of that date decided— correctly, we now believe—that any minority during that period of semantic disorientation and mass hysteria was a probable target for persecution, discriminatory legislation, and even of mob violence. Furthermore the disturbed financial condition of the country and in particular the forced exchange of trust securities for government warrants threatened the solvency of the trust.

"Two courses of action were adopted: the assets of the Foundation were converted into real wealth and distributed widely among members of the Families to be held by them as owners-of-record; and the so-called 'Masquerade' was adopted as a permanent policy. Means were found to simulate the death of any member of the Families who lived to a socially embarrassing age and to provide him with a new identity in another part of the country.

"The wisdom of this later policy, though irksome to some, became evident at once during the Interregnum of the Prophets. The Families at the beginning of the reign of the First Prophet had ninety-seven per cent of their members with publicly avowed ages of less than fifty years. The close public registration enforced by the secret police of the Prophets made changes of public identity difficult, although a few were accomplished with the aid of the revolutionary Cabal.

"Thus, a combination of luck and foresight saved our secret from public disclosure. This was well—we may be sure that things would have gone harshly at that time for any group possessing a prize beyond the power of the Prophet to confiscate.

"The Families took no part as such in the events leading up to the Second American Revolution, but many members participated and served with credit in the Cabal and in the fighting which preceded the fall of New Jerusalem. We took advantage of the period of disorganization which followed to readjust the ages of our kin who had grown conspicuously old. In this we were aided by certain members of the Families who, as members of the Cabal, held key posts in the Reconstruction.

"It was argued by many at the Families' meeting of 2075, the year of the Covenant, that we should reveal ourselves, since civil liberty was firmly re-established. The majority did not agree at that time . . . perhaps through long habits of secrecy and caution. But the renascence of culture in the ensuing fifty years, the steady growth of tolerance and good manners, the semantically sound orientation of education, the increased respect for the custom of privacy and for the dignity of the individual—all of these things led us to believe

9

FUTURE HISTORY

DATES	STORIES	CHARACTERS	TECHNICAL
A.D.	( ) Stories-to-be-told		
	Life-Line	Pinero	
	"Let There Be Light"	Martin	
	(Word Edgewise)	Douglas / Gaines / Blekinsop	
1975	The Roads Must Roll	Harper / Erickson / King	
	Blowups Happen	Lentz / Harriman	Douglas-Martin sun-power screens
	The Man Who Sold the Moon	McIntyre / Cummings	
	Delilah & the Space Rigger	Wingate	
	Space Jockey	Sam Jones	Mechanized roads
	Requiem	Satchel	Commercial rocket travel
	The Long Watch	Rhysling	Helicopters
	Gentlemen, Be Seated	Scudder	
	The Black Pits of Luna	Nehemiah Scudder	
	It's Great to Be Back		
	"—We Also Walk Dogs"		
2000	Ordeal in Space		
	The Green Hills of Earth		Interplanetary travel
	(Fire Down Below!)		
	Logic of Empire		
	(The Sound of His Wings)		atomic cont., artificial radioactives, Uranium 235
	(Eclipse)		
2025	(The Stone Pillow)	Lazarus Long	
2050		Novak / John Lyle / Zeb Jones / Master Peter / Magdelene	Interplanetary travel resumed
	"If This Goes On—"	MacKinnon / "Fader" Randall / Persephone / The "Doctor"	(Hiatus)
2075			Developments in parychometrics and psychodynamics
	Coventry		Limited use of telepathy
2100			
	Misfit	Ford	Interplanetary travel resumed
	Universe (prologue only)	Libby / McCoy / Rhodes / Doyle	Growth of submolar mechanics, atomic cont.
2125	Methuselah's Children		Static submolar engineering (para«tics)
2600	Universe		
	Commonsense		
	(Da Capo)		

10

1951-2600 A.D.

DATA	SOCIOLOGICAL	REMARKS
	THE "CRAZY YEARS"	Considerable technical advance during this period, accompanied by a gradual deterioration of mores, orientation and social institutions, terminating in mass psychoses in the sixth decade, and the Interregnum.
Transatlantic rocket flight	Strike of '66 The "FALSE DAWN," 1960-70 First rocket to the Moon, 1978	
Antipodes rocket service	Luna City founded Space Precautionary Act Harriman's Lunar Corporations	The Interregnum was followed by a period of reconstruction in which the Voorhis financial proposals gave a temporary economic stability and chance for re-orientation. This was ended by the opening of new frontiers and a return to nineteenth-century economy.
	PERIOD OF IMPERIAL EXPLOITATION, 1970-2020 Revolution in Little America Interplanetary exploration and exploitation American-Australasian anschluss	
Bacteriophage The Travel Unit and the Fighting Unit	Rise of religious fanaticism The "New Crusade" Rebellion and independence of Venusian colonists	Three revolutions ended the short period of interplanetary imperialism: Antarctica, U. S., and Venus. Space travel ceased until 2072.
Commercial stereoptics	Religious dictatorship in U. S.	Little research and only minor technical advances during this period. Extreme puritanism. Certain aspects of psychodynamics and psychometrics, mass psychology and social control developed by the priest class.
Booster guns		
Synthetic foods	**THE FIRST HUMAN CIVILIZATION, 2075 et seq.**	Re-establishment of civil liberty. Renascence of scientific research. Resumption of space travel. Luna City refounded. Science of social relations, based on the negative basic statements of semantics. Rigor of epistemology. The Covenant.
Weather control		
Wave mechanics		
The "Barrier"		
Atomic "tailoring," Elements 98-416 Parastatic engineering.		Beginning of the consolidation of the Solar System.
Rigor of colloids Symbiotic research Longevity		First attempt at interstellar exploration. Civil disorder, followed by the end of human adolescence, and beginning of first mature culture.

that the time had at last come when it was becoming safe to reveal ourselves and to take our rightful place as an odd but nonetheless respected minority in society.

"There were compelling reasons to do so. Increasing numbers of us were finding the 'Masquerade' socially intolerable in a new and better society. Not only was it upsetting to pull up roots and seek a new background every few years but also it grated to have to live a lie in a society where frank honesty and fair dealing were habitual with most people. Besides that, the Families as a group had learned many things through our researches in the bio-sciences, things which could be of great benefit to our poor short-lived brethren. We needed freedom to help them.

"These and similar reasons were subject to argument. But the resumption of the custom of positive physical identification made the 'Masquerade' almost untenable. Under the new orientation a sane and peaceful citizen welcomes positive identification under appropriate circumstances even though jealous of his right of privacy at all other times—so we dared not object; it would have aroused curiosity, marked us as an eccentric group, set apart, and thereby have defeated the whole purpose of the 'Masquerade.'

"We necessarily submitted to personal identification. By the time of the meeting of 2125, eleven years ago, it had become extremely difficult to counterfeit new identities for the ever-increasing number of us holding public ages incompatible with personal appearance; we decided on the experiment of letting volunteers from this group up to ten per cent of the total membership of the Families reveal themselves for what they were and observe the consequences, while maintaining all other secrets of the Families' organization.

"The results were regrettably different from our expectations."

Justin Foote stopped talking. The silence had gone on for several moments when a solidly built man of medium height spoke up. His hair was slightly grizzled—unusual in that group—and his face looked space tanned. Mary Sperling had noticed him and had wondered who he was—his live face and gusty laugh had interested her. But any member was free to attend the conclaves of the Families' council; she had thought no more of it.

He said, "Speak up, Bud. What's your report?"

Foote made his answer to the chair. "Our senior psychometrician should give the balance of the report. My remarks were prefatory."

"For the love o'———" the grizzled stranger exclaimed. "Bud, do you mean to stand there and admit that all you had to say were things we already knew?"

12

"My remarks were a foundation . . . and my name is Justin Foote, not 'Bud.' "

Mary Sperling broke in firmly. "Brother," she said to the stranger, "since you are addressing the Families, will you please name yourself? I am sorry to say that I do not recognize you."

"Sorry, Sister. Lazarus Long, speaking for myself."

Mary shook her head. "I still don't place you."

"Sorry again—that's a 'Masquerade' name I took at the time of the First Prophet . . . it tickled me. My Family name is Smith . . . Woodrow Wilson Smith."

" 'Woodrow Wilson Sm——' *How old are you?*"

"Eh? Why, I haven't figured it lately. One hun . . . no, two hundred and—thirteen years. Yeah, that's right, two hundred and thirteen."

There was a sudden, complete silence. Then Mary said quietly, "Did you hear me inquire for anyone older than myself?"

"Yes. But shucks, Sister, you were doing all right. I ain't attended a meeting of the Families in over a century. Been some changes."

"I'll ask you to carry on from here." She started to leave the platform.

"Oh no!" he protested. But she paid no attention and found a seat. He looked around, shrugged and gave in. Sprawling one hip over a corner of the speaker's table he announced, "All right, let's get on with it. Who's next?"

Ralph Schultz of the Schultz Family looked more like a banker than a psychometrician. He was neither shy nor absent-minded and he had a flat, underemphasized way of talking that carried authority. "I was part of the group that proposed ending the 'Masquerade.' I was wrong. I believed that the great majority of our fellow citizens, reared under modern educational methods, could evaluate any data without excessive emotional disturbance. I anticipated that a few abnormal people would dislike us, even hate us; I even predicted that most people would envy us—everybody who enjoys life would like to live a long time. But I did not anticipate any serious trouble. Modern attitudes have done away with inter-racial friction; any who still harbor race prejudice are ashamed to voice it. I believed that our society was so tolerant that we could live peacefully and openly with the short-lived.

"I was wrong.

"The Negro hated and envied the white man as long as the white man enjoyed privileges forbidden the Negro by reason of color. This was a sane, normal reaction. When discrimination was removed, the problem solved itself and cultural

13

assimilation took place. There is a similar tendency on the part of the short-lived to envy the long-lived. We assumed that this expected reaction would be of no social importance in most people once it was made clear that we owe our peculiarity to our genes—no fault nor virtue of our own, just good luck in our ancestry.

"This was mere wishful thinking. By hindsight it is easy to see that correct application of mathematical analysis to the data would have given a different answer, would have spotlighted the false analogy. I do not defend the misjudgment, no defense is possible. We were led astray by our hopes.

"What actually happened was this: we showed our short-lived cousins the greatest boon it is possible for a man to imagine . . . then we told them it could never be theirs. This faced them with an unsolvable dilemma. They have rejected the unbearable facts, they refuse to believe us. Their envy now turns to hate, with an emotional conviction that we are depriving them of their rights . . . deliberately, maliciously.

"That rising hate has now swelled into a flood which threatens the welfare and even the lines of all our revealed brethren . . . and which is potentially as dangerous to the rest of us. The danger is very great and very pressing." He sat down abruptly.

They took it calmly, with the unhurried habit of years. Presently a female delegate stood up. "Eve Barstow, for the Cooper Family. Ralph Schultz, I am a hundred and nineteen years old, older, I believe, than you are. I do not have your talent for mathematics and human behavior but I have known a lot of people. Human beings are inherently good and gentle and kind. Oh, they have their weaknesses but most of them are decent enough if you give them half a chance. I cannot believe that they would hate me and destroy me simply because I have lived a long time. What have you to go on? You admit one mistake—why not two?"

Schultz looked at her soberly and smoothed his kilt. "You're right, Eve. I could easily be wrong again. That's the trouble with psychology; it is a subject so terribly complex, so many unknowns, such involved relationships, that our best efforts sometimes look silly in the bleak light of later facts." He stood up again, faced the others, and again spoke with flat authority. "But I am not making a long-range prediction this time; I am talking about facts, no guesses, not wishful thinking—and with those facts a prediction so short-range that it is like predicting that an egg will break when you see it already on its way to the floor. But Eve is right . . . as far as she went. Individuals *are* kind and decent . . . as individuals and to other individuals. Eve is in no danger from

14

her neighbors and friends, and I am in no danger from mine. But she is in danger from *my* neighbors and friends—and I from hers. Mass psychology is not simply a summation of individual psychologies; that is a prime theorem of social psychodynamics—not just my opinion; no exception has ever been found to this theorem. It is the social mass-action rule, the mob-hysteria law, known and used by military, political, and religious leaders, by advertising men and prophets and propagandists, by rabble rousers and actors and gang leaders, for generations before it was formulated in mathematical symbols. It works. It is working now.

"My colleagues and I began to suspect that a mob-hysteria trend was building up against us several years ago. We did not bring our suspicions to the council for action because we could not prove anything. What we observed then could have been simply the mutterings of the crackpot minority present in even the healthiest society. The trend was at first so minor that we could not be sure it existed, for all social trends are intermixed with other social trends, snarled together like a plate of spaghetti—worse than that, for it takes an abstract topological space of many dimensions (ten or twelve are not uncommon and hardly adequate) to describe mathematically the interplay of social forces. I cannot overemphasize the complexity of the problem.

"So we waited and worried and tried statistical sampling, setting up our statistical universes with great care.

"By the time we were sure, it was almost too late. Sociopsychological trends grow or die by a 'yeast growth' law, a complex power law. We continued to hope that other favorable factors would reverse the trend—Nelson's work in symbiotics, our own contributions to geriatrics, the great public interest in the opening of the Jovian satellites to immigration. Any major break-through offering longer life and greater hope to the short-lived could end the smouldering resentment against us.

"Instead the smouldering has burst into flame, into an uncontrolled forest fire. As nearly as we can measure it, the rate has doubled in the past thirty-seven days and the rate itself is accelerated. I can't guess how far or how fast it will go—and that's why we asked for this emergency session. Because we can expect trouble at any moment." He sat down hard, looking tired.

Eve did not argue with him again and no one else argued with him at all; not only was Ralph Schultz considered expert in his own field but also every one of them, each from his own viewpoint, had seen the grosser aspects of the trend building up against their revealed kin. But, while the acceptance of the problem was unanimous, there were as many opinions about what to do about it as there were people present. Lazarus let the discussion muddle along for two hours before he held up a hand. "We aren't getting anywhere," he stated, "and it looks like we won't get anywhere tonight. Let's take an over-all look at it, hitting just the high spots:

"We can——" He started ticking plans off on his fingers—"do nothing, sit tight, and see what happens.

"We can junk the 'Masquerade' entirely, reveal our full numbers, and demand our rights politically.

"We can sit tight on the surface and use our organization and money to protect our revealed brethren, maybe haul 'em back into the 'Masquerade.'

"We can reveal ourselves and ask for a place to colonize where we can live by ourselves.

"Or we can do something else. I suggest that you sort yourselves out according to those four major points of view —say in the corners of the room, starting clockwise in that far right hand corner—each group hammer out a plan and get it ready to submit to the Families. And those of you who don't favor any of those four things gather in the middle of the room and start scrappin' over just what it is you do think. Now, if I hear no objection, I am going to declare this lodge recessed until midnight tomorrow night. How about it?"

No one spoke up. Lazarus Long's streamlined version of parliamentary procedure had them somewhat startled; they were used to long, leisurely discussions until it became evident that one point of view had become unanimous. Doing things in a hurry was slightly shocking.

But the man's personality was powerful, his years gave him prestige, and his slightly archaic way of speaking added to his patriarchal authority; nobody argued.

"Okay," Lazarus announced, clapping his hands once. "Church is out until tomorrow night." He stepped down from the platform.

Mary Sperling came up to him. "I would like to know you better," she said, looking him in the eyes.

"Sure, Sis. Why not?"

"Are you staying for discussion?"

"No."

"Could you come home with me?"

"Like to. I've no pressing business elsewhere."

"Come then." She led him through the tunnel to the underground pool connecting with Lake Michigan. He widened his eyes at the pseudo-Camden but said nothing until they were submerged.

"Nice little car you've got."

"Yes."

16

"Has some unusual features."

She smiled. "Yes. Among other things, it blows up—quite thoroughly—if anyone tries to investigate it."

"Good." He added, "You a designing engineer, Mary?"

"Me? Heavens, no! Not this past century, at least, and I no longer try to keep up with such things. But you can order a car modified the way this one is through the Families, if you want one. Talk to——"

"Never mind, I've no need for one. I just like gadgets that do what they were designed to do and do it quietly and efficiently. Some good skull sweat in this one."

"Yes." She was busy then, surfacing, making a radar check, and getting them back ashore without attracting notice.

When they reached her apartment she put tobacco and drink close to him, then went to her retiring room, threw off her street clothes and put on a soft loose robe that made her look even smaller and younger than she had looked before. When she rejoined Lazarus, he stood up, struck a cigarette for her, then paused as he handed it to her and gave a gallant and indelicate whistle.

She smiled briefly, took the cigarette, and sat down in a large chair, pulling her feet under her. "Lazarus, you reassure me."

"Don't you own a mirror, girl?"

"Not that," she said impatiently. "You yourself. You know that I have passed the reasonable life expectancy of our people—I've been expecting to die, been resigned to it, for the past ten years. Yet there you sit . . . years and *years* older than I am. You give me hope."

He sat up straight. *"You* expecting to die? Good grief, girl —you look good for another century."

She made a tired gesture. "Don't try to jolly me. You know that appearance has nothing to do with it. Lazarus, I don't *want* to die!"

Lazarus answered soberly, "I wasn't trying to kid you, Sis. You simply don't look like a candidate for corpse."

She shrugged gracefully. "A matter of biotechniques. I'm holding my appearance at the early thirties."

"Or less, I'd say. I guess I'm not up on the latest dodges, Mary. You heard me say that I had not attended a get-together for more than a century. As a matter of fact I've been completely out of touch with the Families the whole time."

"Really? May I ask why?"

"A long story and a dull one. What it amounts to is that I got bored with them. I used to be a delegate to the annual meetings. But they got stuffy and set in their ways—or so it seemed to me. So I wandered off. I spent the Interregnum on

Venus, mostly. I came back for a while after the Covenant was signed but I don't suppose I've spent two years on Earth since then. I like to move around."

Her eyes lit up. "Oh, tell me about it! I've never been out in deep space. Just Luna City, once."

"Sure," he agreed. "Sometime. But I want to hear more about this matter of your appearance. Girl, you sure don't look your age."

"I suppose not. Or, rather, of course I don't. As to how it's done, I can't tell you much. Hormones and symbiotics and gland therapy and some psychotherapy—things like that. What it adds up to is that, for members of the Families, senility is postponed and that senescence can be arrested at least cosmetically." She brooded for a moment. "Once they thought they were on the track of the secret of immortality, the true Fountain of Youth. But it was a mistake. Senility is simply postponed . . . and shortened. About ninety days from the first clear warning—then death from old age." She shivered. "Of course, most of our cousins don't wait—a couple of weeks to make certain of the diagnosis, then euthanasia."

"The hell you say! Well, *I* won't go that way. When the Old Boy comes to get *me*, he'll have to drag me—and I'll be kicking and gouging eyes every step of the way!"

She smiled lopsidedly. "It does me good to hear you talk that way. Lazarus, I wouldn't let my guards down this way with anyone younger than myself. But your example gives me courage."

"We'll outlast the lot of 'em, Mary, never you fear. But about the meeeting tonight: I haven't paid any attention to the news and I've only recently come earthside—does this chap Ralph Schultz know what he is talking about?"

"I think he must. His grandfather was a brilliant man and so is his father."

"I take it you know Ralph."

"Slightly. He is one of my grandchildren."

"That's amusing. He looks older than you do."

"Ralph found it suited him to arrest his appearance at about forty, that's all. His father was my twenty-seventh child. Ralph must be—let me see—oh, eighty or ninety years younger than I am, at least. At that, he is older than some of my children."

"You've done well by the Families, Mary."

"I suppose so. But they've done well by me, too. I've enjoyed having children and the trust benefits for my thirty-odd come to quite a lot. I have every luxury one could want." She shivered again. "I suppose that's why I'm in such a funk —I enjoy life."

"Stop it! I thought my sterling example and boyish grin had cured you of that nonsense."

"Well . . . you've helped."

"Mmm . . . look, Mary, why don't you marry again and have some more squally brats? Keep you too busy to fret."

"What? At my age? Now, really, Lazarus!"

"Nothing wrong with your age. You're younger than I am."

She studied him for a moment. "Lazarus, are you proposing a contract? If so, I wish you would speak more plainly."

His mouth opened and he gulped. "Hey, wait a minute! Take it easy! I was speaking in general terms . . . I'm not the domestic type. Why, every time I've married my wife has grown sick of the sight of me inside of a few years. Not but what I—well, I mean you're a very pretty girl and a man ought to——"

She shut him off by leaning forward and putting a hand over his mouth, while grinning impishly. "I didn't mean to panic you, cousin. Or perhaps I did—men are so funny when they think they are about to be trapped."

"Well——" he said glumly.

"Forget it, dear. Tell me, what plan do you think they will settle on?"

"That bunch tonight?"

"Yes."

"None, of course. They won't get anywhere. Mary, a committee is the only known form of life with a hundred bellies and no brain. But presently somebody with a mind of his own will bulldoze them into accepting his plan. I don't know what it will be."

"Well . . . what course of action do *you* favor?"

"Me? Why, none. Mary, if there is any one thing I have learned in the past couple of centuries, it's this: These things *pass*. Wars and depressions and Prophets and Covenants— they pass. The trick is to stay alive through them."

She nodded thoughtfully. "I think you are right."

"Sure I'm right. It takes a hundred years or so to realize just how good life is." He stood up and stretched. "But right now this growing boy could use some sleep."

"Me, too."

Mary's flat was on the top floor, with a sky view. When she had come back to the lounge she had cut the inside lighting and let the ceiling shutters fold back; they had been sitting, save for an invisible sheet of plastic, under the stars. As Lazarus raised his head in stretching, his eye had rested on his favorite constellation. "Odd," he commented. "Orion seems to have added a fourth star to his belt."

She looked up. "That must be the big ship for the Second Centauri Expedition. See if you can see it move."

"Couldn't tell without instruments."

"I suppose not," she agreed. "Clever of them to build it out in space, isn't it?"

"No other way to do it. It's too big to assemble on Earth. I can doss down right here, Mary. Or do you have a spare room?"

"Your room is the second door on the right. Shout if you can't find everything you need." She put her face up and kissed him goodnight, a quick peck. " 'Night."

Lazarus followed her and went into his own room.

Mary Sperling woke at her usual hour the next day. She got up quietly to keep from waking Lazarus, ducked into her 'fresher, showered and massaged, swallowed a grain of sleep surrogate to make up for the short night, followed it almost as quickly with all the breakfast she permitted her waistline, then punched for the calls she had not bothered to take the night before. The phone played back several calls which she promptly forgot, then she recognized the voice of Bork Vanning. " 'Hello,' " the instrument said. " 'Mary, this is Bork, calling at twenty-one o'clock. I'll be by at ten o'clock tomorrow morning, for a dip in the lake and lunch somewhere. Unless I hear from you it's a date. 'Bye, my dear. Service.' "

"Service," she repeated automatically. Drat the man! Couldn't he take no for an answer? Mary Sperling, you're slipping!—a quarter your age and yet you can't seem to handle him.

Call him and leave word that—no, too late; he'd be here any minute. Bother!

2 When Lazarus went to bed he stepped out of his kilt and chucked it toward a wardrobe . . . which snagged it, shook it out, and hung it up neatly. "Nice catch," he commented, then glanced down at his hairy thighs and smiled wryly; the kilt had concealed a blaster strapped to one thigh, a knife to the other. He was aware of the present gentle custom against personal weapons, but he felt naked without them. Such customs were nonsense anyhow, foolishness from old women—there was no such thing as a "dangerous weapon," there were only dangerous men.

When he came out of the 'fresher, he put his weapons where he could reach them before sprawling in sleep.

He came instantly wide awake with a weapon in each hand . . . then remembered where he was, relaxed, and looked around to see what had wakened him.

It was a murmur of voices through the air duct. Poor soundproofing he decided, and Mary must be entertaining callers—in which case he should not be slug-a-bed. He got up, refreshed himself, strapped his best friends back on his thighs, and went looking for his hostess.

As the door to the lounge dilated noiselessly in front of him the sound of voices became loud and very interesting. The lounge was el-shaped and he was out of sight; he hung back and listened shamelessly. Eavesdropping had saved his skin on several occasions; it worried him not at all—he enjoyed it.

A man was saying, "Mary, you're completely unreasonable! You know you're fond of me, you admit that marriage to me would be to your advantage. So why *won't* you?"

"I told you, Bork. Age difference."

"That's foolish. What do you expect? Adolescent romance? Oh, I admit that I'm not as young as you are . . . but a woman needs an older man to look up to and keep her steady. I'm not too old for you; I'm just at my prime."

Lazarus decided that he already knew this chap well enough to dislike him. Sulky voice——

Mary did not answer. The man went on: "Anyhow, I have a surprise for you on that point. I wish I could tell you now, but . . . well, it's a state secret."

"Then don't tell me. It can't change my mind in any case, Bork."

"Oh, but it would! Mmm . . . I *will* tell you—I know *you* can be trusted."

"Now, Bork, you shouldn't assume that——"

"It doesn't matter; it will be public knowledge in a few days anyhow. Mary . . . *I'll never grow old on you!*"

"What do you mean?" Lazarus decided that her tone was suddenly suspicious.

"Just what I said. Mary, they've found the secret of eternal youth!"

"*What?* Who? How? When?"

"Oh, so now you're interested, eh? Well, I won't keep you waiting. You know these old Johnnies that call themselves the Howard Families?"

"Yes . . . I've heard of them, of course," she admitted slowly. "But what of it? They're fakes."

"Not at all. I *know*. The Administration has been quietly investigating their claims. Some of them are unquestionably more than a hundred years old—and *still young!*"

"That's very hard to believe."

"Nevertheless it's true."

"Well . . . how do they do it?"

"Ah! That's the point. They claim that it is a simple matter of heredity, that they live a long time because they come from long lived stock. But that's preposterous, scientifically

21

incompatible with the established facts. The Administration checked most carefully and the answer is certain: they have the secret of staying young."

"You can't be sure of that."

"Oh, come, Mary! You're a dear girl but you're questioning the expert opinion of the best scientific brains in the world. Never mind. Here's the part that is confidential. We don't have their secret yet—but we will have it shortly. Without any excitement or public notice, they are to be picked up and questioned. We'll get the secret—and you and I will never grow old! What do you think of *that?* Eh?"

Mary answered very slowly, almost inaudibly, "It would be nice if everyone could live a long time."

"Huh? Yes, I suppose it would. But in any case you and I will receive the treatment, whatever it is. Think about *us,* dear. Year after year after year of happy, youthful marriage. Not less than a century. Maybe even——"

"Wait a moment, Bork. This 'secret.' It wouldn't be for everybody?"

"Well, now . . . that's a matter of high policy. Population pressure is a pretty unwieldy problem even now. In practice it might be necessary to restrict it to essential personnel—and their wives. But don't fret your lovely head about it; you and I will have it."

"You mean I'll have it *if* I marry you."

"Mmm . . . that's a nasty way to put it, Mary. I'd do anything in the world for you that I could—because I *love* you. But it would be utterly simple if you were married to me. So say you will."

"Let's let that be for the moment. How do you propose to get this 'secret' out of them?"

Lazarus could almost hear his wise nod. "Oh, they'll talk!"

"Do you mean to say you'd send them to Coventry if they didn't?"

"Coventry? Hm! You don't understand the situation at all, Mary; this isn't any minor social offense. This is *treason*—treason against the whole human race. We'll use means! Ways that the Prophets used . . . if they don't coöperate willingly."

"Do you mean that? Why, that's against the Convenant!"

"Covenant be damned! This is a matter of life and death —do you think we'd let a scrap of paper stand in our way? You can't bother with petty legalities in the fundamental things men live by—not something they will fight to the death for. And that is precisely what this is. These . . . these dog-in-the-manger scoundrels are trying to keep life itself from us. Do you think we'll bow to 'custom' in an emergency like this?"

Mary answered in a hushed and horrified voice: "Do you really think the Council will violate the Covenant?"

"*Think* so? The Action-in-Council was recorded last night. We authorized the Administrator to use 'full expediency.' "

Lazarus strained his ears through a long silence. At last Mary spoke. "Bork——"

"Yes, my dear?"

"You've got to do something about this. You must stop it."

"Stop it? You don't know what you're saying. I couldn't . . . and I would not if I could."

"But you *must*. You must convince the Council. They're making a mistake, a tragic mistake. There is nothing to be gained by trying to coerce those poor people. *There is no secret!*"

"What? You're getting excited, my dear. You're setting your judgment up against some of the best and wisest men on the planet. Believe me, we know what we are doing. We don't relish using harsh methods any more than you do, but it's for the general welfare. Look, I'm sorry I ever brought it up. Naturally you are soft and gentle and warmhearted and I love you for it. Why not marry me and not bother your head about matters of public policy?"

"Marry *you*? Never!"

"Aw, Mary—you're upset. Give me just one good reason why not?"

"I'll tell you why! Because *I* am one of those people you want to persecute!"

There was another pause. "Mary . . . you're not well."

"Not well, am I? I am as well as a person can be at my age. Listen to me, you fool! I have grandsons twice your age. I was here when the First Prophet took over the country. I was here when Harriman launched the first Moon rocket. You weren't even a squalling brat—your *grandparents* hadn't even met, when I was a woman grown and married. And you stand there and glibly propose to push around, even to torture, me and my kind. Marry *you*? I'd rather marry one of my own grandchildren!"

Lazarus shifted his weight and slid his right hand inside the flap of his kilt; he expected trouble at once. You can depend on a woman, he reflected, to blow her top at the wrong moment.

He waited. Bork's answer was cool; the tones of the experienced man of authority replaced those of thwarted passion. "Take it easy, Mary. Sit down, I'll look after you. First I want you to take a sedative. Then I'll get the best psychotherapist in the city—in the whole country. You'll be all right."

"Take your hands off me!"

"Now, Mary . . ."

Lazarus stepped out into the room and pointed at Vanning with his blaster. "This monkey giving you trouble, Sis?"

Vanning jerked his head around. "Who are you?" he demanded indignantly. "What are you doing here?"

Lazarus still addressed Mary. "Say the word, Sis, and I'll cut him into pieces small enough to hide."

"No, Lazarus," she answered with her voice now under control. "Thanks just the same. Please put your gun away. I wouldn't want anything like that to happen."

"Okay." Lazarus holstered the gun but let his hand rest on the grip.

"Who are you?" repeated Vanning. "What's the meaning of this intrusion?"

"I was just about to ask you that, Bud," Lazarus said mildly, "but we'll let it ride. I'm another one of those old Johnnies you're looking for . . . like Mary here."

Vanning looked at him keenly. "I wonder——" he said. He looked back at Mary. "It can't be, it's preposterous. Still . . . it won't hurt to investigate your story. I've plenty to detain you on, in any event, I've never seen a clearer case of anti-social atavism." He moved toward the videophone.

"Better get away from that phone, Bud," Lazarus said quickly, then added to Mary, "I won't touch my gun, Sis. I'll use my knife."

Vanning stopped. "Very well," he said in annoyed tones, "put away that vibroblade. I won't call from here."

"Look again, it ain't a vibroblade. It's steel. Messy."

Vanning turned to Mary Sperling. "I'm leaving. If you are wise, you'll come with me." She shook her head. He looked annoyed, shrugged, and faced Lazarus Long. "As for you, sir, your primitive manners have led you into serious trouble. You will be arrested shortly."

Lazarus glanced up at the ceiling shutters. "Reminds me of a patron in Venusburg who wanted to have me arrested."

"Well?"

"I've outlived him quite a piece."

Vanning opened his mouth to answer—then turned suddenly and left so quickly that the outer door barely had time to clear the end of his nose. As the door snapped closed Lazarus said musingly, "Hardest man to reason with I've met in years. I'll bet he never used an unsterilized spoon in his life."

Mary looked startled, then giggled. He turned toward her. "Glad to see you sounding perky, Mary. Kinda thought you were upset."

"I was. I hadn't known you were listening. I was forced to improvise as I went along."

24

"Did I queer it?"

"No. I'm glad you came in—thanks. But we'll have to hurry now."

"I suppose so. I think he meant it—there'll be a proctor looking for me soon. You, too, maybe."

"That's what I meant. So let's get out of here."

Mary was ready to leave in scant minutes but when they stepped out into the public hall they met a man whose brassard and hypo kit marked him as a proctor. "Service," he said. "I'm looking for a citizen in company with Citizen Mary Sperling. Could you direct me?"

"Sure," agreed Lazarus. "She lives right down there." He pointed at the far end of the corridor. As the peace officer looked in that direction, Lazarus tapped him carefully on the back of the head, a little to the left, with the butt of his blaster, and caught him as he slumped.

Mary helped Lazarus wrestle the awkward mass into her apartment. He knelt over the cop, pawed through his hypo kit, took a loaded injector and gave him a shot. "There," he said, "that'll keep him sleepy for a few hours." Then he blinked thoughtfully at the hypo kit, detached it from the proctor's belt. "This might come in handy again. Anyhow, it won't hurt to take it." As an afterthought he removed the proctor's peace brassard and placed it, too, in his pouch.

They left the apartment again and dropped to the parking level. Lazarus noticed as they rolled up the ramp that Mary had set the North Shore combination. "Where are we going?" she asked.

"The Families' Seat. No place else to go where we won't be checked on. But we'll have to hide somewhere in the country until dark."

Once the car was on beamed control headed north Mary asked to be excused and caught a few minutes sleep. Lazarus watched a few miles of scenery, then nodded himself.

They were awakened by the jangle of the emergency alarm and by the speedster slowing to a stop. Mary reached up and shut off the alarm. "All cars resume local control," intoned a voice. "Proceed at speed twenty to the nearest traffic control tower for inspection. All cars resume local control. Proceed at——"

She switched that off, too. "Well, that's us," Lazarus said cheerfully. "Got any ideas?"

Mary did not answer. She peered out and studied their surroundings. The steel fence separating the high-speed control way they were on from the uncontrolled local-traffic strip lay about fifty yards to their right but no changeover ramp broke the fence for at least a mile ahead—where it did, there would be, of course, the control tower where they were ordered to undergo inspection. She started the car again, operating it manually, and wove through stopped or slowly moving traffic while speeding up. As they got close to the barrier Lazarus felt himself shoved into the cushions; the car surged and lifted, clearing the barrier by inches. She set it down rolling on the far side.

A car was approaching from the north and they were slashing across his lane. The other car was moving no more than ninety but its driver was taken by surprise—he had no reason to expect another car to appear out of nowhere against him on a clear road. Mary was forced to duck left, then right, and left again; the car slewed and reared up on its hind wheel, writhing against the steel grip of its gyros. Mary fought it back into control to the accompaniment of a teeth-shivering grind of herculene against glass as the rear wheel fought for traction.

Lazarus let his jaw muscles relax and breathed out gustily. *"Whew!"* he sighed. "I hope we won't have to do *that* again."

Mary glanced at him, grinning. "Women drivers make you nervous?"

"Oh, no, no, not at all! I just wish you would warn me when something like that is about to happen."

"I didn't know myself," she admitted, then went on worriedly, "I don't know quite what to do now. I thought we could lie quiet out of town until dark . . . but I had to show my hand a little when I took that fence. By now somebody will be reporting it to the tower. Mmm. . . ."

"Why wait until dark?" he asked. "Why not just bounce over to the lake in this Dick Dare contraption of yours and let it swim us home?"

"I don't like to," she fretted. "I've attracted too much attention already. A trimobile faked up to look like a groundster is handy, but . . . well, if anyone sees us taking it under water and the proctors hear of it, somebody is going to guess the answer. Then they'll start fishing—everything from seismo to sonar and Heaven knows what else."

"But isn't the Seat shielded?"

"Of course. But anything that big they can find—if they know what they're looking for and keep looking."

"You're right, of course," Lazarus admitted slowly. "Well, we certainly don't want to lead any nosy proctors to the Families' Seat. Mary, I think we had better ditch your car and get lost." He frowned. "Anywhere but the Seat."

"No, it has to be the Seat," she answered sharply.

"Why? If you chase a fox, he——"

"Quiet a moment! I want to try something." Lazarus shut

up; Mary drove with one hand while she fumbled in the glove compartment.

"Answer," a voice said.

"Life is short——" Mary replied.

They completed the formula. "Listen," Mary went on hurriedly, "I'm in trouble—get a fix on me."

"Okay."

"Is there a sub in the pool?"

"Yes."

"Good! Lock on me and home them in." She explained hurriedly the details of what she wanted, stopping once to ask Lazarus if he could swim. "That's all," she said at last, "but move! We're short on minutes."

"Hold it, Mary!" the voice protested. "You know I can't send a sub out in the daytime, certainly not on a calm day. It's too easy to——"

"Will you, or won't you!"

A third voice cut in. "I was listening, Mary—Ira Barstow. We'll pick you up."

"But——" objected the first voice.

"Stow it, Tommy. Just mind your burners and home me in. See you, Mary."

"Right, Ira!"

While she had been talking to the Seat, Mary had turned off from the local-traffic strip into the unpaved road she had followed the night before, without slowing and apparently without looking. Lazarus gritted his teeth and hung on. They passed a weathered sign reading CONTAMINATED AREA—PROCEED AT YOUR OWN RISK and graced with the conventional purple trefoil. Lazarus blinked at it and shrugged —he could not see how, at the moment, his hazard could be increased by a neutron or so.

Mary slammed the car to a stop in a clump of stunted trees near the abandoned road. The lake lay at their feet, just beyond a low bluff. She unfastened her safety belt, struck a cigarette, and relaxed. "Now we wait. It'll take at least half an hour for them to reach us no matter how hard Ira herds it. Lazarus, do you think we were seen turning off into here?"

"To tell the truth, Mary, I was too busy to look."

"Well . . . nobody ever comes here, except a few reckless boys."

("—and girls," Lazarus added to himself.) Then he went on aloud, "I noted a 'hot' sign back there. How high is the count?"

"That? Oh, pooh. Nothing to worry about unless you decided to build a house here. We're the ones who are hot. If we didn't have to stay close to the communicator, we——"

The communicator spoke. "Okay, Mary. Right in front of you."

She looked startled. "Ira?"

"This is Ira speaking but I'm still at the Seat. Pete Hardy was available in the Evanston pen, so we homed him in on you. Quicker."

"Okay—thanks!" She was turning to speak to Lazarus when he touched her arm.

"Look behind us."

A helicopter was touching down less than a hundred yards from them. Three men burst out of it. They were dressed as proctors.

Mary jerked open the door of the car and threw off her gown in one unbroken motion. She turned and called, "Come on!" as she thrust a hand back inside and tore a stud loose from the instrument panel. She ran.

Lazarus unzipped the belt of his kilt and ran out of it as he followed her to the bluff. She went dancing down it; he came after with slightly more caution, swearing at sharp stones. The blast shook them as the car exploded, but the bluff saved them.

They hit the water together.

The lock in the little submarine was barely big enough for one at a time; Lazarus shoved Mary into it first and tried to slap her when she resisted, and discovered that slapping will not work under water. Then he spent an endless time, or so it seemed, wondering whether or not he could breathe water. "What's a fish got that I ain't got?" he was telling himself, when the outer latch moved under his hand and he was able to wiggle in.

Eleven dragging seconds to blow the lock clear of water and he had a chance to see what damage, if any, the water had done to his blaster.

Mary was speaking urgently to the skipper. "Listen, Pete— there are three proctors back up there with a whirly. My car blew up in their faces just as we hit the water. But if they aren't all dead or injured, there will be a smart boy who will figure out that there was only one place for us to go—under water. We've got to be away from here before they take to the air to look for us."

"It's a losing race," Pete Hardy complained, slapping his controls as he spoke. "Even if it's only a visual search, I'll have to get outside and stay outside the circle of total reflection faster than he can gain altitude—and I can't." But the little sub lunged forward reassuringly.

Mary worried about whether or not to call the Seat from the sub. She decided not to; it would just increase the hazard both to the sub and to the Seat itself. So she calmed herself and waited, huddled small in a passenger seat too cramped for two. Peter Hardy swung wide into deep water, hugging the bottom, picking up the Muskegon-Gary bottom beacons and conned himself in blind.

By the time they surfaced in the pool inside the Seat she had decided against any physical means of communication, even the carefully shielded equipment at the Seat. Instead she hoped to find a telepathic sensitive ready and available among the Families' dependents cared for there. Sensitives were as scarce among healthy members of the Howard Families as they were in the rest of the population, but the very inbreeding which had conserved and reinforced their abnormal longevity had also conserved and reinforced bad genes as well as good; they had an unusually high percentage of physical and mental defectives. Their board of genetic control plugged away at the problem of getting rid of bad strains while conserving the longevity strain, but for many generations they would continue to pay for their long lives with an excess of defectives.

But almost five per cent of these defectives were telepathically sensitive.

Mary went straight to the sanctuary in the Seat where some of these dependents were cared for, with Lazarus Long at her heels. She braced the matron. "Where's Little Stephen? I need him."

"Keep your voice down," the matron scolded. "Rest hour —you can't."

"Janice, I've got to see him," Mary insisted. "This won't wait. I've got to get a message out to all the Families—at once."

The matron planted her hands on her hips. "Take it to the communication office. You can't come here disturbing my children at all hours. I won't have it."

"Janice, please! I don't dare use anything but telepathy. You know I wouldn't do this unnecessarily. Now take me to Stephen."

"It wouldn't do you any good if I did. Little Stephen has had one of his bad spells today."

"Then take me to the strongest sensitive who can possibly work. Quickly, Janice! The safety of every member may depend on it."

"Did the trustees send you?"

"No, no! There wasn't time!"

The matron still looked doubtful. While Lazarus was trying to recall how long it had been since he had socked a lady, she gave in. "All right—you can see Billy, though I shouldn't let you. Mind you, don't tire him out." Still bristling, she led them along a corridor past a series of cheerful rooms and

29

into one of them. Lazarus looked at the thing on the bed and looked away.

The matron went to a cupboard and returned with a hypodermic injector. "Does he work under a hypnotic?" Lazarus asked.

"No," the matron answered coldly, "he has to have a stimulant to be aware of us at all." She swabbed skin on the arm of the gross figure and made the injection. "Go ahead," she said to Mary and lapsed into grim-mouthed silence.

The figure on the bed stirred, its eyes rolled loosely, then seemed to track. It grinned. "Aunt Mary!" it said. "Oooh! Did you bring Billy Boy something?"

"No," she said gently. "Not this time, hon. Aunt Mary was in too much of a hurry. Next time? A surprise? Will that do?"

"All right," it said docilely.

"That's a good boy." She reached out and tousled its hair; Lazarus looked away again. "Now will Billy Boy do something for Aunt Mary? A big, *big* favor?"

"Sure."

"Can you hear your friends?"

"Oh, sure."

"All of them?"

"Uh huh. Mostly they don't say anything," it added.

"Call to them."

There was a very short silence. "They heard me."

"Fine! Now listen carefully, Billy Boy: All the Families—urgent warning! Elder Mary Sperling speaking. Under an Action-in-Council the Administrator is about to arrest every revealed member. The Council directed him to use 'full expedience'—and it is my sober judgment that they are determined to use any means at all, regardless of the Covenant, to try to squeeze out of us the so-called secret of our long lives. They even intend to use the tortures developed by the inquisitors of the Prophets!" Her voice broke. She stopped and pulled herself together. "Now get busy! Find them, warn them, hide them! You may have only minutes left to save them!"

Lazarus touched her arm and whispered; she nodded and went on:

"If any cousin is arrested, rescue him *by any means at all!* Don't try to appeal to the Covenant, don't waste time arguing about justice . . . rescue him! Now *move!*"

She stopped and then spoke in a tired, gentle voice, "Did they hear us, Billy Boy?"

"Sure."

"Are they telling their folks?"

"Uh huh. All but Jimmie-the-Horse. He's mad at me," it added confidentially.

" 'Jimmie-the-Horse'? Where is he?"

"Oh, where he lives."

"In Montreal," put in the matron. "There are two other sensitives there—your message got through. Are you finished?"

"Yes . . ." Mary said doubtfully. "But perhaps we had better have some other Seat relay it back."

"No!"

"But, Janice——"

"I won't permit it. I suppose you had to send it but I want to give Billy the antidote now. So get out."

Lazarus took her arm. "Come on, kid. It either got through or it didn't; you've done your best. A good job, girl."

Mary went on to make a full report to the Resident Secretary; Lazarus left her on business of his own. He retraced his steps, looking for a man who was not too busy to help him; the guards at the pool entrance were the first he found. "Service——" he began.

"Service to you," one of them answered. "Looking for someone?" He glanced curiously at Long's almost complete nakedness, glanced away again—how anybody dressed, or did not dress, was a private matter.

"Sort of," admitted Lazarus. "Say, Bud, do you know of anyone around here who would lend me a kilt?"

"You're looking at one," the guard answered pleasantly. "Take over, Dick—back in a minute." He led Lazarus to bachelors' quarters, outfitted him, helped him to dry his pouch and contents, and made no comment about the arsenal strapped to his hairy thighs. How elders behaved was no business of his and many of them were even touchier about their privacy than most people. He had seen Aunt Mary Sperling arrive stripped for swimming but had not been surprised as he had heard Ira Barstow briefing Pete for the underwater pickup; that the elder with her chose to take a dip in the lake weighed down by hardware did surprise him but not enough to make him forget his manners.

"Anything else you need?" he asked. "Do those shoes fit?"

"Well enough. Thanks a lot, Bud." Lazarus smoothed the borrowed kilt. It was a little too long for him but it comforted him. A loin strap was okay, he supposed—if you were on Venus. But he had never cared much for Venus customs. Damn it, a man liked to be *dressed*. "I feel better," he admitted. "Thanks again. By the way, what's your name?"

"Edmund Hardy, of the Foote Family."

"That so? What's your line?"

"Charles Hardy and Evelyn Foote. Edward Hardy-Alice Johnson and Terence Briggs-Eleanor Weatheral. Oliver——"

31

"That's enough. I sorta thought so. You're one of my great-great-grandsons."

"Why, that's interesting," commented Hardy agreeably. "Gives us a sixteenth of kinship, doesn't it—not counting convergence. May I ask your name?"

"Lazarus Long."

Hardy shook his head. "Some mistake. Not in my line."

"Try Woodrow Wilson Smith instead. It was the one I started with."

"Oh, that one! Yes, surely. But I thought you were . . . uh——"

"Dead? Well, I ain't."

"Oh, I didn't mean that at all," Hardy protested, blushing at the blunt Anglo-Saxon monosyllable. He hastily added, "I'm glad to have run across you, Gran'ther. I've always wanted to hear the straight of the story about the Families' Meeting in 2012."

"That was before you were born, Ed," Lazarus said gruffly, "and don't call me 'Gran'ther.' "

"Sorry, sir—I mean 'Sorry, Lazarus.' Is there any other service I can do for you?"

"I shouldn't have gotten shirty. No—yes, there is, too. Where can I swipe a bite of breakfast? I was sort of rushed this morning."

"Certainly." Hardy took him to the bachelors' pantry, operated the autochef for him, drew coffee for his watch mate and himself, and left. Lazarus consumed his "bite of breakfast"—about three thousand calories of sizzling sausages, eggs, jam, hot breads, coffee with cream, and ancillary items, for he worked on the assumption of always topping off his reserve tanks because you never knew how far you might have to lift before you had another chance to refuel. In due time he sat back, belched, gathered up his dishes and shoved them in the incinerator, then went looking for a newsbox.

He found one in the bachelors' library, off their lounge. The room was empty save for one man who seemed to be about the same age as that suggested by Lazarus' appearance. There the resemblance stopped; the stranger was slender, mild in feature, and was topped off by finespun carroty hair quite unlike the grizzled wiry bush topping Lazarus. The stranger was bending over the news receiver with his eyes pressed to the microviewer.

Lazarus cleared his throat loudly and said, "Howdy."

The man jerked his head up and exclaimed, "Oh! Sorry—I was startled. Do y' a service?"

"I was looking for the newsbox. Mind if we throw it on the screen?"

"Not at all." The smaller man stood up, pressed the rewind

button, and set the controls for projection. "Any particular subject?"

"I wanted to see," said Lazarus, "if there was any news about us—the Families."

"I've been watching for that myself. Perhaps we had better use the sound track and let it hunt."

"Okay," agreed Lazarus, stepping up and changing the setting to audio. "What's the code word?"

" 'Methuselah.' "

Lazarus punched in the setting; the machine chattered and whined as it scanned and rejected the track speeding through it, then it slowed with a triumphant click. "The DAILY DATA," it announced. "The only midwest news service subscribing to every major grid. Leased videochannel to Luna City. Tri-S correspondents throughout the System. First, Fast, and Most! Lincoln, Nebraska—Savant Denounces Oldsters! Dr. Witwell Oscarsen, President Emeritus of Bryan Lyceum, calls for official reconsideration of the status of the kin group styling themselves the 'Howard Families.' 'It is proved,' he says, 'that these people have solved the age-old problem of extending, perhaps indefinitely, the span of human life. For that they are to be commended; it is a worthy and potentially fruitful research. But their claim that their solution is no more than hereditary predisposition defies both science and common sense. Our modern knowledge of the established laws of genetics enables us to deduce with certainty that they are withholding from the public some secret technique or techniques whereby they accomplish their results.

" 'It is contrary to our customs to permit scientific knowledge to be held as a monopoly for the few. When concealing such knowledge strikes at life itself, the action becomes treason to the race. As a citizen, I call on the Administration to act forcefully in this matter and I remind them that the situation is not one which could possibly have been foreseen by the wise men who drew up the Covenant and codified our basic customs. Any custom is man-made and is therefore a finite attempt to describe an infinity of relationships. It follows as the night from day that any custom necessarily has its exceptions. To be bound by them in the face of new——' "

Lazarus pressed the HOLD button. "Had enough of that guy?"

"Yes, I had already heard it." The stranger sighed. "I have rarely heard such complete lack of semantic rigor. It surprises me—Dr. Oscarsen has done sound work in the past."

"Reached his dotage," Lazarus stated, as he told the machine to try again. "Wants what he wants when he wants it —and thinks that constitutes a natural law."

The machine hummed and clicked and again spoke up.

"The DAILY DATA, the only midwest news——"

"Can't we scramble that commercial?" suggested Lazarus.

His companion peered at the control panel. "Doesn't seem to be equipped for it."

"Ensenada, Baja California. Jeffers and Lucy Weatheral today asked for special proctor protection, alleging that a group of citizens had broken into their home, submitted them to personal indignity and committed other asocial acts. The Weatherals are, by their own admission, members of the notorious Howard Families and claim that the alleged incident could be traced to that supposed fact. The district provost points out that they have offered no proof and has taken the matter under advisement. A town mass meeting has been announced for tonight which will air——"

The other man turned toward Lazarus. "Cousin, did we hear what I thought we heard? That is the first case of asocial group violence in more than twenty years . . . yet they reported it like a breakdown in a weather integrator."

"Not quite," Lazarus answered grimly. "The connotations of the words used in describing us were loaded."

"Yes, true, but loaded cleverly. I doubt if there was a word in that dispatch with an emotional index, taken alone, higher than one point five. The newscasters are allowed two zero, you know."

"You a psychometrician?"

"Uh, no. I should have introduced myself. I'm Andrew Jackson Libby."

"Lazarus Long."

"I know. I was at the meeting last night."

" 'Libby . . . Libby,' " Lazarus mused. "Don't seem to place it in the Families. Seems familiar, though."

"My case is a little like yours——"

"Changed it during the Interregnum, eh?"

"Yes and no. I was born after the Second Revolution. But my people had been converted to the New Crusade and had broken with the Families and changed their name. I was a grown man before I knew I was a Member."

"The deuce you say! That's interesting—how did you come to be located . . . if you don't mind my asking?"

"Well, you see I was in the Navy and one of my superior officers——"

"Got it! Got it! I *thought* you were a spaceman. You're Slipstick Libby, the Calculator."

Libby grinned sheepishly. "I have been called that."

"Sure, sure. The last can I piloted was equipped with your paragravitic rectifier. And the control bank used your fractional differential on the steering jets. But I installed that myself—kinda borrowed your patent."

34

Libby seemed undisturbed by the theft. His face lit up. "You are interested in symbolic logic?"

"Only pragmatically. But look, I put a modification on your gadget that derives from the rejected alternatives in your thirteenth equation. It helps like this: suppose you are cruising in a field of density 'x' with an n-order gradient normal to your course and you want to set your optimum course for a projected point of rendezvous capital 'A' at matching-in vector 'rho' using automatic selection the entire jump, then if——"

They drifted entirely away from Basic English as used by earthbound laymen. The newsbox beside them continued to hunt; three times it spoke up, each time Libby touched the rejection button without consciously hearing it.

"I see your point," he said at last. "I had considered a somewhat similar modification but concluded that it was not commercially feasible, too expensive for anyone but enthusiasts such as yourself. But your solution is cheaper than mine."

"How do you figure that?"

"Why, it's obvious from the data. Your device contains sixty-two moving parts, which should require, if we assume standardized fabrication processes, a probable——" Libby hesitated momentarily as if he were programing the problem. "—a probable optimax of five thousand two hundred and eleven operation in manufacture assuming null-therblig automation, whereas mine——"

Lazarus butted in. "Andy," he inquired solicitously, "does your head ever ache?"

Libby looked sheepish again. "There's nothing abnormal about my talent," he protested. "It is theoretically possible to develop it in any normal person."

"Sure," agreed Lazarus, "and you can teach a snake to tap dance once you get shoes on him. Never mind, I'm glad to have fallen in with you. I heard stories about you way back when you were a kid. You were in the Cosmic Construction Corps, weren't you?"

Libby nodded. "Earth-Mars Spot Three."

"Yeah, that was it—chap on Mars gimme the yarn. Trader at Drywater. I knew your maternal grandfather, too. Stiff-necked old coot."

"I suppose he was."

"He was, all right. I had quite a set-to with him at the Meeting in 2012. He had a powerful vocabulary." Lazarus frowned slightly. "Funny thing, Andy . . . I recall that vividly, I've always had a good memory—yet it seems to be getting harder for me to keep things straight. Especially this last century."

"Inescapable mathematical necessity," said Libby.

"Huh? Why?"

"Life experience is linearly additive, but the correlation of memory impressions is an unlimited expansion. If mankind lived as long as a thousand years, it would be necessary to invent some totally different method of memory association in order to be eclectively time-binding. A man would otherwise flounder helplessly in the wealth of his own knowledge, unable to evaluate. Insanity, or feeble-mindedness."

"That so?" Lazarus suddenly looked worried. "Then we'd better get busy on it."

"Oh, it's quite possible of solution."

"Let's work on it. Let's not get caught short."

The newsbox again demanded attention, this time with the buzzer and flashing light of a spot bulletin: "Hearken to the DATA. Flash! High Council Suspends Covenant! Under the Emergency Situation clause of the Covenant an unprecedented Action-in-Council was announced today directing the Administrator to detain and question all members of the so-called Howard Families—*by any means expedient!* The Administrator authorized that the following statement be released by all licensed news outlets: (I quote) 'The suspension of the Covenant's civil guarantees applies only to the group known as the Howard Families except that government agents are empowered to act as circumstances require to apprehend speedily the persons affected by the Action-in-Council. Citizens are urged to tolerate cheerfully any minor inconvenience this may cause them; your right of privacy will be respected in every way possible; your right of free movement may be interrupted temporarily, but full economic restitution will be made.'

"Now, Friends and Citizens, what does this mean?—to you and you and also you! The DAILY DATA brings you now your popular commentator, Albert Reifsnider:

"Reifsnider reporting: Service, Citizens! There is no cause for alarm. To the average free citizen this emergency will be somewhat less troublesome than a low-pressure minimum too big for the weather machines. Take it easy! Relax! Help the proctors when requested and tend to your private affairs. If inconvenienced, don't stand on custom—coöperate with Service!

"That's what it means today. What does it mean tomorrow and the day after that? Next year? It means that your public servants have taken a forthright step to obtain for you the boon of a longer and happier life! Don't get your hopes too high . . . but it looks like the dawn of a new day. Ah, indeed it does! The jealously guarded secret of a selfish few will soon——"

Long raised an eyebrow at Libby, then switched it off.

"I suppose that," Libby said bitterly, "is an example of 'factual detachment in news reporting.' "

Lazarus opened his pouch and struck a cigarette before replying. "Take it easy, Andy. There are bad times and good times. We're overdue for bad times. The people are on the march again . . . this time at us."

3 The burrow known as the Families' Seat became jammed as the day wore on. Members kept trickling in, arriving by tunnels from downstate and from Indiana. As soon as it was dark a traffic jam developed at the underground pool entrance—sporting subs, fake ground cars such as Mary's, ostensible surface cruisers modified to dive, each craft loaded with refugees some half suffocated from lying in hiding on deep bottom most of the day while waiting for a chance to sneak in.

The usual meeting room was much too small to handle the crowd; the resident staff cleared the largest room, the refectory, and removed partitions separating it from the main lounge. There at midnight Lazarus climbed onto a temporary rostrum. "Okay," he announced, "let's pipe it down. You down in front sit on the floor so the rest can see. I was born in 1912. Anybody older?"

He paused, then added, "Nominations for chairman . . . speak up."

Three were proposed; before a fourth could be offered the last man nominated got to his feet. "Axel Johnson, of the Johnson Family. I want my name withdrawn and I suggest that the others do likewise. Lazarus cut through the fog last night; let him handle it. This is no time for Family politics."

The other names were withdrawn; no more were offered. Lazarus said, "Okay if that's the way you want it. Before we get down to arguing, I want a report from the Chief Trustee. How about it, Zack? Any of our kinfolk get nabbed?"

Zaccur Barstow did not need to identify himself; he simply said, "Speaking for the Trustees: our report is not complete, but we do not as yet know that any Member has been arrested. Of the nine thousand two hundred and eighty-five revealed Members, nine thousand one hundred and six had been reported, when I left the communication office ten minutes ago, as having reached hiding, in other Family strongholds, or in the homes of unrevealed Members, or elsewhere. Mary Sperling's warning was amazingly successful in view of how short the time was from the alarm to the public execution of the Action-in-Council—but we still have one hundred and seventy-nine revealed cousins unreported. Probably most of these will trickle in during the next few days. Others are probably safe but unable to get in touch with us."

"Get to the point, Zack," Lazarus insisted. "Any reasonable chance that all of them will make it home safe?"

"Absolutely none."

"Why?"

"Because three of them are known to be in public conveyances between here and the Moon, traveling under their revealed identities. Others we don't know about are almost certainly caught in similar predicaments."

"Question!" A cocky little man near the front stood up and pointed his finger at the Chief Trustee. "Were all those Members now in jeopardy protected by hypnotic injunction?"

"No. There was no——"

"I demand to know why not!"

"Shut up!" bellowed Lazarus. "You're out of order. Nobody's on trial here and we've got no time to waste on spilled milk. Go ahead, Zack."

"Very well. But I will answer the question to this extent: everyone knows that a proposal to protect our secrets by hynotic means was voted down at the Meeting which relaxed the 'Masquerade.' I seem to recall that the cousin now objecting helped then to vote it down."

"That is not true! And I insist that——"

"*PIPE DOWN!*" Lazarus glared at the heckler, then looked him over carefully. "Bud, you strike me as a clear proof that the Foundation should 'a' bred for brains instead of age." Lazarus looked around at the crowd. "Everybody will get his say, but in order as recognized by the chair. If he butts in again, I'm going to gag him with his own teeth—is my ruling sustained?"

There was a murmur of mixed shock and approval; no one objected. Zaccur Barstow went on, "On the advice of Ralph Schultz the trustees have been proceeding quietly for the past three months to persuade revealed Members to undergo hypnotic instruction. We were largely successful." He paused.

"Make it march, Zack," Lazarus urged. "Are we covered? Or not?"

"We are *not*. At least two of our cousins certain to be arrested are not so protected."

Lazarus shrugged. "That tears it. Kinfolk, the game's over. One shot in the arm of babble juice and the 'Masquerade' is over. It's a new situation—or will be in a few hours. What do you propose to do about it?"

In the control room of the Antipodes Rocket *Wallaby*, South Flight, the telecom hummed, went *spung!* and stuck out a tab like an impudent tongue. The copilot rocked forward in his gymbals, pulled out the message and tore it off.

He read it, then reread it. "Skipper, brace yourself."

"Trouble?"

"Read it."

The captain did so, and whistled. "Bloody! I've never arrested anybody. I don't believe I've even *seen* anybody arrested. How do we start?"

"I bow to your superior authority."

"That so?" the captain said in nettled tones. "Now that you're through bowing you can tool aft and make the arrest."

"Uh? That's not what I meant. You're the bloke with the authority. I'll relieve you at the conn."

"You didn't read me. I'm delegating the authority. Carry out your orders."

"Just a moment, Al, I didn't sign up for——"

"Carry out your orders!"

"Aye aye, sir!"

The copilot went aft. The ship had completed its reëntry, was in its long, flat, screaming approach-glide; he was able to walk—he wondered what an arrest in free-fall would be like? Snag him with a butterfly net? He located the passenger by seat check, touched his arm. "Service, sir. There's been a clerical error. May I see your ticket?"

"Why, certainly."

"Would you mind stepping back to the reserve stateroom? It's quieter there and we can both sit down."

"Not at all."

Once they were in the private compartment the chief officer asked the passenger to sit down, then looked annoyed. "Stupid of me!—I've left my lists in the control room." He turned and left. As the door slid to behind him, the passenger heard an unexpected click. Suddenly suspicious, he tried the door. It was locked.

Two proctors came for him at Melbourne. As they escorted him through the skyport he could hear remarks from a curious and surprisingly unfriendly crowd: "There's one of the laddies now!" "Him? My word, he doesn't look *old*." "What price ape glands?" "Don't stare, Herbert." "Why not? Not half bad enough for him."

They took him to the office of the Chief Provost, who invited him to sit down with formal civility. "Now then, sir," the Provost said with a slight local twang, "if you will help us by letting the orderly make a slight injection in your arm——"

"For what purpose?"

"You want to be socially coöperative, I'm sure. It won't hurt you."

"That's beside the point. I insist on an explanation. I am a citizen of the United States."

"So you are, but the Federation has concurrent jurisdiction in any member state—and I am acting under its authority. Now bare your arm, please."

"I refuse. I stand on my civil rights."

"Grab him, lads."

It took four men to do it. Even before the injector touched his skin, his jaw set and a look of sudden agony came into his face. He then sat quietly, listlessly, while the peace officers waited for the drug to take effect. Presently the Provost gently rolled back one of the prisoner's eyelids and said, "I think he's ready. He doesn't weigh over ten stone; it has hit him rather fast. Where's that list of questions?"

A deputy handed it to him; he began, "Horace Foote, do you hear me?"

The man's lips twitched, he seemed about to speak. His mouth opened and blood gushed down his chest.

The Provost bellowed and grabbed the prisoner's head, made quick examination. *Surgeon!* He's bitten his tongue half out of his head!"

The captain of the Luna City Shuttle *Moonbeam* scowled at the message in his hand. "What child's play is this?" He glared at his third officer. "Tell me that, Mister."

The third officer studied the overhead. Fuming, the captain held the message at arm's length, peered at it and read aloud: "—imperative that subject persons be prevented from doing themselves injury. You are directed to render them unconscious without warning them." He shoved the flimsy away from him. "What do they think I'm running? Coventry? Who do they think they are?—telling *me* in *my* ship what I must do with *my* passengers! I won't—so help me, I won't! There's no rule requiring me to . . . is there, Mister?"

The third officer went on silently studying the ship's structure.

The captain stopped pacing. "Purser! *Purser!* Why is that man never around when I want him?"

"I'm here, Captain."

"About time!"

"I've been here all along, sir."

"Don't argue with me. Here—attend to this." He handed the despatch to the purser and left.

A shipfitter, supervised by the purser, the hull officer, and the medical officer, made a slight change in the air-conditioning ducts to one cabin; two worried passengers sloughed off their cares under the influence of a non-lethal dose of sleeping gas.

"Another report, sir."

"Leave it," the Administrator said in a tired voice.

"And Councilor Bork Vanning presents his compliments and requests an interview."

"Tell him that I regret that I am too busy."

"He insists on seeing you, sir."

Administrator Ford answered snappishly, "Then you may tell the Honorable Mr. Vanning that he does not give orders in this office!" The aide said nothing; Administrator Ford pressed his fingertips wearily against his forehead and went on slowly, "No, Gerry, don't tell him that. Be diplomatic . . . but don't let him in."

"Yes, sir."

When he was alone, the Administrator picked up the report. His eye skipped over official heading, date line, and file number: "Synopsis of Interview with Conditionally Proscribed Citizen Arthur Sperling, full transcript attached. Conditions of Interview: Subject received normal dosage of neo-sco., having previously received unmeasured dosage of gaseous hypnotal. Antidote——" How the devil could you cure subordinates of wordiness? Was there something in the soul of a career civil servant that cherished red tape? His eye skipped on down:

"—stated that his name was Arthur Sperling of the Foote Family and gave his age as one hundred thirty-seven years. (Subject's apparent age is forty-five plus-or-minus four: see bio report attached.) Subject admitted that he was a member of the Howard Families. He stated that the Families numbered slightly more than one hundred thousand members. He was asked to correct this and it was suggested to him that the correct number was nearer ten thousand. He persisted in his original statement."

The Administrator stopped and reread this part.

He skipped on down, looking for the key part: "—insisted that his long life was the result of his ancestry and had no other cause. Admitted that artificial means had been used to preserve his youthful appearance but maintained firmly that his life expectancy was inherent, not acquired. It was suggested to him that his elder relatives had subjected him without his knowledge to treatment in his early youth to increase his life span. Subject admitted possibility. On being pressed for names of persons who might have performed, or might be performing, such treatments he returned to his original statement that no such treatments exist.

"He gave the names (surprise association procedure) and in some cases the addresses of nearly two hundred members of his kin group not previously identified as such in our

41

records. (List attached) His strength ebbed under this arduous technique and he sank into full apathy from which he could not be roused by any stimuli within the limits of his estimated tolerance (see Bio Report).

"Conclusions under Expedited Analysis, Kelly-Holmes Approximation Method: Subject does not possess and does not believe in the Search Object. Does not remember experiencing Search Object but is mistaken. Knowledge of Search Object is limited to a small group, of the order of twenty. A member of this star group will be located through not more than triple-concatenation elimination search. (Probability of unity, subject to assumptions: first, that topologic social space is continuous and is included in the physical space of the Western Federation and, second, that at least one concatenative path exists between apprehended subjects and star group. Neither assumption can be verified as of this writing, but the first assumption is strongly supported by statistical analysis of the list of names supplied by Subject of previously unsuspected members of Howard kin group, which analysis also supports Subject's estimate of total size of group, and second assumption when taken negatively postulates that star group holding Search Object has been able to apply it with no social-space of contact, an absurdity.)

"Estimated Time for Search: 71 hrs, plus-or-minus 20 hrs. Prediction but not time estimate vouched for by cognizant bureau. Time estimate will be re——"

Ford slapped the report on a stack cluttering his old-fashioned control desk. The dumb fools! Not to recognize a negative report when they saw one—yet they called themselves *psychographers!*

He buried his face in his hands in utter weariness and frustration.

Lazarus rapped on the table beside him, using the butt of his blaster as a gavel. "Don't interrupt the speaker," he boomed, then added, "Go ahead but cut it short."

Bertram Hardy nodded curtly. "I say again, these mayflies we see around us have no rights that we of the Families are bound to respect. We should deal with them with stealth, with cunning, with guile, and when we eventually consolidate our position . . . with *force!* We are no more obligated to respect their welfare than a hunter is obliged to shout a warning at his quarry. The——"

There was a catcall from the rear of the room. Lazarus again banged for order and tried to spot the source. Hardy ploughed steadily on. "The so-called human race has split in two; it is time we admitted it. On one side, *Homo vivens,* ourselves . . . on the other—*Homo moriturus!* With the great

42

lizards, with the sabertooth tiger and the bison, their day is done. We would no more mix our living blood with theirs than we would attempt to breed with apes. I say temporize with them, tell them any tale, assure them that we will bathe them in the fountain of youth—gain time, so that when these two naturally antagonistic races join battle, *as they inevitably must*, the victory will be ours!"

There was no applause but Lazarus could see wavering uncertainty in many faces. Bertram Hardy's ideas ran counter to thought patterns of many years of gentle living yet his words seemed to ring with destiny. Lazarus did not believe in destiny; he believed in . . . well, never mind—but he wondered how Brother Bertram would look with both arms broken.

Eve Barstow got up. "If that is what Bertram means by the survival of the fittest," she said bitterly, "I'll go live with the asocials in Coventry. However, he has offered a plan; I'll have to offer another plan if I won't take his. I won't accept any plan which would have us live at the expense of our poor transient neighbors. Furthermore it is clear to me now that our mere presence, the simple fact of our rich heritage of life, is damaging to the spirit of our poor neighbor. Our longer years and richer opportunities make his best efforts seem futile to him—any effort save a hopeless struggle against an appointed death. Our mere presence saps his strength, ruins his judgment, fills him with panic fear of death.

"So I propose a plan. Let's disclose ourselves, tell *all* the truth, and ask for our share of the Earth, some little corner where we may live apart. If our poor friends wish to surround it with a great barrier like that around Coventry, so be it—it is better that we never meet face to face."

Some expressions of doubt changed to approval. Ralph Schultz stood up. "Without prejudice to Eve's basic plan, I must advise you that it is my professional opinion that the psychological insulation she proposes cannot be accomplished that easily. As long as we're on this planet they won't be able to put us out of their minds. Modern communications——"

"Then we must move to another planet!" she retorted.

"Where?" demanded Bertram Hardy. "Venus? I'd rather live in a steam bath. Mars? Worn-out and worthless."

"We will rebuild it," she insisted.

"Not in your lifetime nor mine. No, my dear Eve, your tenderheartedness sounds well but it doesn't make sense. There is only one planet in the System fit to live on—we're standing on it."

Something in Bertram Hardy's words set off a response in

Lazarus Long's brain, then the thought escaped him. Something . . . something that he had heard of said just a day or two ago . . . or was it longer than? Somehow it seemed to be associated with his first trip out into space, too, well over a century ago. Thunderation! it was maddening to have his memory play tricks on him like that——

Then he had it—the starship! The interstellar ship they were putting the finishing touches on out there between Earth and Luna. "Folks," he drawled, "before we table this idea of moving to another planet, let's consider all the possibilities." He waited until he had their full attention. "Did you ever stop to think that not all the planets swing around this one Sun?"

Zaccur Barstow broke the silence. "Lazarus . . . are you making a serious suggestion?"

"Dead serious."

"It does not sound so. Perhaps you had better explain."

"I will." Lazarus faced the crowd. "There's a spaceship hanging out there in the sky, a roomy thing, built to make the long jumps between stars. Why don't we take it and go looking for our own piece of real estate?"

Bertram Hardy was first to recover. "I don't know whether our chairman is lightening the gloom with another of his wisecracks or not, but, assuming that he is serious, I'll answer. My objection to Mars applies to this wild scheme ten times over. I understand that the reckless fools who are actually intending to man that ship expect to make the jump in about a century—then maybe their grandchildren will find something, or maybe they won't. Either way, I'm not interested. I don't care to spend a century locked up in a steel tank, nor do I expect to live that long. I won't buy it."

"Hold it," Lazarus told him. "Where's Andy Libby?"

"Here," Libby answered, standing up.

"Come on down front. Slipstick, did you have anything to do with designing the new Centarus ship?"

"No. Neither this one nor the first one."

Lazarus spoke to the crowd. "That settles it. If that ship didn't have Slipstick's finger in the drive design, then she's not as fast as she could be, not by a good big coefficient. Slipstick, better get busy on the problem, son. We're likely to need a solution."

"But, Lazarus, you musn't assume that——"

"Aren't there theoretical possibilities?"

"Well, you know there are, but——"

"Then get that carrot top of yours working on it."

"Well . . . all right." Libby blushed as pink as his hair.

"Just a moment, Lazarus." It was Zaccur Barstow. "I like this proposal and I think we should discuss it at length . . .

not let ourselves be frightened off by Brother Bertram's distaste for it. Even if Brother Libby fails to find a better means of propulsion—and frankly, I don't think he will; I know a little something of field mechanics—even so, I shan't let a century frighten me. By using cold-rest and manning the ship in shifts, most of us should be able to complete one hop. There is——"

"What makes you think," demanded Bertram Hardy, "that they'll let *us* man the ship anyhow?"

"Bert," Lazarus said coldly, "address the chair when you want to sound off. You're not even a Family delegate. Last warning."

"As I was saying," Barstow continued, "there is an appropriateness in the long-lived exploring the stars. A mystic might call it our true vocation." He pondered. "As for the ship Lazarus suggested, perhaps they will not let us have that . . . but the Families are rich. If we need a starship—or ships—we can build them, we can pay for them. I think we had better hope that they will let us do this . . . for it may be that there is no way, not another way of any sort, out of our dilemma which does not include our own extermination."

Barstow spoke these last words softly and slowly, with great sadness. They bit into the company like damp chill. To most of them the problem was so new as not yet to be real; no one had voiced the possible consequence of failing to find a solution satisfactory to the short-lived majority. For their senior trustee to speak soberly of his fear that the Families might be exterminated—hunted down and killed—stirred up in each one the ghost they never mentioned.

"Well," Lazarus said briskly when the silence had grown painful, "before we work this idea over, let's hear what other plan anyone has to offer. Speak up."

A messenger hurried in and spoke to Zaccur Barstow. He looked startled and seemed to ask to have the message repeated. He then hurried across the rostrum to Lazarus, whispered to him. Lazarus looked startled. Barstow hurried out.

Lazarus looked back at the crowd. "We'll take a recess," he announced. "Give you time to think about other plans . . . and time for a stretch and a smoke." He reached for his pouch.

"What's up?" someone called out.

Lazarus struck a cigarette, took a long drag, let it drift out. "We'll have to wait and see," he said. "I don't know. But at least half a dozen of the plans put forward tonight we won't have to bother to vote on. The situation has changed again—how much, I couldn't say."

"What do you mean?"

"Well," Lazarus drawled, "it seems the Federation Administrator wanted to talk to Zack Barstow right away. He asked for him by name . . . *and he called over our secret Families' circuit.*"

"Huh? That's impossible!"

"Yep. So is a baby, son."

4

Zaccur Barstow tried to quiet himself down as he hurried into the phone booth.

At the other end of the same videophone circuit the Honorable Slayton Ford was doing the same thing—trying to calm his nerves. He did not underrate himself. A long and brilliant public career crowned by years as Administrator for the Council and under the Covenant of the Western Administration had made Ford aware of his own superior ability and unmatched experience; no ordinary man could possibly make him feel at a disadvantage in negotiation.

But this was different.

What would a man be like who had lived more than two ordinary lifetimes? Worse than that—a man who had had four or five times the adult experience that Ford himself had had? Slayton Ford knew that his own opinions had changed and changed again since his own boyhood; he knew that the boy he had been, or even the able young man he had been, would be no match for the mature man he had become. So what would this Barstow be like? Presumably he was the most able, the most astute, of a group all of whom had had much more experience than Ford could possibly have—how could he guess such a man's evaluations, intentions, ways of thinking, his possible resources?

Ford was certain of only one thing: he did not intend to trade Manhattan Island for twenty-four dollars and a case of whisky, nor sell humanity's birthright for a mess of pottage.

He studied Barstow's face as the image appeared in his phone. A good face and strong . . . it would be useless to try to bully this man. And the man looked young—why, he looked younger than Ford himself! The subconscious image of the Administrator's own stern and implacable grandfather faded out of his mind and his tension eased off. He said quietly, "You are Citzen Zaccur Barstow?"

"Yes, Mister Administrator."

"You are chief executive of the Howard Families?"

"I am the current speaker trustee of our Families' Foundation. But I am responsible to my cousins rather than in authority over them."

Ford brushed it aside. "I assume that your position carries with it leadership. I can't negotiate with a hundred thousand people."

Barstow did not blink. He saw the power play in the sudden admission that the administration knew the true numbers of the Families and discounted it. He had already adjusted himself to the shock of learning that the Families' secret headquarters was no longer secret and the still more upsetting fact that the Administrator knew how to tap into their private communication system; it simply proved that one or more Members had been caught and forced to talk.

So it was now almost certain that the authorities already knew every important fact about the Families.

Therefore it was useless to try to bluff—just the same, don't volunteer any information; they might not have all the facts this soon.

Barstow answered without noticeable pause. "What is it you wish to discuss with me, sir?"

"The policy of the Administration toward your kin group. The welfare of yourself and your relatives."

Barstow shrugged. "What can we discuss? The Convenant has been tossed aside and you have been given power to do as you like with us—to squeeze a secret out of us that we don't have. What can we do but pray for mercy?"

"Please!" The Administrator gestured his annoyance. "Why fence with me? We have a problem, you and I. Let's discuss it openly and try to reach a solution. Yes?"

Barstow answered slowly, "I would like to . . . and I believe that you would like to, also. But the problem is based on a false assumption, that we, the Howard Families, know how to lengthen human life. We don't."

"Suppose I tell you that I know there is no such secret?"

"Mmm . . . I would like to believe you. But how can you reconcile that with the persecution of my people? You've been harrying us like rats."

Ford made a wry face. "There is an old, old story about a theologian who was asked to reconcile the doctrine of Divine mercy with the doctrine of infant damnation. 'The Almighty,' he explained, 'finds it necessary to do things in His official and public capacity which in His private and personal capacity He deplores.' "

Barstow smiled in spite of himself. "I see the analogy. Is it actually pertinent?"

"I think it is."

"So. You didn't call me simply to make a headsman's apology?"

"No. I hope not. You keep in touch with politics? I'm sure

47

you must; your position would require it." Barstow nodded; Ford explained at length:

Ford's administration had been the longest since the signing of the Covenant; he had lasted through four Councils. Nevertheless his control was now so shaky that he could not risk forcing a vote of confidence—certainly not over the Howard Families. On that issue his nominal majority was already a minority. If he refused the present decision of the Council, forced it to a vote of confidence, Ford would be out of office and the present minority leader would take over as administrator. "You follow me? I can either stay in office and try to cope with this problem while restricted by a Council directive with which I do not agree . . . or I can drop out and let my successor handle it."

"Surely you're not asking my advice?"

"No, no! Not on that. I've made my decision. The Action-in-Council would have been carried out in any case, either by me or by Mr. Vanning—so I decided to do it. The question is: will I have your help, or will I not?"

Barstow hesitated, while rapidly reviewing Ford's political career in his mind. The earlier part of Ford's long administration had been almost a golden age of statesmanship. A wise and practical man, Ford had shaped into workable rules the principles of human freedom set forth by Novak in the language of the Covenant. It had been a period of good will, of prosperous expansion, of civilizing processes which seemed to be permanent, irreversible.

Nevertheless a setback had come and Barstow understood the reasons at least as well as Ford did. Whenever the citizens fix their attention on one issue to the exclusion of others, the situation is ripe for scalawags, demagogues, ambitious men on horseback. The Howard Families, in all innocence, had created the crisis in public morals from which they now suffered, through their own action, taken years earlier, in letting the short-lived learn of their existence. It mattered not at all that the "secret" did not exist; the corrupting effect did exist.

Ford at least understood the true situation——

"We'll help," Barstow answered suddenly.

"Good. What do you suggest?"

Barstow chewed his lip. "Isn't there some way you can stall off this drastic action, this violation of the Covenant itself?"

Ford shook his head. "It's too late."

"Even if you went before the public and told the citizens, face to face, that you knew that——"

Ford cut him short. "I wouldn't last in office long enough to make the speech. Nor would I be believed. Besides that —understand me clearly, Zaccur Barstow—no matter what

48

sympathy I may have personally for you and your people, I would not do so if I could. This whole matter is a cancer eating into vitals of our society; it must be settled. I have had my hand forced, true . . . but there is no turning back. It must be pressed on to a solution."

In at least one respect Barstow was a wise man; he knew that another man could oppose him and not be a villain. Nevertheless he protested, "My people are being persecuted."

"Your people," Ford said forcefully, "are a fraction of a tenth of one per cent of all the people . . . and I must find a solution for all! I've called on you to find out if you have any suggestions toward a solution for everyone. Do you?"

"I'm not sure," Barstow answered slowly. "Suppose I concede that you must go ahead with this ugly business of arresting my people, of questioning them by unlawful means—I suppose I have no choice about that——"

"You have no choice. Neither have I." Ford frowned. "It will be carried out as humanely as I can manage it—I am not a free agent."

"Thank you. But, even though you tell me it would be useless for you yourself to go to the people, nevertheless you have enormous propaganda means at your disposal. Would it be possible, while we stall along, to build up a campaign to convince the people of the true facts? Prove to them that there *is* no secret?"

Ford answered, "Ask yourself: will it work?"

Barstow sighed. "Probably not."

"Nor would I consider it a solution even if it would! The people—even my trusted assistants—are clinging to their belief in a fountain of youth because the only alternative is too bitter to think about. Do you know what it would mean to them? For them to believe the bald truth?"

"Go on."

"Death has been tolerable to me only because Death has been the Great Democrat, treating all alike. But now Death plays favorites. Zaccur Barstow, can you understand the bitter, bitter jealousy of the ordinary man of—oh, say 'fifty'—who looks on one of your sort? Fifty years . . . twenty of them he is a child, he is well past thirty before he is skilled in his profession. He is forty before he is established and respected. For not more than the last ten years of his fifty he has really amounted to something."

Ford learned forward in the screen and spoke with sober emphasis: "And now, when he has reached his goal, what is his prize? His eyes are failing him, his bright young strength is gone, his heart and wind are 'not what they used to be.' He is not senile yet . . . but he feels the chill of the first

49

frost. He knows what is in store for him. He knows—he knows!

"But it was inevitable and each man learned to be resigned to it."

"Now *you* come along," Ford went on bitterly. "You shame him in his weakness, you humble him before his children. He dares not plan for the future; you blithely undertake plans that will not mature for fifty years—for a hundred. No matter what success he has achieved, what excellence he has attained, you will catch up with him, pass him—outlive him. In his weakness you are *kind* to him."

"Is it any wonder that he hates you?"

Barstow raised his head wearily. "Do *you* hate me, Slayton Ford?"

"No. No, I cannot afford to hate anyone. But I can tell you this," Ford added suddenly, "had there been a secret, I would have it out of you if I had to tear you to pieces!"

"Yes. I understand that." Barstow paused to think. "There is little that we of the Howard Families can do. We did not plan it this way; it was planned for us. But there is one thing we can offer."

"Yes?"

Barstow explained.

Ford shook his head. "Medically what you suggest is feasible and I have no doubt that a half interest in your heritage would lengthen the span of human life. But even if women were willing to accept the germ plasm of your men—I do not say that they would—it would be psychic death for all other men. There would be an outbreak of frustration and hatred that would split the human race to ruin. No, no matter what we wish, our customs are what they are. We can't breed men like animals; they won't stand for it."

"I know it," agreed Barstow, "but it is all we have to offer . . . a share in our fortune through artificial impregnation."

"Yes. I suppose I should thank you but I feel no thanks and I shan't. Now let's be practical. Individually you old ones are doubtless honorable, lovable men. But as a group you are as dangerous as carriers of plague. So you must be quarantined."

Barstow nodded. "My cousins and I had already reached that conclusion."

Ford looked relieved. "I'm glad you're being sensible about it."

"We can't help ourselves. Well? A segregated colony? Some remote place that would be a Coventry of our own? Madagascar, perhaps? Or we might take the British Isles, build them up again and spread from there into Europe as the radioactivity died down."

Ford shook his head. "Impossible. That would simply leave the problem for my grandchildren to solve. By that time you and yours would have grown in strength; you might defeat us. No, Zaccur Barstow, you and your kin must leave this planet entirely!"

Barstow looked bleak. "I knew it would come to that. Well, where shall we go?"

"Take your choice of the Solar System. Anywhere you like."

"But *where?* Venus is no prize, but even if we chose it, would they accept us? The Venerians won't take orders from Earth; that was settled in 2020. Yes, they now accept screened immigrants under the Four Planets Convention . . . but would they accept a hundred thousand whom Earth found too dangerous to keep? I doubt it."

"So do I. Better pick another planet."

"What planet? In the whole system there is not another body that will support human life as it is. It would take almost superhuman effort, even with unlimited money and the best of modern engineering, to make the most promising of them fit for habitation."

"Make the effort. We will be generous with help."

"I am sure you would. But is that any better solution in the long run than giving us a reservation on Earth? Are you going to put a stop to space travel?"

Ford sat up suddenly. "Oh! I see your thought. I had not followed it through, but let's face it. Why not? Would it not be better to give up space travel than to let this situation degenerate into open war? It was given up once before."

"Yes, when the Venerians threw off their absentee landlords. But it started up again and Luna City is rebuilt and ten times more tonnage moves through the sky than ever did before. Can you stop it? If you can, will it stay stopped?"

Ford turned it over and over in his mind. He could not stop space travel, no administration could. But could an interdict be placed on whatever planet these oldsters were shipped to? And would it help? One generation, two, three . . . what difference would it make? Ancient Japan had tried some solution like that; the foreign devils had come sailing in anyhow. Cultures could not be kept apart forever, and when they did come in contact, the hardier displaced the weaker; that was a natural law.

A permanent and effective quarantine was impossible. That left only one answer—an ugly one. But Ford was tough-minded; he could accept what was necessary. He started making plans, Barstow's presence in the screen forgotten. Once he gave the Chief Provost the location of the Howard Families headquarters it should be reduced in an hour,

51

two at the most . . . unless they had extraordinary defenses—but anywise it was just a matter of time. From those who would be arrested at their headquarters it should be possible to locate and arrest every other member of their group. With luck he would have them all in twenty-four to forty-eight hours.

The only point left undecided in his mind was whether to liquidate them all, or simply to sterilize them. Either would be a final solution and there was no third solution. But which was the more humane?

Ford knew that this would end his career. He would leave office in disgrace, perhaps be sent to Coventry, but he gave it no thought; he was so constituted as to be unable to weigh his own welfare against his concept of his public duty.

Barstow could not read Ford's mind but he did sense that Ford had reached a decision and he surmised correctly how bad that decision must be or himself and his kin. Now was the time, he decided, to risk his one lone trump.

"Mister Administrator——"

"Eh? Oh, sorry! I was preoccupied." That was a vast understatement; he was shockingly embarrassed to find himself still facing a man he had just condemned to death. He gathered formality about him like a robe. "Thank you, Zaccur Barstow, for talking with me. I am sorry that——"

"Mister Administrator!"

"Yes?"

"I propose that you move us entirely out of the Solar System."

"*What?*" Ford blinked. "Are you speaking seriously?"

Barstow spoke rapidly, persuasively, explaining Lazarus Long's half-conceived scheme, improvising details as he went along, skipping over obstacles and emphasizing advantages.

"It might work," Ford at last said slowly. "There are difficulties you have not mentioned, political difficulties and a terrible hazard of time. Still, it might." He stood up. "Go back to your people. Don't spring this on them yet. I'll talk with you later."

Barstow walked back slowly while wondering what he could tell the Members. They would demand a full report; technically he had no right to refuse. But he was strongly inclined to coöperate with the Administrator as long as there was any chance of a favorable outcome. Suddenly making up his mind, he turned, went to his office, and sent for Lazarus.

"Howdy, Zack," Long said as he came in. "How'd the palaver go?"

"Good and bad," Barstow replied. "Listen——" He gave

him a brief, accurate résumé. "Can you go back in there and tell them something that will hold them?"

"Mmm . . . reckon so."

"Then do it and hurry back here."

They did not like the stall Lazarus gave them. They did not want to keep quiet and they did not want to adjourn the meeting. "Where is Zaccur?"—"We demand a report!"— "Why all the mystification?"

Lazarus shut them up with a roar. "Listen to me, you damned idiots! Zack'll talk when he's ready—don't joggle his elbow. He knows what he's doing."

A man near the back stood up. "I'm going home!"

"Do that," Lazarus urged sweetly. "Give my love to the proctors."

The man looked startled and sat down.

"Anybody else want to go home?" demanded Lazarus. "Don't let me stop you. But it's time you bird-brained dopes realized that you have been outlawed. The only thing that stands between you and the proctors is Zack Barstow's ability to talk sweet to the Administrator. So do as you like . . . the meeting's adjourned."

"Look, Zack," said Lazarus a few minutes later, "let's get this straight. Ford is going to use his extraordinary powers to help us glom onto the big ship and make a getaway. Is that right?"

"He's practically committed to it."

"Hmmm—— He'll have to do this while pretending to the Council that everything he does is just a necessary step in squeezing the 'secret' out of us—he's going to double-cross 'em. That right?"

"I hadn't thought that far ahead. I——"

"But that's true, isn't it?"

"Well . . . yes, it must be true."

"Okay. Now, is our boy Ford bright enough to realize what he is letting himself in for and tough enough to go through with it?"

Barstow reviewed what he knew of Ford and added his impressions from the interview. "Yes," he decided, "he knows and he's strong enough to face it."

"All right. Now how about you, pal? Are *you* up to it, too?" Lazarus' voice was accusing.

"Me? What do you mean?"

"You're planning on double-crossing *your* crowd, too, aren't you? Have you got the guts to go through with it when the going gets tough?"

"I don't understand you, Lazarus," Barstow answered worriedly. "I'm not planning to deceive anyone—at least, no member of the Families."

"Better look at your cards again," Lazarus went on remorselessly. "Your part of the deal is to see to it that every man, woman and child takes part in this exodus. Do you expect to sell the idea to each one of them separately and get a hundred thousand people to agree? *Unanimously?* Shucks, you couldn't get that many to whistle 'Yankee Doddle' unanimously."

"But they will *have* to agree," protested Barstow. "They have no choice. We either emigrate, or they hunt us down and kill us. I'm certain that is what Ford intends to do. And he will."

"Then why didn't you walk into the meeting and tell 'em that? Why did you send me in to give 'em a stall?"

Barstow rubbed a hand across his eyes. "I don't know."

"I'll tell you why," continued Lazarus. "You think better with your hunches than most men do with the tops of their minds. You sent me in there to tell 'em a tale because you knew damn' well the truth wouldn't serve. If you told 'em it was get out or get killed, some would get panicky and some would get stubborn. And some old-woman-in-kilts would decide to go home and stand on his Covenant rights. Then he'd spill the scheme before it ever dawned on him that the government was playing for keeps. That's right, isn't it?"

Barstow shrugged and laughed unhappily. "You're right. I didn't have it figured out but you're absolutely right."

"But you did have it figured out," Lazarus assured him. "You had the right answers. Zack, I like your hunches; that's why I'm stringing along. All right, you and Ford are planning to pull a whizzer on every man jack on this globe—I'm asking you again: *have you got the guts to see it through?*"

5   The Members stood around in groups, fretfully. "I can't understand it," the Resident Archivist was saying to a worried circle around her. "The Senior Trustee never interfered in my work before. But he came bursting into my office with that Lazarus Long behind him and ordered me out."

"What did he say?" asked one of her listeners.

"Well, *I* said, 'May I do you a service, Zaccur Barstow?' and he said, 'Yes, you may. Get out and take your girls with you.' Not a word of ordinary courtesy!"

"A lot you've got to complain about," another voice added gloomily. It was Cecil Hedrick, of the Johnson Family, chief communications engineer. "Lazarus Long paid a call on me, and he was a damned sight less polite."

54

"What did he do?"

"He walks into the communication cell and tells me he is going to take over my board—Zaccur's orders. I told him that nobody could touch my burners but me and my operators, and anyhow, where was his authority? You know what he did? You won't believe it but he pulled a blaster on me."

"You don't mean it!"

"I certainly do. I tell you, that man is dangerous. He ought to go for psycho adjustment. He's an atavism if I ever saw one."

Lazarus Long's face stared out of the screen into that of the Administrator. "Got it all canned?" he demanded.

Ford cut the switch on the facsimulator on his desk. "Got it all," he confirmed.

"Okay," the image of Lazarus replied. "I'm clearing." As the screen went blank Ford spoke into his interoffice circuit. "Have the High Chief Provost report to me at once—in corpus."

The public safety boss showed up as ordered with an expression on his lined face in which annoyance struggled with discipline. He was having the busiest night of his career, yet the Old Man had sent orders to report in the flesh. What the devil were viewphones for, anyway, he thought angrily—and asked himself why he had ever taken up police work. He rebuked his boss by being coldly formal and saluting unnecessarily. "You sent for me, sir."

Ford ignored it. "Yes, thank you. Here." He pressed a stud; a film spool popped out of the facsimulator. "This is a complete list of the Howard Families. Arrest them."

"Yes, sir." The Federation police chief stared at the spool and debated whether or not to ask how it had been obtained—it certainly hadn't come through *his* office . . . did the Old Man have an intelligence service he didn't even know about?

"It's alphabetical, but keyed geographically," the Administrator was saying. "After you put it through sorters, send the —no, *bring* the original back to me. You can stop the psycho interviews, too," he added. "Just bring them in and hold them. I'll give you more instructions later."

The High Chief Provost decided that this was not a good time to show curiosity. "Yes, sir." He saluted stiffly and left.

Ford turned back to his desk controls and sent word that he wanted to see the chiefs of the bureaus of land resources and of transportation control. On afterthought he added the chief of the bureau of consumption logistics.

Back in the Families' Seat a rump session of the trustees was meeting; Barstow was absent. "I don't like it," Andrew

55

Weatherall was saying. "I could understand Zaccur deciding to delay reporting to the Members but I had supposed that he simply wanted to talk to us first. I certainly did expect him to consult us. What do you make of it, Philip?"

Philip Hardy chewed his lip. "I don't know. Zaccur's got a head on his shoulders . . . but it certainly seems to me that he should have called us together and advised with us. Has he spoken with you, Justin?"

"No, he has not," Justin Foote answered frigidly.

"Well, what should we do? We can't very well call him in and demand an accounting unless we are prepared to oust him from office and if he refuses. I, for one, am reluctant to do that."

They were still discussing it when the proctors arrived.

Lazarus heard the commotion and correctly interpreted it—no feat, since he had information that his brethren lacked. He was aware that he should submit peacefully and conspicuously to arrest—set a good example. But old habits die hard; he postponed the inevitable by ducking into the nearest men's 'fresher.

It was a dead end. He glanced at the air duct—no, too small. While thinking he fumbled in his pouch for a cigarette; his hand found a strange object, he pulled it out. It was the brassard he had "borrowed" from the proctor in Chicago.

When the proctor working point of the mop-squad covering that wing of the Seat stuck his head into that 'fresher, he found another "proctor" already there. "Nobody in here," announced Lazarus. "I've checked it."

"How the devil did you get ahead of me?"

"Around your flank. Stoney Island Tunnel and through their air vents." Lazarus trusted that the real cop would be unaware that there was no Stoney Island Tunnel. "Got a cigarette on you?"

"Huh? This is no time to catch a smoke."

"Shucks," said Lazarus, "my legate is a good mile away."

"Maybe so," the proctor replied, "but mine is right behind us."

"So? Well, skip it—I've got something to tell him anyhow." Lazarus started to move past but the proctor did not get out of his way. He was glancing curiously at Lazarus' kilt. Lazarus had turned it inside out and its blue lining made a fair imitation of a proctor's service uniform—if not inspected closely.

"What station did you say you were from?" inquired the proctor.

"This one," answered Lazarus and planted a short jab under the man's breastbone. Lazarus' coach in rough-and-tumble had explained to him that a solar plexus blow was

56

harder to dodge than one to the jaw; the coach had been dead since the roads strike of 1966, his skill lived on.

Lazarus felt more like a cop with a proper uniform kilt and a bandolier of paralysis bombs slung under his left arm. Besides, the proctor's kilt was a better fit. To the right the passage outside led to the Sanctuary and a dead end; he went to the left by Hobson's choice although he knew he would run into his unconscious benefactor's legate. The passage gave into a hall which was crowded with Members herded into a group of proctors. Lazarus ignored his kin and sought out the harassed officer in charge. "Sir," he reported, saluting smartly, "There's sort of a hospital back there. You'll need fifty or sixty stretchers."

"Don't bother me, tell your legate. We've got our hands full."

Lazarus almost did not answer; he had caught Mary Sperling's eye in the crowd—she stared at him and looked away. He caught himself and answered, "Can't tell him, sir. Not available."

"Well, go on outside and tell the first-aid squad."

"Yes, sir." He moved away, swaggering a little, his thumbs hooked in the band of his kilt. He was far down the passage leading to the transbelt tunnel serving the Waukegan outlet when he heard shouts behind him. Two proctors were running to overtake him.

Lazarus stopped in the archway giving into the transbelt tunnel and waited for them. "What's the trouble?" he asked easily as they came up.

"The legate——" began one. He got no further; a paralysis bomb tinkled and popped at his feet. He looked surprised as the radiations wiped all expression from his face; his mate fell across him.

Lazarus waited behind a shoulder of the arch, counted seconds up to fifteen: "Number one jet fire! Number two jet fire! Number three jet fire!"—added a couple to be sure the paralyzing effect had died away. He had cut it finer than he liked. He had not ducked quite fast enough and his left foot tingled from exposure.

He then checked. The two were unconscious, no one else was in sight. He mounted the transbelt. Perhaps they had not been looking for him in his proper person, perhaps no one had given him away. But he did not hang around to find out. One thing he was damn' well certain of, he told himself, if anybody had squealed on him, it wasn't Mary Sperling.

It took two more parabombs and a couple of hundred words of pure fiction to get him out into the open air. Once he was there and out of immediate observation the brassard and the remaining bombs went into his pouch and the bandolier ended up behind some bushes; he then looked up a clothing store in Waukegan.

He sat down in a sales booth and dialed the code for kilts. He let cloth designs flicker past in the screen while he ignored the persuasive voice of the catalogue until a pattern showed up which was distinctly unmilitary and not blue, whereupon he stopped the display and punched an order for his size. He noted the price, tore an open-credit voucher from his wallet, stuck it into the machine and pushed the switch. Then he enjoyed a smoke while the tailoring was done.

Ten minutes later he stuffed the proctor's kilt into the refuse hopper of the sales booth and left, nattily and loudly attired. He had not been in Waukegan the past century but he found a middle-priced autel without drawing attention by asking questions, dialed its registration board for a standard suite and settled down for seven hours of sound sleep.

He breakfasted in his suite, listening with half an ear to the news box; he was interested, in a mild way, in hearing what might be reported concerning the raid on the Families. But it was a detached interest; he had already detached himself from it in his own mind. It had been a mistake, he now realized, to get back in touch with the Families—a darn good thing he was clear of it all with his present public identity totally free of any connection with the whing-ding.

A phrase caught his attention: "—including Zaccur Barstow, alleged to be their tribal chief.

"The prisoners are being shipped to a reservation in Oklahoma, near the ruins of the Okla-Orleans road city about twenty-five miles east of Harriman Memorial Park. The Chief Provost describes it as a 'Little Coventry,' and has ordered all aircraft to avoid it by ten miles laterally. The Administrator could not be reached for a statement but a usually reliable source inside the administration informs us that the mass arrest was accomplished in order to speed up the investigations whereby the administration expects to obtain the 'Secret of the Howard Families'—their techniques for indefinitely prolonging life. This forthright action in arresting and transporting every member of the outlaw group is expected to have a salutary effect in breaking down the resistance of their leaders to the legitimate demands of society. It will bring home forcibly to them that the civil rights enjoyed by decent citizens must not be used as a cloak behind which to damage society as a whole.

"The chattels and holdings of the members of this criminal conspiracy have been declared subject to the Conservator General and will be administered by his agents during the imprisonment of——"

Lazarus switched it off. "Damnation!" he thought. "Don't

fret about things you can't help." Of course, he had expected to be arrested himself . . . but he had escaped. That was that. It wouldn't do the Families any good for him to turn himself in—and besides, he owed the Families nothing, not a tarnation thing.

Anyhow, they were better off all arrested at once and quickly placed under guard. If they had been smelled out one at a time, anything could have happened—lynchings, even pogroms. Lazarus knew from hard experience how close under the skin lay lynch law and mob violence in the most sweetly civilized; that was why he had advised Zack to rig it—that and the fact that Zack and the Administrator had to have the Families in one compact group to stand a chance of carrying out their scheme. They were well off . . . and no skin off his nose.

But he wondered how Zack was getting along, and what he would think of Lazarus' disappearance. And what Mary Sperling thought—it must have been a shock to her when he turned up making a noise like a proctor. He wished he could straighten that out with her.

Not that it mattered what any of them thought. They would all either be light-years away very soon . . . or dead. A closed book.

He turned to the phone and called the post office. "Captain Aaron Sheffield," he announced, and gave his postal number. "Last registered with Goddard Field post office. Will you please have my mail sent to——" He leaned closer and read the code number from the suite's mail receptacle.

"Service," assented the voice of the clerk. "Right away, Captain."

"Thank you."

It would take a couple of hours, he reflected, for his mail to catch up with him—a half hour in trajectory, three times that in fiddle-faddle. Might as well wait here . . . no doubt the search for him had lost itself in the distance but there was nothing in Waukegan he wanted. Once the mail showed up he would hire a U-push-it and scoot down to——

To where? What was he going to do now?

He turned several possibilities over in his mind and came at last to the blank realization that there was nothing, from one end of the Solar System to the other, that he really wanted to do.

It scared him a little. He had once heard, and was inclined to credit, that a loss of interest in living marked the true turning point in the battle between anabolism and catabolism —old age. He suddenly envied normal short-lived people— at least they could go make nuisances of themselves to their children. Filial affection was not customary among Members of the Families; it was not a feasible relationship to maintain for a century or more. And friendship, except between Members, was bound to be regarded as a passing and shallow matter. There was no one whom Lazarus wanted to see.

Wait a minute . . . who was that planter on Venus? The one who knew so many folk songs and who was so funny when he was drunk? He'd go look him up. It would make a nice hop and it would be fun, much as he disliked Venus.

Then he recalled with cold shock that he had not seen the man for—how long? In any case, he was certainly dead by now.

Libby had been right, he mused glumly, when he spoke of the necessity for a new type of memory association for the long-lived. He hoped the lad would push ahead with the necessary research and come up with an answer before Lazarus was reduced to counting on his fingers. He dwelt on the notion for a minute or two before recalling that he was most unlikely ever to see Libby again.

The mail arrived and contained nothing of importance. He was not surprised; he expected no personal letters. The spools of advertising went into the refuse chute; he read only one item, a letter from Pan-Terra Docking Corp. telling him that his convertible cruiser *I Spy* had finished her overhaul and had been moved to a parking dock, rental to start forthwith. As instructed, they had not touched the ship's astrogational controls—was that still the Captain's pleasure?

He decided to pick her up later in the day and head out into space. Anything was better than sitting Earthbound and admitting that he was bored.

Paying his score and finding a jet for hire occupied less than twenty minutes. He took off and headed for Goddard Field, using the low local-traffic level to avoid entering the control pattern with a flight plan. He was not consciously avoiding the police because he had no reason to think that they could be looking for "Captain Sheffield"; it was simply habit, and it would get him to Goddard Field soon enough.

But long before he reached there, while over eastern Kansas, he decided to land and did so.

He picked the field of a town so small as to be unlikely to rate a full-time proctor and there he sought out a phone booth away from the field. Inside it, he hesitated. How did you go about calling up the head man of the entire Federation—and get him? If he simply called Novak Tower and asked for Administrator Ford, he not only would not be put through to him but his call would be switched to the Department of Public Safety for some unwelcome inquiries, sure as taxes.

Well, there was only one way to beat that, and that was to call the Department of Safety himself and, somehow, get the Chief Provost on the screen—after that he would play by ear.

"Department of Civil Safety," a voice answered. "What service, citizen?"

"Service to you," he began in his best control-bridge voice. "I am Captain Sheffield. Give me the Chief." He was not overbearing; his manner simply assumed obedience.

Short silence—— "What is it about, please?"

"I said I was *Captain Sheffield*." This time Lazarus' voice showed restrained annoyance.

Another short pause—— "I'll connect you with the Chief Deputy's office," the voice said doubtfully.

This time the screen came to life. "Yes?" asked the Chief Deputy, looking him over.

"Get me the Chief—hurry."

"What's it about?"

"Good Lord, man—get me the Chief! I'm *Captain Sheffield!*"

The Chief Deputy must be excused for connecting him; he had had no sleep and more confusing things had happened in the last twenty-four hours than he had been able to assimilate. When the High Chief Provost appeared in the screen, Lazarus spoke first. "Oh, there you are! I've had the damnedest time cutting through your red tape. Get me the Old Man and *move!* Use your closed circuit."

"What the devil do you mean? Who are you?"

"Listen, brother," said Lazarus in tones of slow exasperation, "I would not have routed through your damned hidebound department if I hadn't been in a jam. Cut me in to the Old Man. *This is about the Howard Families.*"

The police chief was instantly alert. "Make your report."

"Look," said Lazarus in tired tones, "I know you would like to look over the Old Man's shoulder, but this isn't a good time to try. If you obstruct me and force me to waste two hours by reporting in corpus, I will. But the Old Man will want to know why and you can bet your pretty parade kit, I'll tell him."

The Chief Provost decided to take a chance—cut this character in on a three-way; then, if the Old Man didn't burn this joker off the screen in about three seconds, he'd know he had played safe and guessed lucky. If he did—well, you could always blame it on a cross-up in communications. He set the combo.

Administrator Ford looked flabbergasted when he recognized Lazarus in the screen. "You?" he exclaimed. "How on Earth——Did Zaccur Barstow——"

"*Seal your circuit!*" Lazarus cut in.

The Chief Provost blinked as his screen went dead and

silent. So the Old Man *did* have secret agents outside the department . . . interesting—and not to be forgotten.

Lazarus gave Ford a quick and fairly honest account of how he happened to be at large, then added, "So you see, I could have gone to cover and escaped entirely. In fact I still can. But I want to know this: is the deal with Zaccur Barstow to let us emigrate still on?"

"Yes, it is."

"Have you figured out how you are going to get a hundred thousand people inboard the *New Frontiers* without tipping your hand? You can't trust your own people, you know that."

"I know. The present situation is a temporary expedient while we work it out."

"And I'm the man for the job. I've got to be, I'm the only agent on the loose that either one of you can afford to trust. Now listen——"

Eight minutes later Ford was nodding his head slowly and saying, "It might work. It might. Anyway, you start your preparations. I'll have a letter of credit waiting for you at Goddard."

"Can you cover your tracks on that? I can't flash a letter of credit from the Administrator; people would wonder."

"Credit me with some intelligence. By the time it reaches you it will appear to be a routine banking transaction."

"Sorry. Now how can I get through to you when I need to?"

"Oh, yes—note this code combination." Ford recited it slowly. "That puts you through to my desk without relay. No, don't write it down; memorize it."

"And how can I talk to Zack Barstow?"

"Call me and I'll hook you in. You can't call him directly unless you can arrange a sensitive circuit."

"Even if I could, I can't cart a sensitive around with me. Well, cheerio—I'm clearing."

"Good luck!"

Lazarus left the phone booth with restrained haste and hurried back to reclaim his hired ship. He did not know enough about current police practice to guess whether or not the High Chief Provost had traced the call to the Administrator; he simply took it for granted because he himself would have done so in the Provost's shoes. Therefore the nearest available proctor was probably stepping on his heels —time to move, time to mess up the trail a little.

He took off again and headed west, staying in the local, uncontrolled low level until he reached a cloud bank that walled the western horizon. He then swung back and cut air for Kansas City, staying carefully under the speed limit and flying as low as local traffic regulations permitted. At Kansas City he turned his ship in to the local U-push-it agency and flagged a ground taxi, which carried him down the controlway to Joplin. There he boarded a local jet bus from St. Louis without buying a ticket first, thereby insuring that his flight would not be recorded until the bus's trip records were turned in on the west coast.

Instead of worrying he spent the time making plans.

One hundred thousand people with an average mass of a hundred and fifty—no, make it a hundred and sixty pounds, Lazarus reconsidered—a hundred and sixty each made a load of sixteen million pounds, eight thousand tons. The *I Spy* could boost such a load against one gravity but she would be as logy as baked beans. It was out of the question anyhow; people did not stow like cargo; the *I Spy* could lift that dead weight—but "dead" was the word, for that was what they would be.

He needed a transport.

Buying a passenger ship big enough to ferry the Families from Earth up to where the *New Frontiers* hung in her construction orbit was not difficult; Four Planets Passenger Service would gladly unload such a ship at a fair price. Passenger trade competition being what it was, they were anxious to cut their losses on older ships no longer popular with tourists. But a passenger ship would not do; not only would there be unhealthy curiosity in what he intended to do with such a ship, but—and this settled it—he could not pilot it single-handed. Under the Revised Space Precautionary Act, passenger ships were required to be built for human control throughout on the theory that no automatic safety device could replace human judgment in an emergency.

It would have to be a freighter.

Lazarus knew the best place to find one. Despite efforts to make the Moon colony ecologically self-sufficient, Luna City still imported vastly more tonnage than she exported. On Earth this would have resulted in "empties coming back"; in space transport it was sometimes cheaper to let empties accumulate, especially on Luna where an empty freighter was worth more as metal than it had cost originally as a ship back Earthside.

He left the bus when it landed at Goddard City, went to the space field, paid his bills, and took possession of the *I Spy,* filed a request for earliest available departure for Luna. The slot he was assigned was two days from then, but Lazarus did not let it worry him; he simply went back to the docking company and indicated that he was willing to pay liberally for a swap in departure time. In twenty minutes he had oral assurance that he could boost for Luna that evening.

He spent the remaining several hours in the maddening red tape of interplanetary clearance. He first picked up the letter of credit Ford had promised him and converted it into cash. Lazarus would have been quite willing to use a chunk of the cash to speed up his processing just as he had paid (quite legally) for a swap in slot with another ship. But he found himself unable to do so. Two centuries of survival had taught him that a bribe must be offered as gently and as indirectly as a gallant suggestion is made to a proud lady; in a very few minutes he came to the glum conclusion that civic virtue and public honesty could be run into the ground—the functionaries at Goddard Field seemed utterly innocent of the very notion of cumshaw, squeeze, or the lubricating effect of money in routine transactions. He admired their incorruptibility; he did not have to like it—most especially when filling out useless forms cost him the time he had intended to devote to a gourmet's feast in the Skygate Room.

He even let himself be vaccinated again rather than go back to the *I Spy* and dig out the piece of paper that showed he had been vaccinated on arrival Earthside a few weeks earlier.

Nevertheless, twenty minutes before his revised slot time, he lay at the controls of the *I Spy,* his pouch bulging with stamped papers and his stomach not bulging with the sandwich he had managed to grab. He had worked out the "Hohmann's-S" trajectory he would use; the results had been fed into the autopilot. All the lights on his board were green save the one which would blink green when field control started his count down. He waited in the warm happiness that always filled him when about to boost.

A thought hit him and he raised up against his straps. Then he loosened the chest strap and sat up, reached for his copy of the current *Terra Pilot and Traffic Hazards Supplement.* Mmm . . .

New Frontiers hung in a circular orbit of exactly twenty-four hours, keeping always over meridian 106° west at declination zero at a distance from Earth center of approximately twenty-six thousand miles.

Why not pay her a call, scout out the lay of the land?

The *I Spy,* with tanks topped off and cargo spaces empty, had many mile-seconds of reserve boost. To be sure, the field had cleared him for Luna City, not for the interstellar ship . . . but, with the Moon in its present phase, the deviation from his approved flight pattern would hardly show on a screen, probably would not be noticed until the film record was analyzed at some later time—at which time Lazarus would receive a traffic citation, perhaps even have his license suspended. But traffic tickets had never worried him . . . and it was certainly worthwhile to reconnoitre.

He was already setting up the problem in his ballistic calculator. Aside from checking the orbit elements of the *New Frontiers* in the *Terra Pilot* Lazarus could have done it in his sleep; satellite-matching maneuvers were old hat for any pilot and a doubly-tangent trajectory for a twenty-four hour orbit was one any student pilot knew by heart.

He fed the answers into his autopilot during the count down, finished with three minutes to spare, strapped himself down again and relaxed as the acceleration hit him. When the ship went into free fall, he checked his position and vector via the field's transponder. Satisfied, he locked his board, set the alarm for rendezvous, and went to sleep.

6

About four hours later the alarm woke him. He switched it off; it continued to ring—a glance at his screen showed him why. The Gargantuan cylindrical body of the *New Frontiers* lay close aboard. He switched off the radar alarm circuit as well and completed matching with her by the seat of his pants, not bothering with the ballistic calculator. Before he had completed the maneuver the communications alarm started beeping. He slapped a switch; the rig hunted frequencies and the vision screen came to life. A man looked at him. *"New Frontiers* calling: what ship are you?"

"Private vessel *I Spy*, Captain Sheffield. My compliments to your commanding officer. May I come inboard to pay a call?"

They were pleased to have visitors. The ship was completed save for inspection, trials, and acceptance; the enormous gang which had constructed her had gone to Earth and there was no one aboard but the representatives of the Jordan Foundation and a half dozen engineers employed by the corporation which had been formed to build the ship for the foundation. These few were bored with inactivity, bored with each other, anxious to quit marking time and get back to the pleasures of Earth; a visitor was a welcome diversion.

When the *I Spy's* airlock had been sealed to that of the big ship, Lazarus was met by the engineer in charge—technically "captain" since the *New Frontiers* was a ship under way even though not under power. He introduced himself and took Lazarus on a tour of the ship. They floated through miles of corridors, visited laboratories, storerooms, libraries containing hundreds of thousands of spools, acres of hydroponic tanks for growing food and replenishing oxygen, and comfortable, spacious, even luxurious quarters for a crew colony of ten thousand people. "We believe that the *Vanguard* expedition was somewhat undermanned," the skipper-engineer explained. "The socio-dynamicists calculate that this colony will be able to maintain the basics of our present level of culture."

"Doesn't sound like enough," Lazarus commented. "Aren't there more than ten thousand types of specialization?"

"Oh, certainly! But the idea is to provide experts in all basic arts and indispensable branches of knowledge. Then, as the colony expands, additional specializations can be added through the aid of the reference libraries—anything from tap-dancing to tapestry weaving. That's the general idea though it's out of my line. Interesting subject, no doubt, for those who like it."

"Are you anxious to get started?" asked Lazarus.

The man looked almost shocked. "Me? D'you mean to suggest that *I* would go in this thing? My dear sir, I'm an engineer, not a damn' fool."

"Sorry."

"Oh, I don't mind a resonable amount of spacing when there's a reason for it—I've been to Luna City more times than I can count and I've even been to Venus. But you don't think the man who built the *Mayflower* sailed in her, do you? For my money the only thing that will keep these people who signed up for it from going crazy before they get there is that it's a dead cinch they're all crazy before they start."

Lazarus changed the subject. They did not dally in the main drive space, nor in the armored cell housing the giant atomic converter, once Lazarus learned that they were unmanned, fully-automatic types. The total absence of moving parts in each of these divisions, made possible by recent developments in parastatics, made their inner workings of intellectual interest only, which could wait. What Lazarus did want to see was the control room, and there he lingered, asking endless questions until his host was plainly bored and remaining only out of politeness.

Lazarus finally shut up, not because he minded imposing on this host but because he was confident that he had learned enough about the controls to be willing to chance conning the ship.

He picked up two other important data before he left the ship: in nine Earth days the skeleton crew was planning a weekend on Earth, following which the acceptance trials would be held. But for three days the big ship would be empty, save possibly for a communications operator—Lazarus was too wary to be inquisitive on this point. But there would be no guard left in her because no need for a guard could be imagined. One might as well guard the Mississippi River.

The other thing he learned was how to enter the ship from the outside without help from the inside; he picked that datum up through watching the mail rocket arrive just as he was about to leave the ship.

At Luna City, Joseph McFee, factor for Diana Terminal Corp., subsidiary of Diana Freight Lines, welcomed Lazarus warmly. "Well! Come in, Cap'n, and pull up a chair. What'll you drink?" He was already pouring as he talked—tax-free paint-remover from his own amateur vacuum still. "Haven't seen you in . . . well, too long. Where d'you raise from last and what's the gossip there? Heard any new ones?"

"From Goddard," Lazarus answered and told him what the skipper had said to the V.I.P. McFee answered with the one about the old maid in free fall, which Lazarus pretended not to have heard. Stories led to politics, and McFee expounded his notion of the "only possible solution" to the European questions, a solution predicated on a complicated theory of McFee's as to why the Covenant could not be extended to any culture below a certain level of industrialization. Lazarus did not give a hoot either way but he knew better than to hurry McFee; he nodded at the right places, accepted more of the condemned rocket juice when offered, and waited for the right moment to come to the point.

"Any company ships for sale now, Joe?"

"Are there? I should hope to shout. I've got more steel sitting out on that plain and cluttering my inventory than I've had in ten years. Looking for some? I can make you a sweet price."

"Maybe. Maybe not. Depends on whether you've got what I want."

"You name it, I've got it. Never saw such a dull market. Some days you can't turn an honest credit." McFee frowned. "You know what the trouble is? Well, I'll tell you—it's this Howard Families commotion. Nobody wants to risk any money until he knows where he stands. How can a man make plans when he doesn't know whether to plan for ten years or a hundred? You mark my words: if the administration manages to sweat the secret loose from those babies, you'll see the biggest boom in long-term investments ever. But if not . . . well, long-term holdings won't be worth a peso a dozen and there will be an eat-drink-and-be-merry craze that will make the Reconstruction look like a tea party."

He frowned again. "What kind of metal you looking for?"

"I don't want metal, I want a ship."

McFee's frown disappeared, his eyebrows shot up. "So? What sort?"

"Can't say exactly. Got time to look 'em over with me?"

They suited up and left the dome by North Tunnel, then strolled around grounded ships in the long, easy strides of low gravity. Lazarus soon saw that just two ships had both the lift and the air space needed. One was a tanker and the better buy, but a mental calculation showed him that it lacked deck space, even including the floor plates of the tanks, to accommodate eight thousand tons of passengers. The other was an older ship with cranky piston-type injection meters, but she was fitted for general merchandise and had enough deck space. Her pay load was higher than necessary for the job, since passengers weigh little for the cubage they clutter—but that would make her lively, which might be critically important.

As for the injectors, he could baby them—he had herded worse junk than this.

Lazarus haggled with McFee over terms, not because he wanted to save money but because failure to do so would have been out of character. They finally reached a complicated three-cornered deal in which McFee bought the *I Spy* for himself, Lazarus delivered clear title to it unmortgaged and accepted McFee's unsecured note in payment, then purchased the freighter by endorsing McFee's note back to him and adding cash. McFee in turn would be able to mortgage the *I Spy* at the Commerce Clearance Bank in Luna City, use the proceeds plus cash or credit of his own to redeem his own paper—presumably before his accounts were audited, though Lazarus did not quite mention that.

It was not quite a bribe. Lazarus merely made use of the fact that McFee had long wanted a ship of his own and regarded the *I Spy* as the ideal bachelor's go-buggy for business or pleasure; Lazarus simply held the price down to where McFee could swing the deal. But the arrangements made certain that McFee would not gossip about the deal, at least until he had had time to redeem his note. Lazarus further confused the issue by asking McFee to keep his eyes open for a good buy in trade tobacco . . . which made McFee sure that Captain Sheffield's mysterious new venture involved Venus, that being the only major market for such goods.

Lazarus got the freighter ready for space in only four days through lavish bonuses and overtime payments. At last he dropped Luna City behind him, owner and master of the *City of Chillicothe*. He shortened the name in his mind to *Chili* in honor of a favorite dish he had not tasted in a long time—fat red beans, plenty of chili powder, chunks of meat . . . real meat, not the synthetic pap these youngsters called "meat." He thought about it and his mouth watered.

He had not a care in the world.

As he approached Earth, he called traffic control and asked

for a parking orbit, as he did not wish to put the *Chili* down; it would waste fuel and attract attention. He had no scruples about orbiting without permission but there was a chance that the *Chili* might be spotted, charted, and investigated as a derelict during his absence; it was safer to be legal.

They gave him an orbit; he matched in and steadied down, then set the *Chili's* identification beacon to his own combination, made sure that the radar of the ship's gig could trip it, and took the gig down to the auxiliary small-craft field at Goddard. He was careful to have all necessary papers with him this time; by letting the gig be sealed in bond he avoided customs and was cleared through the space port quickly. He had no destination in mind other than to find a public phone and check in with Zack and Ford—then, if there was time, try to find some real chili. He had not called the Administrator from space because ship-to-ground required relay, and the custom of privacy certainly would not protect them if the mixer who handled the call overheard a mention of the Howard Families.

The Administrator answered his call at once, although it was late at night in the longitude of Novak Tower. From the puffy circles under Ford's eyes Lazarus judged that he had been living at his desk. "Hi," said Lazarus, "better get Zack Barstow on a three-way. I've got things to report."

"So it's you," Ford said grimly. "I thought you had run out on us. Where have you been?"

"Buying a ship," Lazarus answered. "As you knew. Let's get Barstow."

Ford frowned, but turned to his desk. By split screen, Barstow joined them. He seemed surprised to see Lazarus and not altogether relieved. Lazarus spoke quickly:

"What's the matter, pal? Didn't Ford tell you what I was up to?"

"Yes, he did," admitted Barstow, "but we didn't know where you were or what you were doing. Time dragged on and you didn't check in . . . so we decided we had seen the last of you."

"Shucks," complained Lazarus, "you know I wouldn't ever do anything like *that*. Anyhow, here I am and here's what I've done so far——" He told them of the *Chili* and of his reconnaissance of the *New Frontiers*. "Now here's how I see it: sometimes this weekend, while the *New Frontiers* is sitting out there with nobody inboard her, I set the *Chili* down in the prison reservation, we load up in a hurry, rush out to the *New Frontiers*, grab her, and scoot. Mr. Adminstrator, that calls for a lot of help from you. Your proctors will have to look the other way while I land and load. Then we need to sort of slide past the traffic patrol. After that it would be a whole lot better if no naval craft was in a position to do anything drastic about the *New Frontiers*—if there is a communication watch left in her, they may be able to holler for help before we can silence them."

"Give me credit for some foresight," Ford answered sourly. "I know you will have to have a diversion to stand any chance of getting away with it. The scheme is fantastic at the best."

"Not too fantastic," Lazarus disagreed, "if you are willing to use your emergency powers to the limit at the last minute."

"Possibly. But we can't wait four days."

"Why not?"

"The situation won't hold together that long."

"Neither will mine," put in Barstow.

Lazarus looked from one to the other. "Huh? What's the trouble? What's up?"

They explained:

Ford and Barstow were engaged in a presposterously improbable task, that of putting over a complex and subtle fraud, a triple fraud with a different face for the Families, for the public, and for the Federation Council. Each aspect presented unique and apparently insurmountable difficulties.

Ford had no one whom he dared take into his confidence, for even his most trusted personal staff member might be infected with the mania of the delusional Fountain of Youth . . . or might not be, but there was no way to know without compromising the conspiracy. Despite this, he had to convince the Council that the measures he was taking were the best for achieving the Council's purpose.

Besides that, he had to hand out daily news releases to convince the citizens that their government was just about to gain for them the "secret" of living forever. Each day the statements had to be more detailed, the lies more tricky. The people were getting restless at the delay; they were sloughing off the coat of civilization, becoming mob.

The Council was feeling the pressure of the people. Twice Ford had been forced to a vote of confidence; the second he had won by only two votes. "I won't win another one—we've got to *move*."

Barstow's troubles were different but just as sticky. He had to have confederates, because his job was to prepare all the hundred thousand members for the exodus. They had to know, before the time came to embark, if they were to leave quietly and quickly. Nevertheless he did not dare tell them the truth too soon because among so many people there were bound to be some who were stupid and stubborn . . . and it required just one fool to wreck the scheme by spilling it to the proctors guarding them.

Instead he was forced to try to find leaders whom he could trust, convince them, and depend on them to convince others. He needed almost a thousand dependable "herdsmen" to be sure of getting his people to follow him when the time came. Yet the very number of confederates he needed was so great as to make certain that somebody would prove weak.

Worse than that, he needed other confederates for a still touchier purpose. Ford and he had agreed on a scheme, weak at best, for gaining time. They were doling out the techniques used by the Families in delaying the symptoms of senility under the pretense that the sum total of these techniques was the "secret." To put over this fraud Barstow had to have the help of the biochemists, gland therapists, specialists in symbiotics and in metabolism, and other experts among the Families, and these in turn had to be prepared for police interrogation by the Families' most skilled psychotechnicians . . . because they had to be able to put over the fraud even under the influence of babble drugs. The hypnotic false indoctrination required for this was enormously more complex than that necessary for a simple block against talking. Thus far the swindle had worked . . . fairly well. But the discrepancies became more hard to explain each day.

Barstow could not keep these matters juggled much longer. The great mass of the Families, necessarily kept in ignorance, were getting out of hand even faster than the public outside. They were rightfully angry at what had been done to them; they expected anyone in authority to do something about it —and do it now!

Barstow's influence over his kin was melting away as fast as that of Ford over the Council.

"It can't be four days," repeated Ford. "More like twelve hours . . . twenty-four at the outside. The Council meets again tomorrow afternoon."

Barstow looked worried. "I'm not sure I can prepare them in so short a time. I may have trouble getting them aboard."

"Don't worry about it," Ford snapped.

"Why not?"

"Because," Ford said bluntly, "any who stay behind will be dead—if they're lucky."

Barstow said nothing and looked away. It was the first time that either one of them had admitted explicitly that this was no relatively harmless piece of political chicanery but a desperate and nearly hopeless attempt to avoid a massacre . . . and that Ford himself was on both sides of the fence.

"Well," Lazarus broke in briskly, "now that you boys have settled that, let's get on with it. I can ground the *Chili* in——" He stopped and estimated quickly where she would be in orbit, how long it would take him to rendezvous. "—well, by

71

twenty-two Greenwich. Add an hour to play safe. How about seventeen o'clock Oklahoma time tomorrow afternoon? That's today, actually."

The other two seemed relieved. "Good enough," agreed Barstow. "I'll have them in the best shape I can manage."

"All right," agreed Ford, "if that's the fastest it can be done." He thought for a moment. "Barstow, I'll withdraw at once all proctors and government personnel now inside the reservation barrier and shut you off. Once the gate contracts, you can tell them all."

"Right. I'll do my best."

"Anything else before we clear?" asked Lazarus. "Oh, yes—Zack, we'd better pick a place for me to land, or I may shorten a lot of lives with my blast."

"Uh, yes. Make your approach from the west. I'll rig a standard berth marker. Okay?"

"Okay."

"Not okay," denied Ford. "We'll have to give him a pilot beam to come in on."

"Nonsense," objected Lazarus. "I could set her down on top of the Washington Monument."

"Not this time, you couldn't. Don't be surprised at the weather."

As Lazarus approached his rendezvous with the *Chili* he signalled from the gig; the *Chili's* transponder echoed, to his relief—he had little faith in gear he had not personally overhauled and a long search for the *Chili* at this point would have been disastrous.

He figured the relative vector, gunned the gig, flipped, and gunned to brake—homed-in three minutes off estimate, feeling smug. He cradled the gig, hurried inside, and took her down.

Entering the stratosphere and circling two-thirds of the globe took no longer than he had estimated. He used part of the hour's leeway he had allowed himself by being very stingy in his maneuvers in order to spare the worn, obsolescent injection meters. Then he was down in the troposphere and making his approach, with skin temperatures high but not dangerously so. Presently he realized what Ford had meant about the weather. Oklahoma and half of Texas were covered with deep, thick clouds. Lazarus was amazed and somehow pleased; it reminded him of other days, when weather was something experienced rather than controlled. Life had lost some flavor, in his opinion, when the weather engineers had learned how to harness the elements. He hoped that their planet—if they found one!—would have some nice, lively weather.

72

Then he was down in it and too busy to meditate. In spite of her size the freighter bucked and complained. Whew! Ford must have ordered this little charivari the minute the time was set—and, at that, the integrators must have had a big low-pressure area close at hand to build on.

Somewhere a pattern controlman was shouting at him; he switched it off and gave all his attention to his approach radar and the ghostly images in the infra-red rectifier while comparing what they told him with his inertial tracker. The ship passed over a miles-wide scar on the landscape—the ruins of the Okla-Orleans Road City. When Lazarus had last seen it, it had been noisy with life. Of all the mechanical monstrosities the human race had saddled themselves with, he mused, those dinosaurs easily took first prize.

Then the thought was cut short by a squeal from his board; the ship had picked up the pilot beam.

He wheeled her in, cut his last jet as she scraped, and slapped a series of switches; the great cargo ports rumbled open and rain beat in.

Eleanor Johnson huddled into herself, half crouching against the storm, and tried to draw her cloak more tightly about the baby in the crook of her left arm. When the storm had first hit, the child had cried endlessly, stretching her nerves taut. Now it was quiet, but that seemed only new cause for alarm.

She herself had wept, although she had tried not to show it. In all her twenty-seven years she had never been exposed to weather like this; it seemed symbolic of the storm that had overturned her life, swept her away from her cherished first home of her own with its homey old-fashioned fireplace, its shiny service cell, its thermostat which she could set to the temperature she liked without consulting others—a tempest which had swept her away between two grim proctors, arrested like some poor psychotic, and landed her after terrifying indignities here in the cold sticky red clay of this Oklahoma field.

Was it true? Could it possibly be true? Or had she not yet borne her baby at all and this was another of the strange dreams she had while carrying it?

But the rain was too wetly cold, the thunder too loud; she could never have slept through such a dream. Then what the Senior Trustee had told them must be true, too—it had to be true; she had seen the ship ground with her own eyes, its blast bright against the black of the storm. She could no longer see it but the crowd around her moved slowly forward; it must be in front of her. She was close to the outskirts of the crowd; she would be one of the last to get aboard.

It was very necessary to board the ship—Elder Zaccur Barstow had told them with deep solemnness what lay in store for them if they failed to board. She had believed his earnestness; nevertheless she wondered how it could possibly be true—could anyone be so wicked, so deeply and terribly wicked as to want to kill anyone as harmless and helpless as herself and her baby?

She was struck by panic terror—suppose there was no room left by the time she got up to the ship? She clutched her baby more tightly; the child cried again at the pressure.

A woman in the crowd moved closer and spoke to her. "You must be tired. May I carry the baby for a while?"

"No. No, thank you. I'm all right." A flash of lightning showed the woman's face; Eleanor Johnson recognized her— Elder Mary Sperling.

But the kindness of the offer steadied her. She knew now what she must do. If they were filled up and could take no more, she must pass her baby forward, hand to hand over the heads of the crowd. They could not refuse space to anything as little as her baby.

Something brushed her in the dark. The crowd was moving forward again.

When Barstow could see that loading would be finished in a few more minutes he left his post at one of the cargo doors and ran as fast as he could through the splashing sticky mud to the communications shack. Ford had warned him to give notice just before they raised ship; it was necessary to Ford's plan for diversion. Barstow fumbled with an awkward un-powered door, swung it open and rushed in. He set the private combination which should connect him directly to Ford's control desk and pushed the key.

He was answered at once but it was not Ford's face on the screen. Barstow burst out with, "Where is the Administrator? I want to talk with him," before he recognized the face in front of him.

It was a face well known to all the public—Bork Vanning, Leader of the Minority in the Council. "You're talking to the Administrator," Vanning said and grinned coldly. "The new Administrator. Now who the devil are you and why are you calling?"

Barstow thanked all gods, past and present, that recognition was one-sided. He cut the connection with one unaimed blow and plunged out of the building.

Two cargo ports were already closed; stragglers were moving through the other two. Barstow hurried the last of them inside with curses and followed them, slammed pell-mell to the control room. "Raise ship!" he shouted to Lazarus. "Fast!"

"What's all the shootin' fer?" asked Lazarus, but he was already closing and sealing the ports. He tripped the acceleration screamer, waited a scant ten seconds . . . and gave her power.

"Well," he said conversationally six minutes later, "I hope everybody was lying down. If not, we've got some broken bones on our hands. What's that you were saying?"

Barstow told him about his attempt to report to Ford.

Lazarus blinked and whistled a few bars of *Turkey in the Straw*. "It looks like we've run out of minutes. It does look like it." He shut up and gave his attention to his instruments, one eye on his ballistic track, one on radar-aft.

7 Lazarus had his hands full to jockey the *Chili* into just the right position against the side of the *New Frontiers;* the overstrained meters made the smaller craft skittish as a young horse. But he did it. The magnetic anchors clanged home; the gas-tight seals slapped into place; and their ears popped as the pressure in the *Chili* adjusted to that in the giant ship. Lazarus dived for the drop hole in the deck of the control room, pulled himself rapidly hand over hand to the port of contact, and reached the passenger lock of the *New Frontiers* to find himself facing the skipper-engineer.

The man looked at him and snorted. "You again, eh? Why the deuce didn't you answer our challenge? You can't lock onto us without permission; this is private property. What do you mean by it?"

"It means," said Lazarus, "that you and your boys are going back to Earth a few days early—in this ship."

"Why, that's ridiculous!"

"Brother," Lazarus said gently, his blaster suddenly growing out his left fist, "I'd sure hate to hurt you after you were so nice to me . . . but I sure will, unless you knuckle under awful quick."

The official simply stared unbelievingly. Several of his juniors had gathered behind him; one of them sunfished in the air, started to leave. Lazarus winged him in the leg, at low power; he jerked and clutched at nothing. Now you'll have to take care of him," Lazarus observed.

That settled it. The skipper called together his men from the announcing system microphone at the passenger lock; Lazarus counted them as they arrived—twenty-nine, a figure he had been careful to learn on his first visit. He assigned two men to hold each of them. Then he took a look at the man he had shot.

"You aren't really hurt, bub," he decided shortly and turned to the skipper-engineer. "Soon as we transfer you, get some radiation salve on that burn. The Red Cross kit's on the after bulkhead of the control room."

"This is piracy! You can't get away with this."

"Probably not," Lazarus agreed thoughtfully. "But I sort of hope we do." He turned his attention back to his job. "Shake it up there! Don't take all day."

The *Chili* was slowly being emptied. Only the one exit could be used but the pressure of the half hysterical mob behind them forced along those in the bottleneck of the trunk joining the two ships; they came boiling out like bees from a disturbed hive.

Most of them had never been in free fall before this trip; they burst out into the larger space of the giant ship and drifted helplessly, completely disoriented. Lazarus tried to bring order into it by grabbing anyone he could see who seemed to be able to handle himself in zero gravity, ordered him to speed things up by shoving along the helpless ones —shove them anywhere, on back into the big ship, get them out of the way, make room for the thousands more yet to come. When he had conscripted a dozen or so such herdsmen he spotted Barstow in the emerging throne, grabbed him and put him in charge. "Keep 'em moving, just anyhow. I've got to get for'ard to the control room. If you spot Andy Libby, send him after me."

A man broke loose from the stream and approached Barstow. "There's a ship trying to lock onto ours. I saw it through a port."

"Where?" demanded Lazarus.

The man was handicapped by slight knowledge of ships and shipboard terms, but he managed to make himself understood. "I'll be back," Lazarus told Barstow. "Keep 'em moving—and don't let any of those babies get away—our guests there." He holstered his blaster and fought his way back through the swirling mob in the bottleneck.

Number three port seemed to be the one the man had meant. Yes, there was something there. The port had an armor-glass bull's-eye in it, but instead of stars beyond Lazarus saw a lighted space. A ship of some sort had locked against it.

Its occupants either had not tried to open the *Chili's* port or just possibly did not know how. The port was not locked from the inside; there had been no reason to bother. It should have opened easily from either side once pressure was balanced . . . which the tell-tale, shining green by the latch, showed to be the case.

Lazarus was mystified.

Whether it was a traffic control vessel, a Naval craft, or something else, its presence was bad news. But why didn't they simply open the door and walk in? He was tempted to lock the port from the inside, hurry and lock all the others, finish loading and try to run for it.

But his monkey ancestry got the better of him; he could not leave alone something he did not understand. So he compromised by kicking the blind latch into place that would keep them from opening the port from outside, then slithered cautiously alongside the bull's-eye and sneaked a peep with one eye.

He found himself staring at Slayton Ford.

He pulled himself to one side, kicked the blind latch open, pressed the switch to open the port. He waited there, a toe caught in a handihold, blaster in one hand, knife in the other.

One figure emerged. Lazarus saw that it was Ford, pressed the switch again to close the port, kicked the blind latch into place, while never taking his blaster off his visitor. "Now what the hell?" he demanded. "What are you doing here? And who else is here? Patrol?"

"I'm alone."

"Huh?"

"I want to go with you . . . if you'll have me."

Lazarus looked at him and did not answer. Then he went back to the bull's-eye and inspected all that he could see. Ford appeared to be telling the truth, for no one else was in sight. But that was not what held Lazarus' eye.

Why, the ship wasn't a proper deep-space craft at all. It did not have an airlock but merely a seal to let it fasten to a larger ship; Lazarus was staring right into the body of the craft. It looked like—yes, it was a "Joyboat Junior," a little private strato-yacht, suitable only for point-to-point trajectory, or at the most for rendezvous with a satellite provided the satellite could refuel it for the return leg.

There was no fuel for it here. A lightning pilot possibly could land that tin toy without power and still walk away from it . . . provided he had the skill to play Skip-to-M'Lou in and out of the atmosphere while nursing his skin temperatures—but Lazarus wouldn't want to try it. No, sir! He turned to Ford. "Suppose we turned you down. How did you figure on getting back?"

"I didn't figure on it," Ford answered simply.

"Mmm—— Tell me about it, but make it march; we're minus on minutes."

Ford had burned all bridges. Turned out of office only

hours earlier, he had known that, once all the facts came out, life-long imprisonment in Coventry was the best he could hope for—if he managed to avoid mob violence or mind-shattering interrogation.

Arranging the diversion was the thing that finally lost him his thin margin of control. His explanations for his actions were not convincing to the Council. He had excused the storm and the withdrawing of proctors from the reservation as a drastic attempt to break the morale of the Families —a possible excuse but not too plausible. His orders to Naval craft, intended to keep them away from the *New Frontiers*, had apparently not been associated in anyone's mind with the Howard Families affair; nevertheless the apparent lack of sound reason behind them had been seized on by the opposition as another weapon to bring him down. They were watching for anything to catch him out—one question asked in Council concerned certain monies from the Administrator's discretionary fund which had been paid indirectly to one Captain Aaron Sheffield; were these monies in fact expended in the public interest?

Lazarus' eyes widened. "You mean they were onto me?"

"Not quite. Or you wouldn't be here. But they were close behind you. I think they must have had help from a lot of my people at the last."

"Probably. But we made it, so let's not fret. Come on. The minute everybody is out of this ship and into the big girl, we've got to boost." Lazarus turned to leave.

"You're going to let me go along?"

Lazarus checked his progress, twisted to face Ford. "How else?" He had intended at first to send Ford down in the *Chili*. It was not gratitude that changed his mind, but respect. Once he had lost office Ford had gone straight to Huxley Field north of Novak Tower, cleared for the vacation satellite *Monte Carlo*, and had jumped for the *New Frontiers* instead. Lazarus liked that. "Go for broke" took courage and character that most people didn't have. Don't grab a toothbrush, don't wind the cat—just do it! "Of course you're coming along," he said easily. "You're my kind of boy, Slayton."

The *Chili* more than half emptied now but the spaces near the interchange were still jammed with frantic mobs. Lazarus cuffed and shoved his way through, trying not to bruise women and children unnecessarily but not letting the possibility slow him up. He scrambled through the connecting trunk with Ford hanging onto his belt, pulled aside once they were through and paused in front of Barstow.

Barstow stared past him. "Yeah, it's him," Lazarus confirmed. "Don't stare—it's rude. He's going with us. Have you seen Libby?"

"Here I am, Lazarus." Libby separated himself from the throng and approached with the ease of a veteran long used to free fall. He had a small satchel strapped to one wrist.

"Good. Stick around. Zack, how long till you're all loaded?"

"God knows. I can't count them. An hour, maybe."

"Make it less. If you put some husky boys on each side of the hole, they can snatch them through faster than they are coming. We've got to shove out of here a little sooner than is humanly possible. I'm going to the control room. Phone me there the instant you have everybody in, our guests here out, and the *Chili* broken loose. Andy! Slayton! Let's go."

"Lazarus——"

"Later, Andy. We'll talk when we get there."

Lazarus took Slayton Ford with him because he did not know what else to do with him and felt it would be better to keep him out of sight until some plausible excuse could be dreamed up for having him along. So far no one seemed to have looked at him twice, but once they quieted down, Ford's well-known face would demand explanation.

The control room was about a half mile forward of where they had entered the ship. Lazarus knew that there was a passenger belt leading to it but he didn't have time to look for it; he simply took the first passageway leading forward. As soon as they got away from the crowd they made good time even though Ford was not as skilled in the fishlike maneuvers of free fall as were the other two.

Once there, Lazarus spent the enforced wait in explaining to Libby the extremely ingenious but unorthodox controls of the star ship. Libby was fascinated and soon was putting himself through dummy runs. Lazarus turned to Ford. "How about you, Slayton? Wouldn't hurt to have a second relief pilot."

Ford shook his head. "I've been listening but I could never learn it. I'm not a pilot."

"*Huh?* How did you get here?"

"Oh. I do have a license, but I haven't had time to keep in practice. My chauffeur always pilots me. I haven't figured a trajectory in many years."

Lazarus looked him over. "And yet you plotted an orbit rendezvous? With no reserve fuel?"

"Oh, that. I had to."

"I see. The way the cat learned to swim. Well, that's one

way." He turned back to speak to Libby, was interrupted by Barstow's voice over the announcing system:

"Five minutes, Lazarus! Acknowledge."

Lazarus found the microphone, covered the light under it with his hand and answered, "Okay, Zack! Five minutes." Then he said, "Cripes, I haven't even picked a course. What do you think, Andy? Straight out from Earth to shake the busies off our tail? Then pick a destination? How about it, Slayton? Does that fit with what you ordered Navy craft to do?"

"No, Lazarus, no!" protested Libby.

"Huh? Why not?"

"You should head right straight down for the Sun."

"For the Sun? For Pete's sake, why?"

"I tried to tell you when I first saw you. It's because of the space drive you asked me to develop."

"But, Andy, we haven't got it."

"Yes, we have. Here." Libby shoved the satchel he had been carrying toward Lazarus.

Lazarus opened it.

Assembled from odd bits of other equipment, looking more like the product of a boy's workshop than the output of a scientist's laboratory, the gadget which Libby referred to as a "space drive" underwent Lazarus' critical examination. Against the polished sophisticated perfection of the control room it looked uncouth, pathetic, ridiculously inadequate.

Lazarus poked at it tentatively. "What is it?" he asked. "Your model?"

"No, no. That's *it*. That's the space drive."

Lazarus looked at the younger man not unsympathetically. "Son," he asked slowly, "have you come unzipped?"

"No, no, no!" Libby sputtered. "I'm as sane as you are. This is a radically new notion. That's why I want you to take us down near the Sun. If it works at all, it will work best where light pressure is strongest."

"And if it doesn't work," inquired Lazarus, "what does that make us? Sunspots?"

"Not straight down into the Sun. But head for it now and as soon as I can work out the data, I'll give you corrections to warp you into your proper trajectory. I want to pass the Sun in a very flat hyperbola, well inside the orbit of Mercury, as close to the photosphere as this ship can stand. I don't know how close that is, so I couldn't work it out ahead of time. But the data will be here in the ship and there will be time to correlate them as we go."

Lazarus looked again at the giddy little cat's cradle of apparatus. "Andy . . . if you are sure that the gears in your head are still meshed, I'll take a chance. Strap down, both of you." He belted himself into the pilot's couch and called Barstow. "How about it, Zack?"

"*Right now!*"

"Hang on tight!" With one hand Lazarus covered a light in his leftside control panel; acceleration warning shrieked throughout the ship. With the other he covered another; the hemisphere in front of them was suddenly spangled with the starry firmament, and Ford gasped.

Lazarus studied it. A full twenty degrees of it was blanked out by the dark circle of the nightside of Earth. "Got to duck around a corner, Andy. We'll use a little Tennessee windage." He started easily with a quarter gravity, just enough to shake up his passengers and make them cautious, while he started a slow operation of precessing the enormous ship to the direction he needed to shove her in order to get out of Earth's shadow. He raised acceleration to a half gee, then to a gee.

Earth changed suddenly from a black silhouette to a slender silver crescent as the half-degree white disc of the Sun came out from behind her. "I want to clip her about a thousand miles out, Slipstick," Lazarus said tensely, "at two gees. Gimme a temporary vector."

Libby hesitated only momentarily and gave it to him. Lazarus again sounded acceleration warning and boosted to twice Earth-normal gravity. Lazarus was tempted to raise the boost to emergency-full but he dared not do so with a shipload of groundlubbers; even two gees sustained for a long period might be too much of a strain for some of them. Any Naval pursuit craft ordered to intercept them at much higher gee and their selected crews could stand it. But it was just a chance they would have to take . . . and anyhow, he reminded himself, a Navy ship could not maintain a high boost for long; her mile-seconds were strictly limited by her reaction-mass tanks.

The *New Frontiers* had no such old-fashioned limits, no tanks; her converter accepted any mass at all, turned it into pure radiant energy. Anything would serve—meteors, cosmic dust, stray atoms gathered in by her sweep field, or anything from the ship herself, such as garbage, dead bodies, deck sweepings, anything at all. Mass was energy. In dying, each tortured gram gave up nine hundred million trillion ergs of thrust.

The crescent of Earth waxed and swelled and slid off toward the left edge of the hemispherical screen while the Sun remained dead ahead. A little more than twenty minutes later, when they were at closest approach and the crescent, now at half phase, was sliding out of the bowl screen, the ship-to-ship circuit came to life. "*New Frontiers!*" a forceful

81

voice sounded. "Maneuver to orbit and lay to! This is an of-ficial traffic control order."

Lazarus shut it off. "Anyhow," he said cheerfully, "if they try to catch us, they won't like chasing us down into the Sun! Andy, it's a clear road now and time we corrected, maybe. You want to compute it? Or will you feed me the data?"

"I'll compute it," Libby answered. He had already discov-ered that the ship's characteristics pertinent to astrogation, including her "black body" behavior, were available at both piloting stations. Armed with this and with the running data from instruments he set out to calculate the hyperboloid by which he intended to pass the Sun. He made a half-hearted attempt to use the ship's ballistic calculator but it baffled him; it was a design he was not used to, having no moving parts of any sort, even in the exterior controls. So he gave it up as a waste of time and fell back on the strange talent for figures lodged in his brain. His brain had no moving parts, either, but he was used to it.

Lazarus decided to check on their popularity rating. He switched on the ship-to-ship again, found that it was still an-grily squawking, although a little more faintly. They knew his own name now—one of his names—which caused him to decide that the boys in the *Chili* must have called traffic con-trol almost at once. He tut-tutted sadly when he learned that "Captain Sheffield's" license to pilot had been suspended. He shut it off and tried the Naval frequencies . . . then shut them off also when he was able to raise nothing but code and scramble, except that the words "New Frontiers" came through once in clear.

He said something about "Sticks and stones may break my bones——" and tried another line of investigation. Both by long-range radar and by paragravitic detector he could tell that there were ships in their neighborhood but this alone told him very little; there were bound to be ships this close to Earth and he had no easy way to distinguish, from these data alone, an unarmed liner or freighter about her lawful occasions from a Naval cruiser in angry pursuit.

But the *New Frontiers* had more resources for analyzing what was around her than had an ordinary ship; she had been specially equipped to cope unassisted with any imagina-ble strange conditions. The hemispherical control room in which they lay was an enormous multi-screened television receiver which could duplicate the starry heavens either in view-aft or view-forward at the selection of the pilot. But it also had other circuits, much more subtle; simultaneously or separately it could act as an enormous radar screen as well, displaying on it the blips of any body within radar range.

82

But that was just a starter. Its inhuman senses could apply differential analysis to doppler data and display the result in a visual analog. Lazarus studied his lefthand control bank, tried to remember everything he had been told about it, made a change in the set up.

The simulated stars and even the Sun faded to dimness; about a dozen lights shined brightly.

He ordered the board to check them for angular rate; the bright lights turned cherry red, became little comets trailing off to pink tails—all but one, which remained white and grew no tail. He studied the others for a moment, decided that their vectors were such that they would remain forever strangers, and ordered the board to check the line-of-sight doppler on the one with a steady bearing.

It faded to violet, ran halfway through the spectrum and held steady at blue-green. Lazarus thought a moment, subtracted from the inquiry their own two gees of boost; it turned white again. Satisfied he tried the same tests with view-aft.

"Lazarus——"

"Yeah, Lib?"

"Will it interfere with what you are doing if I give you the corrections now?"

"Not at all. I was just taking a look-see. If this magic lantern knows what it's talking about, they didn't manage to get a pursuit job on our tail in time."

"Good. Well, here are the figures . . ."

"Feed 'em in yourself, will you? Take the conn for a while. I want to see about some coffee and sandwiches. How about you? Feel like some breakfast?"

Libby nodded absent-mindedly, already starting to revise the ship's trajectory. Ford spoke up eagerly, the first word he had uttered in a long time. "Let me get it. I'd be glad to." He seemed pathetically anxious to be useful."

"Mmm . . . you might get into some kind of trouble, Slayton. No matter what sort of a selling job Zack did, your name is probably 'Mud' with most of the members. I'll phone aft and raise somebody."

"Probably nobody would recognize me under these circumstances," Ford argued. "Anyway, it's a legitimate errand—I can explain that."

Lazarus saw from his face that it was necessary to the man's morale. "Okay . . . if you can handle yourself under two gees."

Ford struggled heavily up out of the acceleration couch he was in. "I've got space legs. What kind of sandwiches?"

"I'd say corned beef, but it would probably be some damned substitute. Make mine cheese, with rye if they've got it, and use plenty of mustard. And a gallon of coffee. What are you having, Andy?"

"Me? Oh, anything that is convenient."

Ford started to leave, bracing himself heavily against double weight, then he added, "Oh—it might save time if you could tell me where to go."

"Brother," said Lazarus, "if this ship isn't pretty well crammed with food, we've all made a terrible mistake. Scout around. You'll find some."

Down, down, down toward the Sun, with speed increasing by sixty-four feet per second for every second elapsed. Down and still down for fifteen endless hours of double weight. During this time they traveled seventeen million miles and reached the inconceivable speed of six hundred and forty miles per second. The figures mean little—think instead of New York to Chicago, a half hour's journey even by stratomail, done in a single heartbeat.

Barstow had a rough time during heavy weight. For all of the others it was a time to lie down, try hopelessly to sleep, breathe painfully and seek new positions in which to try to rest from the burdens of their own bodies. But Zaccur Barstow was driven by his sense of responsibility; he kept going though the Old Man of the Sea sat on his neck and raised his weight to three hundred and fifty pounds.

Not that he could do anything for them, except crawl wearily from one compartment to another and ask about their welfare. Nothing could be done, no organization to relieve their misery was possible, while high boost continued. They lay where they could, men, women, and children crowded together like cattle being shipped, without even room to stretch out, in spaces never intended for such extreme overcrowding.

The only good thing about it, Barstow reflected wearily, was that they were all too miserable to worry about anything but the dragging minutes. They were too beaten down to make trouble. Later on there would be doubts raised, he was sure, about the wisdom of fleeing; there would be embarrassing questions asked about Ford's presence in the ship, about Lazarus' peculiar and sometimes shady actions, about his own contradictory role. But not yet.

He really must, he decided reluctantly, organize a propaganda campaign before trouble could grow. If it did—and it surely would if he didn't move to offset it, and . . . well, that would be the last straw. It would be.

He eyed a ladder in front of him, set his teeth, and struggled up to the next deck. Picking his way through the bodies there he almost stepped on a woman who was clutching a baby too tightly to her. Barstow noticed that the infant was wet and soiled and he thought of ordering its mother to take care of the matter, since she seemed to be awake. But he let it go—so far as he knew there was not a clean diaper in millions of miles. Or there might be ten thousand of them on the deck above . . . which seemed almost as far away.

He plodded on without speaking to her. Eleanor Johnson had not been aware of his concern. After the first great relief at realizing that she and her baby were safe inside the ship she had consigned all her worries to her elders and now felt nothing but the apathy of emotional reaction and of inescapable weight. Baby had cried when that awful weight had hit them, then had become quiet, too quiet. She had roused herself enough to listen for its heartbeat; then, sure that he was alive, she had sunk back into stupor.

Fifteen hours out, with the orbit of Venus only four hours away, Libby cut the boost. The ship plunged on, in free fall, her terrific speed still mounting under the steadily increasing pull of the Sun. Lazarus was awakened by no weight. He glanced at the copilot's couch and said, "On the curve?"

"As plotted."

Lazarus looked him over. "Okay, I've got it. Now get out of here and get some sleep. Boy, you look like a used towel."

"I'll just stay here and rest."

"You will like hell. You haven't slept even when I had the conn; if you stay here, you'll be watching instruments and figuring. So beat it! Slayton, chuck him out."

Libby smiled shyly and left. He found the spaces abaft the control room swarming with floating bodies but he managed to find an unused corner, passed his kilt belt through a handihold, and slept at once.

Free fall should have been as great a relief to everyone else; it was not, except to the fraction of one per cent who were salted spacemen. Free-fall nausea, like seasickness, is a joke only to those not affected; it would take a Dante to describe a hundred thousand cases of it. There were anti-nausea drugs aboard, but they were not found at once; there were medical men among the Families, but they were sick, too. The misery went on.

Barstow, himself long since used to free flight, floated forward to the control room to pray relief for the less fortunate. "They're in bad shape," he told Lazarus. "Can't you put spin on the ship and give them some let-up? It would help a lot."

"And it would make maneuvering difficult, too. Sorry. Look, Zack, a lively ship will be more important to them in a pinch than just keeping their suppers down. Nobody dies from seasickness anyhow . . . they just wish they could."

The ship plunged on down, still gaining speed as it fell toward the Sun. The few who felt able continued slowly to assist the enormous majority who were ill.

Libby continued to sleep, the luxurious return-to-the-womb sleep of those who have learned to enjoy free fall. He had had almost no sleep since the day the Families had been arrested; his overly active mind had spent all its time worrying the problem of a new space drive.

The big ship precessed around him; he stirred gently and did not awake. It steadied in a new attitude and the acceleration warning brought him instantly awake. He oriented himself, placed himself flat against the after bulkhead, and waited; weight hit him almost at once—three gees this time and he knew that something was badly wrong. He had gone almost a quarter mile aft before he found a hide-away; nevertheless he struggled to his feet and started the unlikely task of trying to climb that quarter mile—now straight up—at three times his proper weight, while blaming himself for having let Lazarus talk him into leaving the control room.

He managed only a portion of the trip . . . but an heroic portion, one about equal to climbing the stairs of a ten-story building while carrying a man on each shoulder . . . when resumption of free fall relieved him. He zipped the rest of the way like a salmon returning home and was in the control room quickly. "What happened?"

Lazarus said regretfully, "Had to vector, Andy." Slayton Ford said nothing but looked worried.

"Yes, I know. But why?" Libby was already strapping himself against the copilot's couch while studying the astrogational situation.

"Red lights on the screen." Lazarus described the display, giving coördinates and relative vectors.

Libby nodded thoughtfully. "Naval craft. No commercial vessels would be in such trajectories. A minelaying bracket."

"That's what I figured. I didn't have time to consult you; I had to use enough mile-seconds to be sure they wouldn't have boost enough to reposition on us."

"Yes, you had to." Libby looked worried. "I thought we were free of any possible Naval interference."

"They're not ours," put in Slayton Ford. "They can't be ours no matter what orders have been given since I—uh, since I left. They must be Venerian craft."

"Yeah," agreed Lazarus, "they must be. Your pal, the new Administrator, hollered to Venus for help and they gave it to him—just a friendly gesture of interplanetary good will."

Libby was hardly listening. He was examining data and processing it through the calculator inside his skull. "Lazarus . . . this new orbit isn't too good."

"I know," Lazarus agreed sadly. "I had to duck . . . so I ducked the only direction they left open to me—closer to the Sun."

"Too close, perhaps."

The Sun is not a large star, nor is it very hot. But it is hot with reference to men, hot enough to strike them down dead if they are careless about tropic noonday ninety-two million miles away from it, hot enough that we who are reared under its rays nevertheless dare not look directly at it.

At a distance of two and a half million miles the Sun beats out with a flare fourteen hundred times as bright as the worst ever endured in Death Valley, the Sahara, or Aden. Such radiance would not be perceived as heat or light; it would be death more sudden than the full power of a blaster. The Sun is a hydrogen bomb, a naturally occuring one; the *New Frontiers* was skirting the limits of its circle of total destruction.

It was hot inside the ship. The Families were protected against instant radiant death by the armored walls but the air temperature continued to mount. They were relieved of the misery of free fall but they were doubly uncomfortable, both from heat and from the fact that the bulkheads slanted crazily; there was no level place to stand or lie. The ship was both spinning on its axis and accelerating now; it was never intended to do both at once and the addition of the two accelerations, angular and linear, make "down" the direction where outer and after bulkheads met. The ship was being spun through necessity to permit some of the impinging radiant energy to re-radiate on the "cold" side. The forward acceleration was equally from necessity, a forlorn-hope maneuver to pass the Sun as far out as possible and as fast as possible, in order to spend least time at perihelion, the point of closest approach.

It was hot in the control room. Even Lazarus had voluntarily shed his kilt and shucked down to Venus styles. Metal was hot to the touch. On the great stellarium screen an enormous circle of blackness marked where the Sun's disc should have been; the receptors had cut out automatically at such a ridiculous demand.

Lazarus repeated Libby's last words. " 'Thirty-seven minutes to perihelion.' We can't take it, Andy. The ship can't take it."

"I know. I never intended us to pass this close."

"Of course you didn't. Maybe I shouldn't have maneuvered. Maybe we would have missed the mines anyway. Oh, well——" Lazarus squared his shoulders and filed it with the might-have-beens. "It looks to me, son, about time to try out your gadget." He poked a thumb at Libby's uncouth-looking "space drive." "You say that all you have to do is to hook up that one connection?"

"That is what is intended. Attach that one lead to any portion of the mass to be affected. Of course I don't really know that it will work," Libby admitted. "There is no way to test it."

"Suppose it doesn't?"

"There are three possibilities," Libby answered methodically. "In the first place, nothing may happen."

"In which case we fry."

"In the second place, we and the ship may cease to exist as matter as we know it."

"Dead, you mean. But probably a pleasanter way."

"I suppose so. I don't know what death is. In the third place, if my hypotheses are correct, we will recede from the Sun at a speed just under that of light."

Lazarus eyed the gadget and wiped sweat from his shoulders. "It's getting hotter, Andy. Hook it up—and it had better be good!"

Andy hooked it up.

"Go ahead," urged Lazarus. "Push the button, throw the switch, cut the beam. Make it march."

"I have," Libby insisted. "Look at the Sun."

"Huh? *Oh!*"

The great circle of blackness which had marked the position of the Sun on the star-speckled stellarium was shrinking rapidly. In a dozen heartbeats it lost half its diameter; twenty seconds later it had dwindled to a quarter of its original width.

"It worked," Lazarus said softly. "Look at it, Slayton! Sign me up as a purple baboon—it *worked!*"

"I rather thought it would," Libby answered seriously. "It should, you know."

"Hmm—— That may be evident to you, Andy. It's not to me. How fast are we going?"

"Relative to what?"

"Uh, relative to the Sun."

"I haven't had opportunity to measure it, but it seems to be just under the speed of light. It can't be greater."

"Why not? Aside from theoretical considerations."

"We still see." Libby pointed at the stellarium bowl.

"Yeah, so we do," Lazarus mused. "Hey! We shouldn't be able to. I ought to doppler out."

Libby looked blank, then smiled. "But it dopplers right back in. Over on that side, toward the Sun, we're seeing by short radiations stretched to visibility. On the opposite side we're picking up something around radio wavelengths dopplered down to light."

"And in between?"

"Quit pulling my leg, Lazarus. I'm sure you can work out relatively vector additions quite as well as I can."

"*You* work it out," Lazarus said firmly. "I'm just going to sit here and admire it. Eh, Slayton?"

"Yes. Yes indeed."

Libby smiled politely. "We might as well quit wasting mass on the main drive." He sounded the warner, then cut the drive. "Now we can return to normal conditions." He started to disconnect his gadget.

Lazarus said hastily, "Hold it, Andy! We aren't even outside the orbit of Mercury yet. Why put on the brakes?"

"Why, this won't stop us. We have acquired velocity; we will keep it."

Lazarus pulled at his cheek and stared. "Ordinarily I would agree with you. First Law of Motion. But with this pseudo-speed I'm not so sure. We got it for nothing and we haven't paid for it—in energy, I mean. You seem to have declared a holiday with respect to inertia; when the holiday is over, won't all that free speed go back where it came from?"

"I don't think so," Libby answered. "Our velocity isn't 'pseudo' anything; it's as real as velocity can be. You are attempting to apply verbal anthropomorphic logic to a field in which it is not pertinent. You would not expect us to be transported instantaneously back to the lower gravitational potential from which we started, would you?"

"Back to where you hooked in your space drive? No, we've moved."

"And we'll keep on moving. Our newly acquired gravitational potential energy of greater height above the Sun is no more real than our present kinetic energy of velocity. They both exist."

Lazarus looked baffled. The expression did not suit him. "I guess you've got me, Andy. No matter how I slice it, we seemed to have picked up energy from somewhere. But *where?* When I went to school, they taught me to honor the Flag, vote the straight party ticket, and believe in the law of conservation of energy. Seems like you're violated it. How about it?"

"Don't worry about it," suggested Libby. "The so-called law of conservation of energy was merely a working hypothesis, unproved and unprovable, used to describe gross phenomena. Its terms apply only to the older, dynamic concept of the world. In a plenum conceived as a static grid of relationships, a 'violation' of that 'law' is nothing more startling than a discontinuous function, to be noted and described. That's what I did. I saw a discontinuity in the mathematical model of the aspect of mass-energy called inertia. I applied it. The mathematical model turned out to be similar to the real world. That was the only hazard, really—one never knows that a mathematical model is similar to the real world until you try it."

"Yeah, yeah, sure, you can't tell the taste till you bite it—but, Andy, I still don't see what *caused* it!" He turned toward Ford. "Do you, Slayton?"

Ford shook his head. "No. I would like to know . . . but I doubt if I could understand it."

"You and me both. Well, Andy?"

Now Libby looked baffled. "But, Lazarus, causality has nothing to do with the real plenum. A fact simply *is*. Causality is merely an old-fashioned postulate of a pre-scientific philosophy."

"I guess," Lazarus said slowly, "I'm old-fashioned."

Libby said nothing. He disconnected his apparatus.

The disc of black continued to shrink. When it had shrunk to about one sixth its greatest diameter, it changed suddenly from black to shining white, as the ship's distance from the Sun again was great enough to permit the receptors to manage the load.

Lazarus tried to work out in his head the kinetic energy of the ship—one-half the square of the velocity of light (minus a pinch, he corrected) times the mighty tonnage of the *New Frontiers*. The answer did not comfort him, whether he called it ergs or apples.

8 "First things first," interrupted Barstow. "I'm as fascinated by the amazing scientific aspects of our present situation as any of you, but we've got work to do. We've got to plan a pattern for daily living at once. So let's table mathematical physics and talk about organization."

He was not speaking to the trustees but to his own personal lieutenants, the key people in helping him put over the complex maneuvers which had made their escape possible—Ralph Schultz, Eve Barstow, Mary Sperling, Justin Foote, Clive Johnson, about a dozen others.

Lazarus and Libby were there. Lazarus had left Slayton Ford to guard the control room, with orders to turn away all visitors and, above all, not to let anyone touch the controls. It was a make-work job, it being Lazarus' notion of temporary occupational therapy. He had sensed in Ford a mental condition that he did not like. Ford seemed to have withdrawn into himself. He answered when spoken to, but that was all. It worried Lazarus.

"We need an executive," Barstow went on, "someone who, for the time being, will have very broad powers to give orders and have them carried out. He'll have to make decisions, organize us, assign duties and responsibilities, get the internal economy of the ship working. It's a big job and I would like to have our brethren hold an election and do it democratically. That'll have to wait; somebody has to give orders now. We're wasting food and the ship is—well, I wish you could have seen the 'fresher I tried to use today."

"Zaccur . . ."

"Yes, Eve?"

"It seems to me that the thing to do is to put it up to the trustees. We haven't any authority; we were just an emergency group for something that is finished now."

"Ahrrumph——" It was Justin Foote, in tones as dry and formal as his face. "I differ somewhat from our sister. The trustees are not conversant with the full background; it would take time we can ill afford to put them into the picture, as it were, before they would be able to judge the matter. Furthermore, being one of the trustees myself, I am able to say without bias that the trustees, as an organized group, can have no jurisdiction because legally they no longer exist."

Lazarus looked interested. "How do you figure that, Justin?"

"Thusly: the board of trustees were the custodians of a foundation which existed as a part of and in relation to a society. The trustees were never a government; their sole duties had to do with relations between the Families and the rest of that society. With the ending of relationship between the Families and terrestrial society, the board of trustees, *ipso facto*, ceases to exist. It is one with history. Now we in this ship are not yet a society, we are an anarchistic group. This present assemblage has as much—or as little—authority to initiate a society as has any part group."

Lazarus cheered and clapped. "Justin," he applauded, "that is the neatest piece of verbal juggling I've heard in a century. Let's get together sometime and have a go at solipsism."

Justin Foote looked pained. "Obviously——" he began.

"Nope! Not another word! You've convinced me, don't spoil it. If that's how it is, let's get busy and pick a bull moose. How about you, Zack? You look like the logical candidate."

Barstow shook his head. "I know my limitations. I'm an engineer, not a political executive; the Families were just a hobby with me. We need an expert in social adminstration."

When Barstow had convinced them that he meant it, other names were proposed and their qualifications debated at

91

length. In a group as large as the Families there were many who had specialized in political science, many who had served in public office with credit.

Lazarus listened; he knew four of the candidates. At last he got Eve Barstow aside and whispered with her. She looked startled, then thoughtful, finally nodded.

She asked for the floor. "I have a candidate to propose," she began in her always gentle tones, "who might not ordinarily occur to you, but who is incomparably better fitted, by temperament, training, and experience, to do this job than is anyone as yet proposed. For civil administrator of the ship I nominate Slayton Ford."

They were flabbergasted into silence, then everybody tried to talk at once. "Has Eve lost her mind? Ford is back on Earth!"—"No, no, he's not. I've seen him—*here*—in the ship."—"But it's out of the question!"—*"Him?* The Families would never accept him!"—"Even so, he's not one of us."

Eve patiently kept the floor until they quieted. "I know my nomination sounds ridiculous and I admit the difficulties. But consider the advantages. We all know Slayton Ford by reputation and by performance. You know, every member of the Families knows, that Ford is a genius in his field. It is going to be hard enough to work out plans for living together in this badly overcrowded ship; the best talent we can draw on will be no more than enough."

Her words impressed them because Ford was that rare thing in history, a statesman whose worth was almost universally acknowledged in his own lifetime. Contemporary historians credited him with having saved the Western Federation in at least two of its major development crises; it was his misfortune rather than his personal failure that his career was wrecked on a crisis not solvable by ordinary means.

"Eve," said Zaccur Barstow, "I agree with your opinion of Ford and I myself would be glad to have him as our executive. But how about all of the others? To the Families—everyone except ourselves here present—Mr. Administrator Ford symbolizes the persecution they have suffered. I think that makes him an impossible candidate."

Eve was gently stubborn. "I don't think so. We've already agreed that we will have to work up a campaign to explain away a lot of embarrassing facts about the last few days. Why don't we do it thoroughly and convince them that Ford is a martyr who sacrificed himself to save them? He is, you know."

"Mmm . . . yes, he is. He didn't sacrifice himself primarily on our account, but there is no doubt in my mind that his personal sacrifice saved us. But whether or not we can convince the others, convince them strongly enough that they will accept him and take orders from him . . . when he is now a sort of personal devil to them—well, I just don't know. I think we need expert advice. How about it, Ralph? Could it be done?"

Ralph Schultz hesitated. "The truth of a proposition has little or nothing to do with its psychodynamics. The notion that 'truth will prevail' is merely a pious wish; history doesn't show it. The fact that Ford really is a martyr to whom we owe gratitude is irrelevant to the purely technical question you put to me." He stopped to think. "But the proposition *per se* has certain sentimentally dramatic aspects which lend it to propaganda manipulation, even in the face of the currently accepted strong counterproposition. Yes . . . yes, I think it could be sold."

"How long would it take you to put it over?"

"Mmm . . . the social space involved is both 'tight' and 'hot' in the jargon we use; I should be able to get a high positive 'k' factor on the chain reaction—if it works at all. But it's an unsurveyed field and I don't know what spontaneous rumors are running around the ship. If you decide to do this, I'll want to prepare some rumors before we adjourn, rumors to repair Ford's reputation—then about twelve hours from now I can release another one that Ford is actually aboard . . . because he intended from the first to throw his lot in with us."

"Uh, I hardly think he did, Ralph."

"Are you *sure*, Zaccur?"

"No, but—— Well . . ."

"You see? The truth about his original intentions is a secret between him and his God. You don't know and neither do I. But the dynamics of the proposition are a separate matter. Zaccur, by the time my rumor gets back to you three or four times, even you will begin to wonder." The psychometrician paused to stare at nothing while he consulted an intuition refined by almost a century of mathematical study of human behavior. "Yes, it will work. If you all want to do it, you will be able to make a public announcement inside of twenty-four hours."

"I so move!" someone called out.

A few minutes later Barstow had Lazarus fetch Ford to the meeting place. Lazarus did not explain to him why his presence was required; Ford entered the compartment like a man come to judgment, one with a bitter certainty that the outcome will be against him. His manner showed fortitude but not hope. His eyes were unhappy.

93

Lazarus had studied those eyes during the long hours they had been shut up together in the control room. They bore an expression Lazarus had seen many times before in his long life. The condemned man who has lost his final appeal, the fully resolved suicide, little furry things exhausted and defeated by struggle with the unrelenting steel of traps—the eyes of each of these hold a single expression, born of hopeless conviction that his time has run out.

Ford's eyes had it.

Lazarus had seen it grow and had been puzzled by it. To be sure, they were all in a dangerous spot, but Ford no more than the rest. Besides, awareness of danger brings a *live* expression; why should Ford's eyes hold the signal of death?

Lazarus finally decided that it could only be because Ford had reached the dead-end state of mind where suicide is necessary. But why? Lazarus mulled it over during the long watches in the control room and reconstructed the logic of it to his own satisfaction. Back on Earth, Ford had been important among his own kind, the short-lived. His paramount position had rendered him then almost immune to the feeling of defeated inferiority which the long-lived stirred up in normal men. But now he was the *only* ephemeral in a race of Methuselahs.

Ford had neither the experience of the elders nor the expectations of the young; he felt inferior to them both, hopelessly outclassed. Correct or not, he felt himself to be a useless pensioner, an impotent object of charity.

To a person of Ford's busy useful background the situation was intolerable. His very pride and strength of character were driving him to suicide.

As he came into the conference room Ford's glance sought out Zaccur Barstow. "You sent for me, sir?"

"Yes, Mr. Administrator." Barstow explained briefly the situation and the responsibility they wanted him to assume. "You are under no compulsion," he concluded, "but we need your services if you are willing to serve. Will you?"

Lazarus' heart felt light as he watched Ford's expression change to amazement. "Do you really mean that?" Ford answered slowly. "You're not joking with me?"

"Most certainly we mean it!"

Ford did not answer at once and when he did, his answer seemed irrelevant. "May I sit down?"

A place was found for him; he settled heavily into the chair and covered his face with his hands. No one spoke. Presently he raised his head and said in a steady voice, "If that is your will, I will do my best to carry out your wishes."

The ship required a captain as well as a civil administrator.

Lazarus had been, up to that time, her captain in a very practical, piratical sense but he balked when Barstow proposed that it be made a formal title. "Huh *uh!* Not me. I may just spend this trip playing checkers. Libby's your man. Serious-minded, conscientious, former naval officer—just the type for the job."

Libby blushed as eyes turned toward him. "Now, really," he protested, "while it is true that I have had to command ships in the course of my duties, it has never suited me. I am a staff officer by temperament. I don't *feel* like a commanding officer."

"Don't see how you can duck out of it," Lazarus persisted. "You invented the go-fast gadget and you are the only one who understands how it works. You've got yourself a job, boy."

"But that does not follow at all," pleaded Libby. "I am perfectly willing to be astrogator, for that is consonant with my talents. But I very much prefer to serve under a commanding officer."

Lazarus was smugly pleased then to see how Slayton Ford immediately moved in and took charge; the sick man was gone, here again was the executive. "It isn't a matter of your personal preference, Commander Libby; we each must do what we can. I have agreed to direct social and civil organization; that is consonant with *my* training. But I can't command the ship as a ship; I'm not trained for it. You are. You must do it."

Libby blushed pinker and stammered. "I would if I were the only one. But there are hundreds of spacemen among the Families and dozens of them certainly have more experience and talent for command than I have. If you'll look for him, you'll find the right man."

Ford said, "What do you think, Lazarus?"

"Um. Andy's got something. A captain puts spine into his ship . . . or doesn't, as the case may be. If Libby doesn't hanker to command, maybe we'd better look around."

Justin Foote had a microed roster with him but there was no scanner at hand with which to sort it. Nevertheless the memories of the dozen and more present produced many candidates. They finally settled on Captain Rufus "Ruthless" King.

Libby was explaining the consequences of his light-pressure drive to his new commanding officer. "The loci of our attainable destinations is contained in a sheaf of paraboloids having their apices tangent to our present course. This assumes that acceleration by means of the ship's normal drive will always be applied so that the magnitude our present

95

vector, just under the speed of light, will be held constant. This will require that the ship be slowly precessed during the entire maneuvering acceleration. But it will not be too fussy because of the enormous difference in magnitude between our present vector and the maneuvering vectors being impressed on it. One may think of it roughly as accelerating at right angles to our course."

"Yes, yes, I see that," Captain King cut in, "but why do you assume that the resultant vectors must always be equal to our present vector?"

"Why, it need not be if the Captain decides otherwise," Libby answered, looking puzzled, "but to apply a component that would reduce the resultant vector below our present speed would simply be to cause us to backtrack a little without increasing the scope of our present loci of possible destinations. The effect would only increase our flight time, to generations, even to centuries, if the resultant——"

"Certainly, certainly! I understand basic ballistics, Mister. But why do you reject the other alternative? Why not increase our speed? Why can't I accelerate directly along my present course if I choose?"

Libby looked worried. "The Captain may, if he so orders. But it would be an attempt to exceed the speed of light. That has been assumed to be impossible——"

"That's exactly what I was driving at. 'Assumed.' I've always wondered if that assumption was justified. Now seems like a good time to find out."

Libby hesitated, his sense of duty struggling against the ecstatic temptations of scientific curiosity. "If this were a research ship, Captain, I would be anxious to try it. I can't visualize what the conditions would be if we did pass the speed of light, but it seems to me that we would be cut off entirely from the electromagnetic spectrum insofar as other bodies are concerned. How could we see to astrogate?" Libby had more than theory to worry him; they were "seeing" now only by electronic vision. To the human eye itself the hemisphere behind them along their track was a vasty black; the shortest radiations had dopplered to wavelengths too long for the eye. In the forward direction stars could still be seen but their visible "light" was made up of longest Hertzian waves crowded in by the ship's incomprehensible speed. Dark "radio stars" shined at first magnitude; stars poor in radio wavelengths had faded to obscurity. The familiar constellations were changed beyond easy recognition. The fact that they were seeing by vision distorted by Doppler's effect was confirmed by spectrum analysis; Fraunhofer's lines had not merely shifted toward the violet end, they had passed beyond, out of sight, and previously unknown patterns replaced them.

"Hmm . . ." King replied. "I see what you mean. But I'd certainly like to try it, damme if I wouldn't! But I admit it's out of the question with passengers inboard. Very well, prepare for me roughed courses to type 'G' stars lying inside this trumpet-flower locus of yours and not too far away. Say ten light-years for your first search."

"Yes, sir. I have. I can't offer anything in that range in the 'G' types."

"So? Lonely out here, isn't it? Well?"

"We have Tau Ceti inside the locus at eleven light-years."

"A G5, eh? Not too good."

"No, sir. But we have a true Sol type, a G2—catalog ZD9817. But it's more than twice as far away."

Captain King chewed a knuckle. "I suppose I'll have to put it up to the elders. How much subjective time advantage are we enjoying?"

"I don't know, sir."

"Eh? Well, work it out! Or give me the data and I will. I don't claim to be the mathematician you are, but any cadet could solve that one. The equations are simple enough."

"So they are, sir. But I don't have the data to substitute in the time-contraction equation . . . because I have no way now to measure the ship's speed. The violet shift is useless to use; we don't know what the lines mean. I'm afraid we must wait until we have worked up a much longer baseline."

King sighed. "Mister, I sometimes wonder why I got into this business. Well, are you willing to venture a best guess? Long time? Short time?"

"Uh . . . a long time, sir. Years."

"So? Well, I've sweated it out in worse ships. Years, eh? Play any chess?"

"I have, sir." Libby did not mention that he had given up the game long ago for lack of adequate competition.

"Looks like we'd have plenty of time to play. King's pawn to king four."

"King's knight to bishop three."

"An unorthodox player, eh? Well, I'll answer you later. I suppose I had better try to sell them the G2 even though it takes longer . . . and I suppose I had better caution Ford to start some contests and things. Can't have 'em getting coffin fever."

"Yes, sir. Did I mention deceleration time? It works out to just under one Earth year, subjective, at a negative one gee, to slow us to stellar speeds."

"Eh? We'll decelerate the same way we accelerated—with your light-pressure drive."

97

Libby shook his head. "I'm sorry, sir. The drawback of the light-pressure drive is that it makes no difference what your previous course and speed may be; if you go inertialess in the near neighborhood of a star, its light pressure kicks you away from it like a cork hit by stream of water. Your previous momentum is canceled out when you cancel your inertia."

"Well," King conceded, "let's assume that we will follow your schedule. I can't argue with you yet; there are still some things about that gadget of yours that I don't understand."

"There are lots of things about it," Libby answered seriously, "that I don't understand either."

The ship had flicked by Earth's orbit less than ten minutes after Libby cut in his space drive. Lazarus and he had discussed the esoteric physical aspects of it all the way to the orbit of Mars—less than a quarter hour. Jupiter's path was far distant when Barstow called the organization conference. But it killed an hour to find them all in the crowded ship; by the time he called them to order they were a billion miles out, beyond the orbit of Saturn—elapsed time from "*Go!*" less than an hour and a half.

But the blocks get longer after Saturn. Uranus found them still in discussion. Nevertheless Ford's name was agreed on and he had accepted before the ship was as far from the Sun as is Neptune. King had been named captain, had toured his new command with Lazarus as guide, and was already in conference with his astrogator when the ship passed the orbit of Pluto nearly four billion miles deep into space, but still less than six hours after the Sun's light had blasted them away.

Even then they were not outside the Solar System, but between them and the stars lay nothing but the winter homes of Sol's comets and hiding places of hypothetical trans-Plutonian planets—space in which the Sun holds options but can hardly be said to own in fee simple. But even the nearest stars were still light-years away. *New Frontiers* was headed for them at a pace which crowded the heels of light—weather cold, track fast.

Out, out, and still farther out . . . out to the lonely depths where world lines are almost straight, undistorted by gravitation. Each day, each month . . . each year . . . their headlong flight took them farther from all humanity.

1 The ship lunged on, alone in the desert of night, each light-year as empty as the last. The Families built up a way of life in her.

The *New Frontiers* was approximately cylindrical. When not under acceleration, she was spun on her axis to give pseudo-weight to passengers near the outer skin of the ship; the outer or "lower" compartments were living quarters while the innermost or "upper" compartments were storerooms and so forth. 'Tween compartments were shops, hydroponic farms and such. Along the axis, fore to aft, were the control room, the converter, and the main drive.

The design will be recognized as similar to that of the larger free-flight interplanetary ships in use today, but it is necessary to bear in mind her enormous size. She was a city, with ample room for a colony of twenty thousand, which would have allowed the planned complement of ten thousand to double their numbers during the long voyage to Proxima Centauri.

Thus, big as she was, the hundred thousand and more of the Families found themselves overcrowded fivefold.

They put up with it only long enough to rig for cold-sleep. By converting some recreation space on the lower levels to storage, room was squeezed out for the purpose. Somnolents require about one per cent the living room needed by active, functioning humans; in time the ship was roomy enough for those still awake. Volunteers for cold-sleep were not numerous at first—these people were more than commonly aware of death because of their unique heritage; cold-sleep seemed too much like the Last Sleep. But the great discomfort of extreme overcrowding combined with the equally extreme monotony of the endless voyage changed their minds rapidly enough to provide a steady supply for the little death as fast as they could be accommodated.

Those who remained awake were kept humping simply to get the work done—the ship's housekeeping, tending the hydroponic farms and the ship's auxiliary machinery and, most especially, caring for the somnolents themselves. Biomechanicians have worked out complex empirical formulas describing body deterioration and the measures which must be taken to offset it under various conditions of impressed acceleration, ambient temperature, the drugs used, and other factors such as metabolic age, body mass, sex, and so forth.

By using the upper, low-weight compartments, deterioration caused by acceleration (that is to say, the simple weight of body tissues on themselves, the wear that leads to flat feet or bed sores) could be held to a minimum. But all the care of the somnolents had to be done by hand—turning them, massaging them, checking on blood sugar, testing the slow-motion heart actions, all the tests and services necessary to make sure that extremely reduced metabolism does not slide over into death. Aside from a dozen stalls in the ships infirmary she had not been designed for cold-sleep passengers; no automatic machinery had been provided. All this tedious care of tens of thousands of somnolents had to be done by hand.

Eleanor Johnson ran across her friend, Nancy Weatheral, in Refectory 9-D—called "The Club" by its habitués, less flattering things by those who avoided it. Most of its frequenters were young and noisy. Lazarus was the only elder who ate there often. He did not mind noise, he enjoyed it.

Eleanor swooped down on her friend and kissed the back of her neck. "Nancy! So you are awake again! My, I'm glad to see you!"

Nancy disentangled herself. "H'lo, babe. Don't spill my coffee."

"Well! Aren't you glad to see *me*?"

"Of course I am. But you forget that while it's been a year to you, it's only yesterday to me. And I'm still sleepy."

"How long have you been awake, Nancy?"

"A couple of hours. How's that kid of yours?"

"Oh, he's fine!" Eleanor Johnson's face brightened. "You wouldn't know him—he's shot up fast this past year. Almost up to my shoulder and looking more like his father every day."

Nancy changed the subject. Eleanor's friends made a point of keeping Eleanor's deceased husband out of the conversation. "What have you been doing while I was snoozing? Still teaching primary?"

"Yes. Or rather 'No.' I stay with the age group my Hubert is in. He's in junior secondary now."

"Why don't you catch a few months' sleep and skip some of that drudgery, Eleanor? You'll make an old woman out of yourself if you keep it up."

"No," Eleanor refused, "not until Hubert is old enough not to need me."

"Don't be sentimental. Half the female volunteers are women with young children. I don't blame 'em a bit. Look at me—from my point of view the trip so far has lasted only seven months. I could do the rest of it standing on my head."

Eleanor looked stubborn. "No, thank you. That may be

all right for you, but I am doing very nicely as I am."

Lazarus had been sitting at the same counter doing drastic damage to a sirloin steak surrogate. "She's afraid she'll miss something," he explained. "I don't blame her. So am I."

Nancy changed her tack. "Then have another child, Eleanor. That'll get you relieved from routine duties."

"It takes two to arrange that," Eleanor pointed out.

"That's no hazard. Here's Lazarus, for example. He'd make a plus father."

Eleanor dimpled. Lazarus blushed under his permanent tan. "As a matter of fact," Eleanor stated evenly, "I proposed to him and was turned down."

Nancy sputtered into her coffee and looked quickly from Lazarus to Eleanor. "Sorry. I didn't know."

"No harm," answered Eleanor. "It's simply because I am one of his granddaughters, four times removed."

"But . . ." Nancy fought a losing fight with the custom of privacy. "Well, goodness me, that's well within the limits of permissible consanguinity. What's the hitch? Or should I shut up?"

"You should," Eleanor agreed.

Lazarus shifted uncomfortably. "I know I'm old-fashioned," he admitted, "but I soaked up some of my ideas a long time ago. Genetics or no genetics, I just wouldn't feel *right* marrying one of my own grandchildren."

Nancy looked amazed. "I'll say you're old-fashioned!" She added, "Or maybe you're just shy. I'm tempted to propose to you myself and find out."

Lazarus glared at her. "Go ahead and see what a surprise you get!"

Nancy looked him over coolly. "Mmm . . ." she meditated.

Lazarus tried to outstare her, finally dropped his eyes. "I'll have to ask you ladies to excuse me," he said nervously. "Work to do."

Eleanor laid a gentle hand on his arm. "Don't go, Lazarus. Nancy is a cat and can't help it. Tell her about the plans for landing."

"What's that? Are we going to land? When? Where?"

Lazarus, willing to be mollified, told her. The type G2, or Sol-type star, toward which they had bent their course years earlier was now less than a light-year away—a little over seven light-months—and it was now possible to infer by para-interferometric methods that the star (ZD9817, or simply "our" star) had planets of some sort.

In another month, when the star would be a half light-year away, deceleration would commence. Spin would be taken off the ship and for one year she would boost back—

wards at one gravity, ending near the star at interplanetary rather than interstellar speed, and a search would be made for a planet fit to support human life. The search would be quick and easy as the only planets they were interested in would shine out brilliantly then, like Venus from Earth; they were not interested in elusive cold planets, like Neptune or Pluto, lurking in distant shadows, nor in sorched cinders like Mercury, hiding in the flaming skirts of the mother star.

If no Earthlike planet was to be had, then they must continue on down really close to the strange sun and again be kicked away by light pressure, to resume hunting for a home elsewhere—with the difference that this time, not harassed by police, they could select a new course with care.

Lazarus explained that the *New Frontiers* would not actually land in either case; she was too big to land, her weight would wreck her. Instead, if they found a planet, she would be thrown into a parking orbit around her and exploring parties would be sent down in ship's boats.

As soon as face permitted Lazarus left the two young women and went to the laboratory where the Families continued their researches in metabolism and gerontology. He expected to find Mary Sperling there; the brush with Nancy Weatheral had made him feel a need for her company. If he ever did marry again, he thought to himself, Mary was more his style. Not that he seriously considered it; he felt that a liaison between Mary and himself would have a ridiculous flavor of lavender and old lace.

Mary Sperling, finding herself cooped up in the ship and not wishing to accept the symbolic death of cold-sleep, had turned her fear of death into constructive channels by volunteering to be a laboratory assistant in the continuing research into longevity. She was not a trained biologist but she had deft fingers and an agile mind; the patient years of the trip had shaped her into a valuable assistant to Dr. Gordon Hardy, chief of the research.

Lazarous found her servicing the deathless tissue of chicken heart known to the laboratory crew as "Mrs. 'Awkins." Mrs. 'Awkins was older than any member of the Familes save possibly Lazarus himself; she was a growing piece of the original tissue obtained by the Families from the Rockefeller Institute in the twentieth century, and the tissues had been alive since early in the twentieth century even then. Dr. Hardy and his predecessors had kept their bit of it alive for more than two centuries now, using the Carrel-Lindbergh-O'Shaug techniques—and still Mrs. 'Awkins flourished.

Gordon Hardy had insisted on taking the tissue and the apparatus which cherished it with him to the reservation when he was arrested; he had been equally stubborn about taking the living tissue along during the escape in the *Chili.* Now Mrs. 'Awkins still lived and grew in the *New Fontiers,* fifty or sixty pounds of her—blind, deaf, and brainless, but still alive.

Mary Sperling was reducing her size. "Hello, Lazarus," she greeted him. "Stand back. I've got the tank open."

He watched her slice off excess tissue. "Mary," he mused, "what keeps that silly thing alive?"

"You've got the question inverted," she answered, not looking up; "the proper form is: why should it die? Why shouldn't it go on forever?"

"I wish to the Devil it would die!" came the voice of Dr. Hardy from behind them. "Then we could observe and find out why."

"You'll never find out why from Mrs. 'Awkins, boss," Mary answered, hands and eyes still busy. "The key to the matter is in the gonads—she hasn't any."

"Hummph! What do you know about it?"

"A woman's intuition. What do *you* know about it?"

"Nothing, absolutely nothing!—which puts me ahead of you and your intuition."

"Maybe. At least," Mary added slyly, "I knew you before you were housebroken."

"A typical female argument. Mary, that lump of muscle cackled and laid eggs before either one of us was born, yet it doesn't know anything." He scowled at it. "Lazarus, I'd gladly trade it for one pair of carp, male and female."

"Why carp?" asked Lazarus.

"Because carp don't seem to die. They get killed, or eaten, or starve to death, or succumb to infection, but so far as we know they don't die."

"Why not?"

"That's what I was trying to find out when we were rushed off on this damned safari. They have unusual intestinal flora and it may have something to do with that. But I think it has to do with the fact that they never stop growing."

Mary said something inaudibly. Hardy said, "What are you muttering about? Another intuition?"

"I said, 'Amebas don't die.' You said yourself that every ameba now alive has been alive for, oh, fifty million years or so. Yet they don't grow indefinitely larger and they certainly can't have intestinal flora."

"No guts," said Lazarus and blinked.

"What a terrible pun, Lazarus. But what I said is true. They don't die. They just twin and keep on living."

"Guts or no guts," Hardy said impatiently, "there may be a structural parallel. But I'm frustrated for lack of experimental subjects. Which reminds me: Lazarus, I'm glad you dropped in. I want you to do me a favor."

"Speak up. I might be feeling mellow."

"You're an interesting case yourself, you know. You didn't follow our genetic pattern; you anticipated it. I don't want your body to go into the converter; I want to examine it."

Lazarus snorted. " 'Sall right with me, bud. But you'd better tell your successor what to look for—you may not live that long. And I'll bet you anything that you like that nobody'll find it by poking around in my cadaver!"

The planet they had hoped for was there when they looked for it, green, lush, and young, and looking as much like Earth as another planet could. Not only was it Earthlike but the rest of the system duplicated roughly the pattern of the Solar System—small terrestrial planets near this sun, large Jovian planets farther out. Cosmologists had never been able to account for the Solar System; they had alternated between theories of origin whch had failed to stand up and "sound" mathematico-physical "proofs" that such a system could never have originated in the first place. Yet here was another enough like it to suggest that its paradoxes were not unique, might even be common.

But more startling and even more stimulating and certainly more disturbing was another fact brought out by telescopic observation as they got close to the planet. The planet held life . . . intelligent life . . . civilized life.

Their cities could be seen. Their engineering works, strange in form and purpose, were huge enough to be seen from space just as ours can be seen.

Nevertheless, though it might mean that they must again pursue their weary hegira, the dominant race did not appear to have crowded the available living space. There might be room for their little colony on those broad continents. If a colony was welcome——

"To tell the truth," Captain King fretted, "I hadn't expected anything like this. Primitive aborigines perhaps, and we certainly could expect dangerous animals, but I suppose I unconsciously assumed that man was the only really civilized race. We're going to have to be very cautious."

King made up a scouting party headed by Lazarus; he had come to have confidence in Lazarus' practical sense and will to survive. King wanted to head the party himself, but his concept of his duty as a ship's captain forced him to forego it. But Slayton Ford could go; Lazarus chose him and Ralph Schultz and his lieutenants. The rest of the party were specialists—biochemist, geologist, ecologist, stereographer, several sorts of psychologists and sociologists to study the natives including one authority in McKelvy's structural theory of communication whose task would be to find some way to talk with the natives.

No weapons——

King flatly refused to arm them. "Your scouting party is expendable," he told Lazarus bluntly; "for we cannot risk offending them by any sort of fighting for any reason, even in self-defense. You are ambassadors, not soldiers. Don't forget it."

Lazarus returned to his stateroom, came back and gravely delivered to King one blaster. He neglected to mention the one still strapped to his leg under his kilt.

As King was about to tell them to man the boat and carry out their orders they were interrupted by Janice Schmidt, chief nurse to the Families' congenital defectives. She pushed her way past and demanded the Captain's attention.

Only a nurse could have obtained it at that moment; she had professional stubbornness to match his and half a century more practice at being balky. He glared at her. "'What's the meaning of this interruption?"

"Captain, I must speak with you about one of my children."

"Nurse, you are decidedly out of order. Get out. See me in my office—after taking it up with the Chief Surgeon."

She put her hands on her hips. "You'll see me now. This is the landing party, isn't it? I've got something you have to hear before they leave."

King started to speak, changed his mind, merely said, "Make it brief."

She did so. Hans Weatheral, a youth of some ninety years and still adolescent in appearance through a hyper-active thymus gland, was one of her charges. He had inferior but not moronic mentality, a chornic apathy, and a neuro-muscular deficiency which made him too weak to feed himself—and an acute sensitivity to telepathy.

He had told Janice that he knew all about the planet around which they orbited. His friends on the planet had told him about it . . . and they were expecting him.

The departure of the landing boat was delayed while King and Lazarus investigated. Hans was matter of fact about his information and what little they could check of what he said was correct. But he was not too helpful about his "friends." "Oh, just people," he said, shrugging at their stupidity. "Much like back home. Nice people. Go to work, go to school, go to church. Have kids and enjoy themselves. You'll like them."

But he was quite clear about one point: his friends were expecting him; therefore he must go along.

Against his wishes and his better judgment Lazarus saw added to his party Hans Weatheral, Janice Schmidt, and a stretcher for Hans.

When the party returned three days later Lazarus made a long private report to King while the specialist reports were being analyzed and combined. "It's amazingly like Earth, Skipper, enough to make you homesick. But it's also different enough to give you the willies—like looking at your own face in the mirror and having it turn out to have three eyes and no nose. Unsettling."

"But how about the natives?"

"Let me tell it. We made a quick swing of the day side, for a bare eyes look. Nothing you haven't seen through the 'scopes. Then I put her down where Hans told me to, in a clearing near the center of one of their cities. I wouldn't have picked the place myself; I would have preferred to land in the bush and reconnoitre. But you told me to play Hans' hunches."

"You were free to use your judgment," King reminded him.

"Yes, yes. Anyhow we did it. By the time the techs had sampled the air and checked for hazards there was quite a crowd around us. They—well, you've seen the stereographs."

"Yes. Incredibly android."

"Android, hell! They're *men*. Not humans, but men just the same." Lazarus looked puzzled. "I don't like it."

King did not argue. The pictures had shown bipeds seven to eight feet tall, bilaterally symmetric, possessed of internal skeletal framework, distinct heads, lens-and-camera eyes. Those eyes were their most human and appealing features; they were large, limpid, and tragic, like those of a Saint Bernard dog.

It was well to concentrate on the eyes; their other features were not as tolerable. King looked away from the loose, toothless mouths, the bifurcated upper lips. He decided that it might take a long, long time to learn to be fond of these creatures. "Go ahead," he told Lazarus.

"We opened up and I stepped out alone, with my hands empty and trying to look friendly and peaceable. Three of them stepped forward—eagerly, I would say. But they lost interest in me at once; they seemed to be waiting for somebody else to come out. So I gave orders to carry Hans out.

"Skipper, you wouldn't believe it. They fawned over Hans like a long lost brother. No, that doesn't describe it. More like a king returning home in triumph. They were polite enough with the rest of us, in an offhand way, but they fairly slobbered over Hans." Lazarus hesitated. "Skipper?

106

Do you believe in reincarnation?"

"Not exactly. I'm open-minded about it. I've read the report of the Frawling Committee, of course."

"I've never had any use for the notion myself. But how else could you account for the reception they gave Hans?"

"I don't account for it. Get on with your report. Do you think it is going to be possible for us to colonize here?"

"Oh," said Lazarus, "they left no doubt on that point. You see, Hans really can talk to them, telepathically. Hans tells us that their gods have authorized us to live here and the natives have already made plans to receive us."

"Eh?"

"That's right. They want us."

"Well! That's a relief."

"Is it?"

King studied Lazarus' glum features. "You've made a report favorable on every point. Why the sour look?"

"I don't know. I'd just rather we found a planet of our own. Skipper, anything this easy has a hitch in it."

2   The Jockaira (or Zhacheira, as some prefer) turned an entire city over to the colonists.
    Such astounding coöperation, plus the sudden discovery by almost every member of the Howard Families that he was sick for the feel of dirt under foot and free air in his lungs, greatly speeded the removal from ship to ground. It had been anticipated that at least an Earth year would be needed for such transition and that somnolents would be waked only as fast as they could be accommodated dirtside. But the limiting factor now was the scanty ability of the ship's boats to transfer a hundred thousand people as they were roused.

The Jockaira city was not designed to fit the needs of human beings. The Jockaira were not human beings, their physical requirements were somewhat different, and their cultural needs as expressed in engineering were vastly different. But a city, any city, is a machine to accomplish certain practical ends: shelter, food supply, sanitation, communication; the internal logic of these prime requirements, as applied by different creatures to different environments, will produce an unlimited number of answers. But, as applied by any race of warm-blooded, oxygen-breathing androidal creatures to a particular environment, the results, although strange, are necessarily such that Terran humans can use them. In some ways the Jockaira city looked as wild as a pararealist painting, but humans have lived in igloos, grass shacks, and even in the cybernautomated burrow under Antarctica; these humans could and did move into the Jockaira city—and of course at once set about reshaping it to suit them better.

It was not difficult even though there much to be done. There were buildings already standing—shelters with roofs on them, the artificial cave basic to all human shelter requirements. It did not matter what the Jockaira had used such a structure for; humans could use it for almost anything: sleeping, recreation, eating, storage, production. There were actual "caves" as well, for the Jockaira dig in more than we do. But humans easily turn troglodyte on occasion, in New York as readily as in Antarctica.

There was fresh potable water piped in for drinking and for limited washing. A major lack lay in plumbing; the city had no over-all drainage system. The "Jocks" did not water-bathe and their personal sanitation requirements differed from ours and were taken care of differently. A major effort had to be made to jury-rig equivalents of shipboard refreshers and adapt them to hook in with Jockaira disposal arrangements. Minimum necessity ruled; baths would remain a rationed luxury until water supply and disposal could be increased at least tenfold. But baths are not a necessity.

But such efforts at modification were minor compared with the crash program to set up hydroponic farming, since most of the somnolents could not be waked until a food supply was assured. The do-it-now crowd wanted to tear out every bit of hydroponic equipment in the *New Frontiers* at once, ship it down dirtside, set it up and get going, while depending on stored supplies during the change-over; a more cautious minority wanted to move only a pilot plant while continuing to grow food in the ship; they pointed out that unsuspected fungus or virus on the strange planet could result in disaster . . . starvation.

The minority, strongly led by Ford and Barstow and supported by Captain King, prevailed; one of the ship's hydroponic farms was drained and put out of service. Its machinery was broken down into parts small enough to load into ship's boats.

But even this never reached dirtside. The planet's native farm products turned out to be suitable for human food and the Jockaira seemed almost pantingly anxious to give them away. Instead, efforts were turned to establishing Earth crops in native soil in order to supplement Jockaira foodstuffs with sorts the humans were used to. The Jockaira moved in and almost took over that effort; they were superb "natural" farmers (they had no need for synthetics on their undepleted planet) and seemed delighted to attempt to raise anything their guests wanted.

Ford transferred his civil headquarters to the city as soon as a food supply for more than a pioneer group was assured, while King remained in the ship. Sleepers were awakened and ferried to the ground as fast as facilities were made ready for them and their services could be used. Despite assured food, shelter, and drinking water, much needed to be done to provide minimum comfort and decency. The two cultures were basically different. The Jockaira seemed always anxious to be endlessly helpful but they were often obviously baffled at what the humans tried to do. The Jockaira culture did not seem to include the idea of privacy; the buildings of the city had no partitions in them which were not loadbearing—and few that were; they tended to use columns or posts. They could not understand why the humans would break up these lovely open spaces into cubicles and passageways; they simply could not comprehend why any individual would ever wish to be alone for any purpose whatsoever.

Apparently (this is not certain for abstract communication with them never reached a subtle level) they decided eventually that being alone held a religious significance for Earth people. In any case they were again helpful; they provided thin sheets of material which could be shaped into partitions—with their tools and only with their tools. The stuff frustrated human engineers almost to nervous collapse. No corrosive known to our technology affected it; even the reactions that would break down the rugged fluorine plastics used in handling uranium compounds had no effect on it. Diamond saws went to pieces on it, heat did not melt it, cold did not make it brittle. It stopped light, sound, and all radiation they were equipped to try on it. Its tensile strength could not be defined because they could not break it. Yet Jockaira tools, even when handled by humans, could cut it, shape it, reweld it.

The human engineers simply had to get used to such frustrations. From the criterion of control over environment through techology the Jockaira were as civilized as humans. But their developments had been along other lines.

The important differences between the two cultures went much deeper than engineering technology. Although ubiquitously friendly and helpful the Jockaira were *not* human. They thought differently, they evaluated differently; their social structure and language structure reflected their unhuman quality and both were incomprehensible to human beings.

Oliver Johnson, the semantician who had charge of developing a common language, found his immediate task made absurdly easy by the channel of communication through

Hans Weatheral. "Of course," he explained to Slayton Ford and to Lazarus, "Hans isn't exactly a genius; he just misses being a moron. That limits the words I can translate through him to ideas he can understand. But it does give me a basic vocabulary to build on."

"Isn't that enough?" asked Ford. "It seems to me that I have heard that eight hundred words will do to convey any idea."

"There's some truth in that," admitted Johnson. "Less than a thousand words will cover all ordinary situations. I have selected not quite seven hundred of their terms, operationals and substantives, to give us a working *lingua franca*. But subtle distinctions and fine discriminations will have to wait until we know them better and understand them. A short vocabulary cannot handle high abstractions."

"Shucks," said Lazarus, "seven hundred words ought to be enough. Me, I don't intend to make love to 'em, or try to discuss poetry."

This opinion seemed to be justified; most of the members picked up basic Jockairan in two weeks to a month after being ferried down and chattered in it with their hosts as if they had talked it all their lives. All of the Earthmen had had the usual sound grounding in mnemonics and semantics; a short-vocabulary auxiliary language was quickly learned under the stimulus of need and the circumstance of plenty of chance to practice—except, of course, by the usual percentage of unshakable provincials who felt that it was up to "the natives" to learn English.

The Jockaria did not learn English. In the first place not one of them showed the slightest interest. Nor was it reasonable to expect their millions to learn the language of a few thousand. But in any case the split upper lip of a Jockaira could not cope with "m," "p," and "b," whereas the gutturals, sibilants, dentals, and clicks they did use could be approximated by the human throat.

Lazarus was forced to revise his early bad impression of the Jockaira. It was impossible not to like them once the strangeness of their appearance had worn off. They were so hospitable, so generous, so friendly, so anxious to please. He became particularly attached to Kreel Sarloo, who acted as a sort of liaison officer between the Families and the Jockaira. Sarloo held a position among his own people which could be translated roughly as "chief," "father," "priest," or "leader" of the Kreel family or tribe. He invited Lazarus to visit him in the Jockaira city nearest the colony. "My people will like to see you and smell your skin," he said. "It will be a happy-making thing. The gods will be pleased."

Sarloo seemed almost unable to form a sentence without

making reference to his gods. Lazarus did not mind; to another's religion he was tolerantly indifferent. "I will come, Sarloo, old bean. It will be a happy-making thing for me, too."

Sarloo took him in the common vehicle of the Jockaira, a wheelless wain shaped much like a soup bowl, which moved quietly and rapidly over the ground, skimming the surface in apparent contact. Lazarus squatted on the floor of the vessel while Sarloo caused it to speed along at a rate that made Lazarus' eyes water.

"Sarloo," Lazarus asked, shouting to make himself heard against the wind, "how does this thing work? What moves it?"

"The gods breathe on the——" Sarloo used a word not in their common language. "——and cause it to need to change its place."

Lazarus started to ask for a fuller explanation, then shut up. There had been something familiar about that answer and he now placed it; he had once given a very similar answer to one of the water people of Venus when he was asked to explain the diesel engine used in an early type of swamp tractor. Lazarus had not meant to be mysterious; he had simply been tongue-tied by inadequate common language.

Well, there was a way to get around that——

"Sarloo, I want to see pictures of what happens inside," Lazarus persisted, pointing. "You have pictures?"

"Pictures are," Sarloo acknowledged, "in the temple. You must not enter the temple." His great eyes looked mournfully at Lazarus, giving him a strong feeling that the Jockaira chief grieved over his friend's lack of grace. Lazarus hastily dropped the subject.

But the thought of Venerians brought another puzzler to mind. The water people, cut off from the outside world by the eternal clouds of Venus, simply did not believe in astronomy. The arrival of Earthmen had caused them to readjust their concept of the cosmos a little, but there was reason to believe that their revised explanation was no closer to the truth. Lazarus wondered what the Jockaira thought about visitors from space. They had shown no surprise—or had they?

"Sarloo," he asked, "do you know where my brothers and I come from?"

"I know," Sarloo answered. "You come from a distant sun—so distant that many seasons would come and go while light traveled that long journey."

Lazarus felt mildly astonished. "Who told you that?"

"The gods tell us. Your brother Libby spoke on it."

Lazarus was willing to lay long odds that the gods had not

111

got around to mentioning it until after Libby explained it to Kreel Sarloo. But he held his peace. He still wanted to ask Sarloo if he had been surprised to have visitors arrive from the skies but he could think of no Jockairan term for surprise or wonder. He was still trying to phrase the question when Sarloo spoke again:

"The fathers of my people flew through the skies as you did, but that was before the coming of the gods. The gods, in their wisdom, bade us stop."

And that, thought Lazarus, is one damn' big lie, from pure swank. There was not the slightest indication that the Jockaira had ever been off the surface of their planet.

At Sarloo's home that evening Lazarus sat through a long session of what he assumed was entertainment for the guest of honor, himself. He squatted beside Sarloo on a raised portion of the floor of the vast common room of the clan Kreel and listened to two hours of howling that might have been intended as singing. Lazarus felt that better music would result from stepping on the tails of fifty assorted dogs but he tried to take it in the spirit in which it seemed to be offered.

Libby, Lazarus recalled, insisted that this mass howling which the Jockaira were wont to indulge in was, in fact, music, and that men could learn to enjoy it by studying its interval relationships.

Lazarus doubted it.

But he had to admit that Libby understood the Jockaira better than he did in some ways. Libby had been delighted to discover that the Jockaira were excellent and subtle mathematicians. In particular they had a grasp of number that paralleled his own wild talent. Their arithmetics were incredibly involved for normal humans. A number, any number large or small, was to them a unique entity, to be grasped in itself and not merely as a grouping of smaller numbers. In consequence they used any convenient positional or exponential notation with any base, rational, irrational, or variable —or none at all.

It was supreme luck, Lazarus mused, that Libby was available to act as mathematical interpreter between the Jockaira and the Families, else it would have been impossible to grasp a lot of the new technologies the Jockaira were showing them.

He wondered why the Jockaira showed no interest in learning human technologies they were offered in return?

The howling discords died away and Lazarus brought his thoughts back to the scene around him. Food was brought in; the Kreel family tackled it with the same jostling enthusiasm with which Jockaira did everything. Dignity, thought

112

Lazarus, is an idea which never caught on here. A large bowl, fully two feet across and brimful of an amorphous mess, was placed in front of Kreel Sarloo. A dozen Kreels crowded around it and started grabbing, giving no precedence to their senior. But Sarloo casually slapped a few of them out of the way and plunged a hand into the dish, brought forth a gob of the ration and rapidly kneaded it into a ball in the palm of his double-thumbed hand. Done, he shoved it towards Lazarus' mouth.

Lazarus was not squeamish but he had to remind himself, first, that food for Jockaira was food for men, and second, that he could not catch anything from them anyhow, before he could bring himself to try the proffered morsel.

He took a large bite. Mmmm . . . not too bad—rather bland and sticky, no particular flavor. Not good, either, but it could be swallowed. Grimly determined to uphold the honor of his race, he ate on, while promising himself a proper meal in the near future. When he felt that to swallow another mouthful would be to invite physical and social disaster, he thought of a possible way out. Reaching into the common plate he scooped up a large handful of the stuff, molded it into a ball and offered it to Sarloo.

It was inspired diplomacy. For the rest of the meal Lazarus fed Sarloo, fed him until his arms were tired, until he marveled at his host's ability to tuck it away.

After eating they slept and Lazarus slept with the family, literally. They slept where they had eaten, without beds and disposed as casually as leaves on a path or puppies in a pen. To his surprise, Lazarus slept well and did not wake until false suns in the cavern roof glowed in mysterious sympathy to new dawn. Sarloo was still asleep near him and giving out most humanlike snores. Lazarus found that one infant Jockaira was cuddled spoon fashion against his own stomach.

He felt a movement behind his back, a rustle at his thigh. He turned cautiously and found that another Jockaira— a six-year-old in human equivalence—had extracted his blaster from its holster and was now gazing curiously into its muzzle.

With hasty caution Lazarus removed the deadly toy from the child's unwilling fingers, noted with relief that the safety was still on, and reholstered it. Lazarus received a reproachful look; the kid seemed about to cry. "Hush," whispered Lazarus, "you'll wake your old man. Here——" He gathered the child into his left arm and cradled it against his side. The little Jockaira snuggled up to him, laid a soft moist mouth against his hide, and promptly went to sleep.

Lazarus looked down at him. "You're a cute little devil," he said softly. "I could grow right fond of you if I could ever get used to your smell."

Some of the incidents between the two races would have been funny had they not been charged with potential trouble: for example, the case of Eleanor Johnson's son Hubert. This gangling adolescent was a confirmed sidewalk superintendent. One day he was watching two technicians, one human and one Jockaira, adapt a Jockaira power source to the needs of Earth-type machinery. The Jockaira was apparently amused by the boy and, in an obviously friendly spirit, picked him up.

Hubert began to scream.

His mother, never far from him, joined battle. She lacked strength and skill to do the utter destruction she was bent on; the big nonhuman was unhurt, but it created a nasty situation.

Administrator Ford and Oliver Johnson tried very hard to explain the incident to the amazed Jockaira. Fortunately, they seemed grieved rather than vengeful.

Ford then called in Eleanor Johnson. "You have endangered the entire colony by your stupidity——"

"But I——"

"Keep *quiet!* If you hadn't spoiled the boy rotten, he would have behaved himself. If you weren't a maudlin fool, you would have kept your hands to yourself. The boy goes to the regular development classes henceforth and you are to let him alone. At the slightest sign of animosity on your part toward any of the natives, I'll have you subjected to a few years' cold-rest. Now get out!"

Ford was forced to use almost as strong measures on Janice Schmidt. The interest shown in Hans Weatheral by the Jockaira extended to all of the telepathic defectives. The natives seemed to be reduced to a state of quivering adoration by the mere fact that these could communicate with them directly. Kreel Sarloo informed Ford that he wanted the sensitives to be housed separately from the other defectives in the evacuated temple of the Earthmen's city and that the Jockaira wished to wait on them personally. It was more of an order than a request.

Janice Schmidt submitted ungracefully to Ford's insistence that the Jockaira be humored in the matter in return for all that they had done, and Jockaria nurses took over under her jealous eyes.

Every sensitive of intelligence level higher than the semi-moronic Hans Weatheral promptly developed spontaneous and extreme psychoses while being attended by Jockaira.

114

So Ford had another headache to straighten out. Janice Schmidt was more powerfully and more intelligently vindictive than was Eleanor Johnson. Ford was forced to bind Janice over to keep the peace under the threat of retiring her completely from the care of her beloved "children." Kreel Sarloo, distressed and apparently shaken to his core, accepted a compromise whereby Janice and her junior nurses resumed care of the poor psychotics while Jockaira continued to minister to sensitives of moron level and below.

But the greatest difficulty arose over . . . surnames.

Jockaira each had an individual name and a surname. Surnames were limited in number, much as they were in the Families. A native's surname referred equally to his tribe and to the temple in which he worshipped.

Kreel Sarloo took up the matter with Ford. "High Father of the Strange Brothers," he said, "the time has come for you and your children to choose your surnames." (The rendition of Sarloo's speech into English necessarily contains inherent errors.)

Ford was used to difficulties in understanding the Jockaira. "Sarloo, brother and friend," he answered, "I hear your words but I do not understand. Speak more fully."

Sarloo began over. "Strange brother, the seasons come and the seasons go and there is a time of ripening. The gods tell us that you, the Strange Brothers, have reached the time in your education (?) when you must select your tribe and your temple. I have come to arrange with you the preparations (ceremonies?) by which each will choose his surname. I speak for the gods in this. But let me say for myself that it would make me happy if you, my brother Ford, were to choose the temple Kreel."

Ford stalled while he tried to understand what was implied. "I am happy that you wish me to have your surname. But my people already have their own surnames."

Sarloo dismissed that with a flip of his lips. "Their present surnames are words and nothing more. Now they must choose their real surnames, each the name of his temple and of the god whom he will worship. Children grow up and are no longer children."

Ford decided that he needed advice. "Must this be done at once?"

"Not today, but in the near future. The gods are patient."

Ford called in Zaccur Barstow, Oliver Johnson, Lazarus Long, and Ralph Schultz, and described the interview. Johnson played back the recording of the conversation and strained to catch the sense of the words. He prepared several possible translations but failed to throw any new light on the matter.

"It looks," said Lazarus, "like a case of join the church or get out."

"Yes," agreed Zaccur Barstow, "that much seems to come through plainly. Well, I think we can afford to go through the motions. Very few of our people have religious prejudices strong enough to forbid their paying lip service to the native gods in the interests of the general welfare."

"I imagine you are correct," Ford said. "I, for one, have no objection to adding Kreel to my name and taking part in their genuflections if it will help us to live in peace." He frowned. "But I would not want to see our culture submerged in theirs."

"You can forget that," Ralph Schultz assured him. "No matter what we have to do to please them, there is absolutely no chance of any real cultural assimilation. Our brains are not like theirs—just how different I am only beginning to guess."

"Yeah," said Lazarus, " 'just how different.' "

Ford turned to Lazarus. "What do you mean by that? What's troubling you?"

"Nothing. Only," he added, "I never did share the general enthusiasm for this place."

They agreed that one man should take the plunge first, then report back. Lazarus tried to grab the assignment on seniority, Schultz claimed it as a professional right; Ford overruled them and appointed himself, asserting that it was his duty as the responsible executive.

Lazarus went with him to the doors of the temple where the induction was to take place. Ford was as bare of clothing as the Jockaira, but Lazarus, since he was not to enter the temple, was able to wear his kilt. Many of the colonists, sunstarved after years in the ship, went bare when it suited them, just as the Jockaira did. But Lazarus never did. Not only did his habits run counter to it, but a blaster is an extremely conspicuous object on a bare thigh.

Kreel Sarloo greeted them and escorted Ford inside. Lazarus called out after them, "Keep your chin up, pal!"

He waited. He struck a cigarette and smoked it. He walked up and down. He had no way to judge how long it would be; it seemed, in consequence, much longer than it was.

At last the doors slid back and natives crowded out through them. They seemed curiously worked up about something and none of them came near Lazarus. The press that still existed in the great doorway separated, formed an aisle, and a figure came running headlong through it and out into the open.

Lazarus recognized Ford.

Ford did not stop where Lazarus waited but plunged

blindly on past. He tripped and fell down. Lazarus hurried to him.

Ford made no effort to get up. He lay sprawled face down, his shoulders heaving violently, his frame shaking with sobs.

Lazarus knelt by him and shook him. "Slayton," he demanded, "what's happened? What's wrong with you?" Ford turned wet and horror-stricken eyes to him, checking his sobs momentarily. He did not speak but he seemed to recognize Lazarus. He flung himself on Lazarus, clung to him, wept more violently than before.

Lazarus wrenched himself free and slapped Ford hard. "Snap out of it!" he ordered. "Tell me what's the matter."

Ford jerked his head at the slap and stopped his outcries but he said nothing. His eyes looked dazed. A shadow fell across Lazarus' line of sight; he spun around, covering with his blaster. Kreel Sarloo stood a few feet away and did not come closer—not because of the weapon; he had never seen one before.

"You!" said Lazarus. "For the—— What did you do to him?"

He checked himself and switched to speech that Sarloo could understand. "What has happened to my brother Ford?"

"Take him away," said Sarloo, his lips twitching. "This is a bad thing. This is a very bad thing."

"You're telling me!" said Lazarus. He did not bother to translate.

3 The same conference as before, minus its chairman, met as quickly as possible. Lazarus told his story, Shultz reported on Ford's condition. "The medical staff can't find anything wrong with him. All I can say with certainty is that the Administrator is suffering from an undiagnosed extreme psychosis. We can't get into communication with him."

"Won't he talk at all?" asked Barstow.

"A word or two, on subjects as simple as food or water. Any attempt to reach the cause of his trouble drives him into incoherent hysteria."

"No diagnosis?"

"Well, if you want an unprofessional guess in loose language, I'd say he was scared out of his wits. But," Shultz added, "I've seen fear syndromes before. Never anything like this."

"I have," Lazarus said suddenly.

"You have? Where? What were the circumstances?"

"Once," said Lazarus, "when I was a kid, a couple of hundred years back, I caught a grown coyote and penned him up. I had a notion I could train him to be a hunting dog. It didn't work.

"Ford acts just the way that coyote did."

An unpleasant silence followed. Schultz broke it with, "I don't quite see what you mean. What is the parallel?"

"Well," Lazarus answered slowly, "this is just my guess. Slayton is the only one who knows the true answer and he can't talk. But here's my opinion: we've had these Jockaira doped out all wrong from scratch. We made the mistake of thinking that because they looked like us, in a general way, and were about as civilized as we are, that they were *people*. But they aren't people at all. They are . . . *domestic animals*.

"Wait a minute now!" he added. "Don't get in a rush. There are people on this planet, right enough. Real people. They lived in the temples and the Jockaira called them gods. They *are* gods!"

Lazarus pushed on before anyone could interrupt. "I know what you're thinking. Forget it. I'm not going metaphysical on you; I'm just putting it the best I can. I mean that there is something living in those temples and whatever it is, it is such heap big medicine that it can pinch-hit for gods, so you might as well call 'em that. Whatever they are, they are the true dominant race on this planet—its *people!* To them, the rest of us, Jocks or us, are just animals, wild or tame. We made the mistake of assuming that a local religion was merely superstition. It ain't."

Barstow said slowly, "And you think this accounts for what happened to Ford?"

"I do. He met one, the one called Kreel, and it drove him crazy."

"I take it," said Schultz, "that it is your theory that any man exposed to this . . . this *presence* . . . would become phychotic?"

"Not exactly," answered Lazarus. "What scares me a damn' sight more is the fear that I might *not* go crazy!"

That same day the Jockaira withdrew all contact with the Earthmen. It was well that they did so, else there would have been violence. Fear hung over the city, fear of horror worse than death, fear of some terrible nameless thing, the mere knowledge of which could turn a man into a broken mindless animal. The Jockaira no longer seemed harmless friends, rather clownish despite their scientific attainments, but puppets, decoys, bait for the unseen potent beings who lurked in the "temples."

There was no need to vote on it; with the single-mindedness of a crowd stampeding from a burning building the

Earthmen wanted to leave this terrible place. Zaccur Barstow assumed command. "Get King on the screen. Tell him to send down every boat at once. We'll get out of here as fast as we can." He ran his fingers worriedly through his hair. "What's the most we can load each trip, Lazarus? How long will the evacuation take?"

Lazarus muttered.

"What did you say?"

"I said, 'It ain't a case of how long; it's a case of will we be let.' Those things in the temples may want more domestic animals—us!"

Lazarus was needed as a boat pilot but he was needed more urgently for his ability to manage a crowd. Zaccur Barstow was telling him to conscript a group of emergency police when Lazarus looked past Zaccur's shoulder and exclaimed, "Oh oh! Hold it, Zack—school's out."

Zaccur turned his head quickly and saw, approaching with stately dignity across the council hall, Kreel Sarloo. No one got in his way.

They soon found out why. Zaccur moved forward to greet him, found himself stopped about ten feet from the Jockaira. No clue to the cause; just that—stopped.

"I greet you, unhappy brother," Sarloo began.

"I greet you, Kreel Sarloo."

"The gods have spoken. Your kind can never be civilized (?). You and your brothers are to leave this world."

Lazarus let out a deep sigh of relief.

"We are leaving, Kreel Sarloo," Zaccur answered soberly.

"The gods require that you leave. Send your brother Libby to me."

Zaccur sent for Libby, then turned back to Sarloo. But the Jockaira had nothing more to say to them; he seemed indifferent to their presence. They waited.

Libby arrived. Sarloo held him in a long conversation. Barstow and Lazarus were both in easy earshot and could see their lips move, but heard nothing. Lazarus found the circumstance very disquieting. Damn my eyes, he thought, I could figure several ways to pull that trick with the right equipment but I'll bet none of 'em is the right answer—and I don't see any equipment.

The silent discussion ended, Sarloo stalked off without farewell. Libby turned to the others and spoke; now his voice could be heard. "Sarloo tells me," he began, brow wrinkled in puzzlement, "that we are to go to a planet, uh, over thirty-two light-years from here. The gods have decided it." He stopped and bit his lip.

"Don't fret about it," advised Lazarus. "Just be glad they

119

want us to leave. My guess is that they could have squashed us flat just as easily. Once we're out in space we'll pick our own destination."

"I suppose so. But the thing that puzzles me is that he mentioned a time about three hours away as being our departure from this system."

"Why, that's utterly unreasonable," protested Barstow. "Impossible. We haven't the boats to do it."

Lazarus said nothing. He was ceasing to have opinions.

Zaccur changed his opinion quickly. Lazarus acquired one, born of experience. While urging his cousins toward the field where embarkation was proceeding, he found himself lifted up, free of the ground. He struggled, his arms and legs met no resistance but the ground dropped away. He closed his eyes, counted ten jets, opened them again. He was at least two miles in the air.

Below him, boiling up from the city like bats from a cave, were uncountable numbers of dots and shapes, dark against the sunlit ground. Some were close enough for him to see that they were men, Earthmen, the Families.

The horizon dipped down, the planet became a sphere, the sky turned black. Yet his breathing seemed normal, his blood vessels did not burst.

They were sucked into clusters around the open ports of the *New Frontiers* like bees swarming around a queen. Once inside the ship Lazarus gave himself over to a case of the shakes. *Whew!* he sighed to himself, watch that first step —it's a honey!

Libby sought out Captain King as soon as he was inboard and had recovered his nerve. He delivered Sarloo's message.

King seemed undecided. "I don't know," he said. "You know more about the natives than I do, inasmuch as I have hardly put foot to ground. But between ourselves, Mister, the way they sent my passengers back has me talking to myself. That was the most remarkable evolution I have ever seen performed."

"I might add that it was remarkable to experience, sir," Libby answered unhumorously. "Personally I would prefer to take up ski jumping. I'm glad you had the ship's access ports open."

"I didn't," said King tersely. "They were opened for me."

They went to the control room with the intention of getting the ship under boost and placing a long distance between it and the planet from which they had been evicted; thereafter they would consider destination and course. "This planet that Sarloo described to you," said King, "does it belong to a G-type star?"

"Yes," Libby confirmed, "an Earth-type planet accompanying a Sol-type star. I have its coördinates and could identify from the catalogues. But we can forget it; it is too far away."

"So . . ." King activated the vision system for the stellarium. Then neither of them said anything for several long moments. The images of the heavenly bodies told their own story.

With no orders from King, with no hands at the controls, the *New Frontiers* was on her long way again, headed out, as if she had a mind of her own.

"I can't tell you much," admitted Libby some hours later to a group consisting of King, Zaccur Barstow, and Lazarus Long. "I was able to determine, before we passed the speed of light—or appeared to—that our course then was compatible with the idea that we have been headed toward the star named by Kreel Sarloo as the destination ordered for us by his gods. We continued to accelerate and the stars faded out. I no longer have any astrogational reference points and I am unable to say where we are or where we are going."

"Loosen up, Andy," suggested Lazarus. "Make a guess."

"Well . . . if our world line is a smooth function—*if* it is, and I have no data—then we may arrive in the neighborhood of star PK3722, where Kreel Sarloo said we were going."

"Rummph!" Lazarus turned to King. "Have you tried slowing down?"

"Yes," King said shortly. "The controls are dead."

"Mmmm . . . Andy, when do we get there?"

Libby shrugged helplessly. "I have no frame of reference. What is time without a space reference?"

Time and space, inseparable and one—— Libby thought about it long after the others had left. To be sure, he had the space framework of the ship itself and therefore there necessarily was ship's time. Clocks in the ship ticked or hummed or simply marched; people grew hungry, fed themselves, got tired, rested. Radioactives deteriorated, physicochemical processes moved toward states of greater entropy, his own consciousness perceived duration.

But the background of the stars, against which every timed function in the history of man had been measured, was gone. So far as his eyes or any instrument in the ship could tell him, they had become unrelated to the rest of the universe.

What universe?

There was no universe. It was gone.

Did they move? Can there be motion when there is nothing to move past?

Yet the false weight achieved by the spin of the ship persisted. Spin with reference to *what?* thought Libby. Could it be that space held a true, absolute, nonrelational texture of its own, like that postulated for the long-discarded "ether" that the classic Michelson-Morley experiments had failed to detect? No, more than that—had denied the very possibility of its existence?

—had for that matter denied the possibility of speed greater than light. Had the ship actually passed the speed of light? Was it not more likely that this was a coffin, with ghosts as passengers, going nowhere at no time?

But Libby itched between his shoulder blades and was forced to scratch; his left leg had gone to sleep; his stomach was beginning to speak insistently for food—if this was death, he decided, it did not seem materially different from life.

With renewed tranquility, he left the control room and headed for his favorite refectory, while starting to grapple with the problem of inventing a new mathematics which would include all the new phenomenia. The mystery of how the hypothetical gods of the Jockaira had teleported the Families from ground to ship he discarded. There had been no opportunity to obtain significant data, *measured* data; the best that any honest scientist could do, with epistemological rigor, was to include a note that recorded the fact and stated that it was unexplained. It *was* a fact; here he was who shortly before had been on the planet; even now Schultz's assistants were overworked trying to administer depressant drugs to the thousands who had gone to pieces emotionally under the outrageous experience.

But Libby could not explain it and, lacking data, felt no urge to try. What he did want to do was to deal with world lines in a plenum, the basic problem of field physics.

Aside from his penchant for mathematics Libby was a simple person. He preferred the noisy atmosphere of the "Club," refectory 9-D, for reasons different from those of Lazarus. The company of people younger than himself reassured him; Lazarus was the only elder he felt easy with.

Food, he learned, was not immediately available at the Club; the commissary was still adjusting to the sudden change. But Lazarus was there and others whom he knew; Nancy Weatheral scrunched over and made room for him. "You're just the man I want to see," she said. "Lazarus is being most helpful. Where are we going this time and when do we get there?"

Libby explained the dilemma as well as he could. Nancy wrinkled her nose. "That's a pretty prospect, I must say! Well, I guess that means back to the grind for little Nancy."

"What do you mean?"

"Have you ever taken care of a somnolent? No, of course you haven't. It gets tiresome. Turn them over, bend their arms, twiddle their tootsies, move their heads, close the tank and move on to the next one. I get so sick of human bodies that I'm tempted to take a vow of chastity."

"Don't commit yourself too far," advised Lazarus.

"Why would you care, you old false alarm?"

Eleanor Johnson spoke up. "I'm *glad* to be in the ship again. Those slimy Jockaira—ugh!"

Nancy shrugged. "You're prejudiced, Eleanor. The Jocks are okay, in their way. Sure, they aren't exactly like us, but neither are dogs. You don't dislike dogs, do you?"

"That's what they are," Lazarus said soberly. "Dogs."

"Huh?"

"I don't mean that they are anything like dogs in most ways—they aren't even vaguely canine and they certainly are our equals and possibly our superiors in some things . . . but they are dogs just the same. Those things they call their 'gods' are simply their masters, their owners. We couldn't be domesticated, so the owners chucked us out."

Libby was thinking of the inexplicable telekinesis the Jockaira—or their masters—had used. "I wonder what it would have been like," he said thoughtfully, "if they had been able to domesticate us. They could have taught us a lot of wonderful things."

"Forget it," Lazarus said sharply. "It's not a man's place to be property."

"What is a man's place?"

"It's a man's business to be what he is . . . and be it in style!" Lazarus got up. "Got to go."

Libby started to leave also, but Nancy stopped him. "Don't go. I want to ask you some questions. What year is it back on Earth?"

Libby started to answer, closed his mouth. He started to answer a second time, finally said, "I don't know how to answer that question. It's like saying, 'How high is up?'"

"I know I probably phrased it wrong," admitted Nancy. "I didn't do very well in basic physics, but I did gather the idea that time is relative and simultaneity is an idea which applies only to two points close together in the same framework. But just the same, I want to know something. We've traveled a lot faster and farther than anyone ever did before, haven't we? Don't our clocks slow down, or something?"

Libby got that completely baffled look which mathematical physicists wear whenever laymen try to talk about physics in nonmathematical language. "You're referring to the Lorentz-FitzGerald contraction. But, if you'll pardon me, anything one says about it in words is necessarily nonsense."

"Why?" she insisted.

"Because . . . well, because the language is inappropriate. The formulae used to describe the effect loosely called a contraction presuppose that the observer is part of the phenomenon. But verbal language contains the implicit assumption that we can stand outside the whole business and watch what goes on. The mathematical language denies the very possibility of any such outside viewpoint. Every observer has his own world line; he can't get outside it for a detached viewpoint."

"But suppose he did? Suppose we could see Earth right now?"

"There I go again," Libby said miserably. "I tried to talk about it in words and all I did was to add to the confusion. There is no way to measure time in any absolute sense when two events are separated in a continuum. All you can measure is interval."

"Well, what is interval? So much space and so much time."

"No, no, no! It isn't that at all. Interval is . . . well, it's interval. I can write down formulae about it and show you how we use it, but it can't be defined in words. Look, Nancy, can you write the score for a full orchestration of a symphony in words?"

"No. Well, maybe you could but it would take thousands of times as long."

"And musicians still could play it until you put it back into musical notation. That's what I meant," Libby went on, "when I said that the language was inappropriate. I got into a difficulty like this once before in trying to describe the light-pressure drive. I was asked why, since the drive depends on loss of inertia, we people inside the ship had felt no loss of inertia. There was no answer, in words. Inertia isn't a word; it is a mathematical concept used in *mathematically* certain aspects of a plenum. I was stuck."

Nancy looked baffled but persisted doggedly. "My question still means something, even if I didn't phrase it right. You can't just tell me to run along and play. Suppose we turned around and went back the way we came, all the way to Earth, exactly the same trip but in reverse—just double the ship's time it has been so far. All right, what year would it be on Earth when we got there?"

"It would be . . . let me see, now——" The almost automatic processes of Libby's brain started running off the unbelievably huge and complex problem in accelerations, intervals, difform motion. He was approaching the answer in a warm glow of mathematical revery when the problem suddenly fell to pieces on him, became indeterminate. He abruptly realized that the problem had an unlimited number of equally valid answers.

But that was impossible. In the real world, not the fantasy world of mathematics, such a situation was absurd. Nancy's question had to have just one answer, unique and real.

Could the whole beautiful structure of relativity be an absurdity? Or did it mean that it was physically impossible ever to back-track an interstellar distance?

"I'll have to give some thought to that one," Libby said hastily and left before Nancy could object.

But solitude and contemplation gave him no clue to the problem. It was not a failure of his mathematical ability; he was capable, he knew, of devising a mathematical description of any group of facts, whatever they might be. His difficulty lay in having too few facts. Until some observer traversed interstellar distances at speeds approximating the speed of light *and returned to the planet from which he had started* there could be no answer. Mathematics alone has no content, gives no answers.

Libby found himself wondering if the hills of his native Ozarks were still green, if the smell of wood smoke still clung to the trees in the autumn, then he recalled that the question lacked any meaning by any rules he knew of. He surrendered to an attack of homesickness such as he had not experienced since he was a youth in the Cosmic Construction Corps, making his first deep-space jump.

This feeling of doubt and uncertainty, the feeling of lostness and nostalgia, spread throughout the ship. On the first leg of their journey the Families had had the incentive that had kept the covered wagons crawling across the plains. But now they were going nowhere, one day led only to the next. Their long lives were become a meaningless burden.

Ira Howard, whose fortune established the Howard Foundation, was born in 1825 and died in 1873—of old age. He sold groceries to the Forty-niners in San Francisco, became a wholesale sutler in the American War of the Secession, multiplied his fortune during the tragic Reconstruction.

Howard was deathly afraid of dying. He hired the best doctors of his time to prolong his life. Nevertheless old age plucked him when most men are still young. But his will commanded that his money be used "to lengthen human life." The administrators of the trust found no way to carry out his wishes other than by seeking out persons whose family trees showed congenital predispositions toward long life and then inducing them to reproduce in kind. Their

125

method anticipated the work of Burbank; they may or may not have known of the illuminating researches of the Monk Gregor Mendel.

Mary Sperling put down the book she had been reading when Lazarus entered her stateroom. He picked it up. "What are you reading, Sis? 'Ecclesiastes.' Hmm . . . I didn't know you were religious." He read aloud:

" 'Yea, though he live a thousand years twice told, yet hath he seen no good: do not all go to one place?'

"Pretty grim stuff, Mary. Can't you find something more cheerful? Even in The Preacher?" His eyes skipped on down. "How about this one? 'For to him that is joined to all the living there is hope——' Or . . . mmmm, not too many cheerful spots. Try this: 'Therefore remove sorrow from thy heart, and put away evil from thy flesh: for childhood and youth are vanity.' That's more my style; I wouldn't be young again for overtime wages."

"I would."

"Mary, what's eating you? I find you sitting here, reading the most depressing book in the Bible, nothing but death and funerals. Why?"

She passed a hand wearily across her eyes. "Lazarus, I'm getting old. What else is there to think about?"

"You? Why, you're fresh as a daisy!"

She looked at him. She knew that he lied; her mirror showed her the greying hair, the relaxed skin; she felt it in her bones. Yet Lazarus was older than she . . . although she knew, from what she had learned of biology during the years she had assisted in the longevity research, that Lazarus should never have lived to be as old as he was now. When he was born the program had reached only the third generation, too few generations to eliminate the less durable strains —except through some wildly unlikely chance shuffling of genes.

But there he stood. "Lazarus," she asked, "how long do you expect to live?"

"Me? Now that's an odd question. I mind a time when I asked a chap that very same question—about me, I mean, not about him. Ever hear of Dr. Hugo Pinero?"

" 'Pinero . . . Pinero . . .' Oh, yes, 'Pinero the Charlatan.' "

"Mary, he was no charlatan. He could do it, no foolin'. He could predict accurately when a man would die."

"But—— Go ahead. What did he tell you?"

"Just a minute. I want you to realize that he was no fake. His predictions checked out right on the button—if he hadn't died, the life insurance companies would have been ruined. That was before you were born, but I was there and I know.

Anyhow, Pinero took my reading and it seemed to bother him. So he took it again. Then he returned my money."

"What did he say?"

"Couldn't get a word out of him. He looked at me and he looked at his machine and he just frowned and clammed up. So I can't rightly answer your question."

"But what do *you* think about it, Lazarus? Surely you don't expect just to go on forever?"

"Mary," he said softly, "I'm not planning on dying. I'm not giving it any thought at all."

There was silence. At last she said, "Lazarus, I don't want to die. But what is the purpose of our long lives? We don't seem to grow wiser as we grow older. Are we simply hanging on after our time has passed? Loitering in the kindergarten when we should be moving on? Must we die and be born again?"

"I don't know," said Lazarus, "and I don't have any way to find out . . . and I'm damned if I see any sense in my worrying about it. Or you either. I propose to hang onto this life as long as I can and learn as much as I can. Maybe wisdom and understanding are reserved for a later existence and maybe they aren't for us at all, ever. Either way, I'm satisfied to be living and enjoying it. Mary my sweet, carp that old diem!—it's only game in town."

The ship slipped back into the same monotonous routine that had obtained during the weary years of the first jump. Most of the Members went into cold-rest; the others tended them, tended the ship, tended the hydroponds. Among the somnolents was Slayton Ford; cold-rest was a common last-resort therapy for functional psychoses.

The flight to star PK3722 took seventeen months and three days, ship's time.

The ships officers had as little choice about the journey's end as about its beginning. A few hours before their arrival star images flashed back into being in the stellarium screens and the ship rapidly decelerated to interplanetary speeds. No feeling of slowing down was experienced; whatever mysterious forces were acting on them acted on all masses alike. The *New Frontiers* slipped into an orbit around a live green planet some hundred million miles from its sun; shortly Libby reported to Captain King that they were in a stable parking orbit.

Cautiously King tried the controls, dead since their departure. The ship surged; their ghostly pilot had left them.

Libby decided that the simile was incorrect; this trip had undoubtedly been planned for them but it was not necessary to assume that anyone or anything had shepherded them here.

Libby suspected that the "gods" of the dog-people saw the plenum as static; their deportation was an accomplished fact to them before regrettably studded with unknowns—but there were no appropriate words. Inadequately and incorrectly put into words, his concept was that of a "cosmic cam," a world line shaped for them which ran out of normal space and back into it; when the ship reached the end of its "cam" it returned to normal operation.

He tried to explain his concept to Lazarus and to the Captain, but he did not do well. He lacked data and also had not had time to refine his mathematical description into elegance; it satisfied neither him nor them.

Neither King nor Lazarus had time to give the matter much thought. Barstow's face appeared on an interstation viewscreen. "Captain!" he called out. "Can you come aft to lock seven? We have visitors!"

Barstow had exaggerated; there was only one. The creature reminded Lazarus of a child in fancy dress, masqueraded as a rabbit. The little thing was more android than were the Jockaira, though possibly not mammalian. It was unclothed but not naked, for its childlike body was beautifully clothed in short sleek golden fur. Its eyes were bright and seemed both merry and intelligent.

But King was too bemused to note such detail. A voice, a thought, was ringing in his head: ". . . so you are the group leader . . ." it said. ". . . welcome to our world . . . we have been expecting you . . . the (*blank*) told us of your coming . . ."

Controlled telepathy——

A creature, a race, so gentle, so civilized, so free from enemies, from all danger and strife that they could afford to share their thoughts with others—to share more than their thoughts; these creatures were so gentle and so generous that they were offering the humans a homestead on their planet. This was why this messenger had come: to make that offer.

To King's mind this seemed remarkably like the prize package that had been offered by the Jockaira; he wondered what the boobytrap might be in this proposition.

The messenger seemed to read his thought. ". . . look into our hearts . . . we hold no malice toward you . . . we share your love of life and we love the life in you . . ."

"We thank you," King answered formally and aloud. "We will have to confer." He turned to speak to Barstow, glanced back. The messenger was gone.

The Captain said to Lazarus, "Where did he go?"

"Huh? Don't ask me."

"But you were in front of the lock."

"I was checking the tell-tales. There's no boat sealed on outside this lock—so they show. I was wondering if they were working right. They are. How did he get into the ship? Where's his rig?"

"How did he *leave*?"

"Not past me!"

"Zaccur, he came in through this lock, didn't he?"

"I don't know."

"But he certainly went out through it."

"Nope," denied Lazarus. "This lock hasn't been opened. The deep-space seals are still in place. See for yourself."

King did. "You don't suppose," he said slowly, "that he can pass through——"

"Don't look at me," said Lazarus. "I've got no more prejudices in the matter than the Red Queen. Where does a phone image go when you cut the circuit?" He left, whistling softly to himself. King did not recognize the tune. Its words, which Lazarus did not sing, started with:

> *"Last night I saw upon the stair*
> *A little man who wasn't there——"*

4.
There was no catch to the offer. The people of the planet—they had no name since they had no spoken language and the Earthmen simply called them "The Little People"—the little creatures really did welcome them and help them. They convinced the Families of this without difficulty for there was no trouble in communication such as there had been with the Jockaira. The Little People could make even subtle thoughts known directly to the Earthmen and in turn could sense correctly any thought directed at them. They appeared either to ignore or not to be able to read any thought not directed at them; communication with them was as controlled as spoken speech. Nor did the Earthmen acquire any telepathic powers among themselves.

Their planet was even more like Earth than was the planet of the Jockaira. It was a little larger than Earth but had a slightly lower surface gravitation, suggesting a lower average density—the Little People made slight use of metals in their culture, which may be indicative.

The planet rode upright in its orbit; it had not the rakish tilt of Earth's axis. Its orbit was nearly circular; aphelion differed from perhelion by less than one per cent. There were no seasons.

Nor was there a great heavy moon, such as Earth has, to wrestle its oceans about and to disturb the isostatic balance of its crust. Its hills were low, its winds were gentle, its seas were placid. To Lazarus' disappointment, their new home had no lively weather; it hardly had weather at all; it had climate, and that of the sort that California patriots would have the rest of the Earth believe exists in their part of the globe.

But on the planet of the Little People it really exists.

They indicated to the Earth people where they were to land, a wide sandy stretch of beach running down to the sea. Back of the low break of the bank lay mile on mile of lush meadowland, broken by irregular clumps of bushes and trees. The landscape had a careless neatness, as if it were a planned park, although there was no evidence of cultivation.

It was here, a messenger told the first scouting party, that they were welcome to live.

There seemed always to be one of the Little People present when his help might be useful—not with the jostling inescapable overhelpfulness of the Jockaira, but with the unobtrusive readiness to hand of a phone or a pouch knife. The one who accompanied the first party of explorers confused Lazarus and Barstow by assuming casually that he had met them before, that he had visited them in the ship. Since his fur was rich mahogany rather than golden, Barstow attributed the error to misunderstanding, with a mental reservation that these people might possibly be capable of chameleonlike changes in color. Lazarus reserved his judgment.

Barstow asked their guide whether or not his people had any preferences as to where and how the Earthmen were to erect buildings. The question had been bothering him because a preliminary survey from the ship had disclosed no cities. It seemed likely that the natives lived underground —in which case he wanted to avoid getting off on the wrong foot by starting something which the local government might regard as a slum.

He spoke aloud in words directed at their guide, they having learned already that such was the best way to insure that the natives would pick up the thought.

In the answer that the little being flashed back Barstow caught the emotion of surprise. ". . . must you sully the sweet countryside with interruptions? . . . to what purpose do you need to form buildings? . . ."

"We need buildings for many purposes," Barstow explained. "We need them as daily shelter, as places to sleep at night. We need them to grow our food and prepare it for eating." He considered trying to explain the processes of hydroponic farming, of food processing, and of cooking, then dropped it, trusting to the subtle sense of telepathy to let his "listener" understand. "We need buildings for many other uses, for workshops and laboratories, to house the machines whereby we communicate, for almost everything we do in our everyday life."

". . . be patient with me . . ." the thought came, ". . . since I know so little of your ways . . . but tell me . . . do you prefer to sleep in such as *that*? . . ." He gestured toward the ship's boats they had come down in, where their bulges showed above the low bank. The thought he used for the boats was too strong to be bound by a word; to Lazarus' mind came a thought of a dead, constricted space—a jail that had once harbored him, a smelly public phone booth.

"It is our custom."

The creature leaned down and patted the turf. ". . . is this not a good place to sleep? . . ."

Lazarus admitted to himself that it was. The ground was covered with a soft spring turf, grasslike but finer than grass, softer, more even, and set more closely together. Lazarus took off his sandals and let his bare feet enjoy it, toes spread and working. It was, he decided, more like a heavy fur rug than a lawn.

". . . as for food . . ." their guide went on, ". . . why struggle for that which the good soil gives freely? . . . come with me . . ."

He took them across a reach of meadow to where low bushy trees hung over a meandering brook. The "leaves" were growths the size of a man's hand, irregular in shape, and an inch or more in thickness. The little person broke off one and nibbled at it daintily.

Lazarus plucked one and examined it. It broke easily, like a well-baked cake. The inside was creamy yellow, spongy but crisp, and had a strong pleasant odor, reminiscent of mangoes.

"Lazarus, don't eat that!" warned Barstow. "It hasn't been analyzed."

". . . it is harmonious with your body . . ."

Lazarus sniffed it again. "I'm willing to be a test case, Zack."

"Oh, well——" Barstow shrugged. "I warned you. You will anyhow."

Lazarus did. The stuff was oddly pleasing, firm enough to suit the teeth, piquant though elusive in flavor. It settled down happily in his stomach and made itself at home.

Barstow refused to let anyone else try the fruit until its effect on Lazaus was established. Lazarus took advantage of his exposed and privileged position to make a full meal —the best, he decided, that he had had in years.

". . . will you tell me what you are in the habit of eating? . . ." inquired their little friend. Barstow started to reply

131

but was checked by the creature's thought: ". . . all of you . . . think about it . . ." no further thought message came from him for a few moments, then he flashed, ". . . that is enough . . . my wives will take care of it . . ."

Lazarus was not sure the image meant "wives" but some similar close relationship was implied. It had not yet been established that the Little People were bisexual—or what.

Lazarus slept that night out under the stars and let their clean impersonal light rinse from him the claustrophobia of the ship. The constellations here were distorted out of easy recognition, although he could recognize, he decided, the cool blue of Vega and the orange glow of Antares. The one certainty was the Milky Way, spilling its cloudy arch across the sky just as at home. The Sun, he knew, could not be visible to the naked eye even if he knew where to look for it; its low absolute magnitude would not show up across the light-years. Have to get hold of Andy, he thought sleepily, work out its coördinates and pick it out with instruments. He fell asleep before it could occur to him to wonder why he should bother.

Since no shelter was needed at night they landed everyone as fast as boats could shuttle them down. The crowds were dumped on the friendly soil and allowed to rest, picnic fashion, until the colony could be organized. At first they ate supplies brought down from the ship, but Lazarus' continued good health caused the rule against taking chances with natural native foods to be relaxed shortly. After that they ate mostly of the boundless largesse of the plants and used ship's food only to vary their diets.

Several days after the last of them had been landed Lazarus was exploring alone some distance from the camp. He came across one of the Little People; the native greeted him with the same assumption of earlier acquaintance which all of them seemed to show and led Lazarus to a grove of low trees still farther from base. He indicated to Lazarus that he wanted him to eat.

Lazarus was not particularly hungry but he felt compelled to humor such friendliness, so he plucked and ate.

He almost choked in his astonishment. Mashed potatoes and brown gravy!

". . . didn't we get it right? . . ." came an anxious thought.

"Bub," Lazarus said solemnly, "I don't know what you planned to do, but this is just fine!"

A warm burst of pleasure invaded his mind. ". . . try the next tree . . ."

Lazarus did so, with cautious eagerness. Fresh brown bread and sweet butter seemed to be the combination, though a dash of ice cream seemed to have crept in from somewhere. He was hardly surprised when the third tree gave strong evidence of having both mushrooms and charcoal-broiled steak in its ancestry. ". . . we used your thought images almost entirely . . ." explained his companion. ". . . they were much stronger than those of any of your wives . . ."

Lazarus did not bother to explain that he was not married. The little person added, ". . . there has not yet been time to simulate the appearances and colors your thoughts showed . . . does it matter much to you? . . ."

Lazarus gravely assured him that it mattered very little.

When he returned to the base, he had considerable difficulty in convincing others of the seriousness of his report.

One who benefited greatly from the easy, lotus-land quality of their new home was Slayton Ford. He had awakened from cold rest apparently recovered from his breakdown except in one respect: he had no recollection of whatever it was he had experienced in the temple of Kreel. Ralph Schultz considered this a healthy adjustment to an intolerable experience and dismissed him as a patient.

Ford seemed younger and happier than he had appeared before his breakdown. He no longer held formal office among the Members—indeed there was little government of any sort; the Families lived in cheerful easy-going anarchy on this favored planet—but he was still addressed by his title and continued to be treated as an elder, one whose advice was sought, whose judgment was deferred to, along with Zaccur Barstow, Lazarus, Captain King, and others. The Families paid little heed to calendar ages; close friends might differ by a century. For years they had benefited from his skilled administration; now they continued to treat him as an elder statesman, even though two-thirds of them were older than was he.

The endless picnic stretched into weeks, into months. After being long shut up in the ship, sleeping or working, the temptation to take a long vacation was too strong to resist and there was nothing to forbid it. Food in abundance, ready to eat and easy to handle, grew almost everywhere; the water in the numerous streams was clean and potable. As for clothing, they had plenty if they wanted to dress but the need was esthetic rather than utilitarian; the Elysian climate made clothing for protection as silly as suits for swimming. Those who liked clothes wore them; bracelets and beads and flowers in the hair were quite enough for most of them and not nearly so much nuisance if one chose to take a dip in the sea.

Lazarus stuck to his kilt.

The culture and degree of enlightenment of the Little

People was difficult to understand all at once, because their ways were subtle. Since they lacked outward signs, in Earth terms, of high scientific attainment—no great buildings, no complex mechanical transportation machines, no throbbing power plants—it was easy to mistake them for Mother Nature's children, living in a Garden of Eden.

Only one-eighth of an iceberg shows above water.

Their knowledge of physical science was not inferior to that of the colonists; it was incredibly superior. They toured the ship's boats with polite interest, but confounded their guides by inquiring why things were done *this* way rather than *that?*—and the way suggested invariably proved to be simpler and more efficient than Earth technique . . . when the astounded human technicians managed to understand what they were driving at.

The Little People understood machinery and all that machinery implies, but they simply had little use for it. They obviously did not need it for communication and had little need for it for transportation (although the full reason for that was not at once evident), and they had very little need for machinery in any of their activities. But when they had a specific need for a mechanical device they were quite capable of inventing, building it, using it once, and destroying it, performing the whole process with a smooth coöperation quite foreign to that of men.

But in biology their preëminence was the most startling. The Little People were masters in the manipulation of life forms. Developing plants in a matter of days which bore fruit duplicating not only in flavor but in nutrition values the foods humans were used to was not a miracle to them but a routine task any of their biotechnicians could handle. They did it more easily than an Earth horticulturist breeds for a certain strain of color or shape in a flower.

But their methods were different from those of any human plant breeder. Be it said for them that they did try to explain their methods, but the explanations simply did not come through. In our terms, they claimed to "think" a plant into the shape and character they desired. Whatever they meant by that, it is certainly true that they could take a dormant seedling plant and, without touching it or operating on it in any way perceptible to their human students, cause it to bloom and burgeon into maturity in the space of a few hours —with new characteristics not found in the parent line . . . and which bred true thereafter.

However the Little People differed from Earthmen only in degree with respect to scientific attainments. In an utterly basic sense they differed from humans in kind.

They were not individuals.

134

No single body of a native housed a discrete individual. Their individuals were multi-bodied; they had group "souls." The basic unit of their society was a telepathic rapport group of many parts. The number of bodies and brains housing one individual ran as high as ninety or more and was never less than thirty-odd.

The colonists began to understand much that had been utterly puzzling about the Little People only after they learned this fact. There is much reason to believe that the Little People found the Earthmen equally puzzling, that they, too, had assumed that their pattern of existence must be mirrored in others. The eventual discovery of the true facts on each side, brought about mutual misunderstandings over identity, seemed to arouse horror in the minds of the Little People. They withdrew themselves from the neighborhood of the Families' settlement and remained away for several days.

At length a messenger entered the camp site and sought out Barstow. ". . . we are sorry we shunned you . . . in our haste we mistook your fortune for your fault . . . we wish to help you . . . we offer to teach you that you may become like ourselves . . ."

Barstow pondered how to answer this generous overture. "We thank you for your wish to help us," he said at last, "but what you call our misfortune seems to be a necessary part of our makeup. Our ways are not your ways. I do not think we could understand your ways."

The thought that came back to him was very troubled. ". . . we have aided the beasts of the air and of the ground to cease their strife . . . but if you do not wish our help we will not thrust it on you . . ."

The messenger went away, leaving Zaccur Barstow troubled in his mind. Perhaps, he thought, he had been hasty in answering without taking time to consult the elders. Telepathy was certainly not a gift to be scorned; perhaps the Little People could train them in telepathy without any loss of human individualism. But what he knew of the sensitives among the Families did not encourage such hope; there was not a one of them who was emotionally healthy, many of them were mentally deficient as well—it did not seem like a safe path for humans.

It could be discussed later, he decided; no need to hurry.

"No need to hurry" was the spirit throughout the settlement. There was no need to strive, little that had to be done and rarely any rush about that little. The sun was warm and pleasant, each day was much like the next, and there was always the day after that. The Members, predisposed by their inheritance to take a long view of things, began to take

135

an eternal view. Time no longer mattered. Even the longevity research, which had continued throughout their memories, languished. Gordon Hardy tabled his current experimentation to pursue the vastly more fruitful occupation of learning what the Little People knew of the nature of life. He was forced to take it slowly, spending long hours in digesting new knowledge. As time trickled on, he was hardly aware that his hours of contemplation were becoming longer, his bursts of active study less frequent.

One thing he did learn, and its implications opened up whole new fields of thought: the Little People had, in one sense, conquered death.

Since each of their egos was shared among many bodies, the death of one body involved no death for the ego. All memory experiences of that body remained intact, the personality associated with it was not lost, and the physical loss could be made up by letting a young native "marry" into the group. But a group ego, one of the personalities which spoke to the Earthmen, could not die, save possibly by the destruction of every body it lived in. They simply went on, apparently forever.

Their young, up to the time of "marriage" or group assimilation, seemed to have little personality and only rudimentary or possibly instinctive mental processes. Their elders expected no more of them in the way of intelligent behavior than a human expects of a child still in the womb. There were always many such uncompleted persons attached to any ego group; they were cared for like dearly beloved pets or helpless babies, although they were often as large and as apparently mature to Earth eyes as were their elders.

Lazarus grew bored with paradise more quickly than did the majority of his cousins. "It can't always," he complained to Libby, who was lying near him on the fine grass, "be time for tea."

"What's fretting you, Lazarus?"

"Nothing in particular." Lazarus set the point of his knife on his right elbow, flipped it with his other hand, watched it bury its point in the ground. "It's just that this place reminds me of a well-run zoo. It's got about as much future." He grunted scornfully. "It's 'Never-Never Land.'"

"But what in particular is worrying you?"

"Nothing. That's what worries me. Honest to goodness, Andy, don't you see anything wrong in being turned out to pasture like this?"

Libby grinned sheepishly. "I guess it's my hillbilly blood. 'When it don't rain, the roof don't leak; when it rains, I cain't

136

fix it nohow,' " he quoted. "Seems to me we're doing tolerably well. What irks you?"

"Well——" Lazarus' pale-blue eyes stared far away; he paused in his idle play with his knife. "When I was a young man a long time ago, I was beached in the South Seas——"

"Hawaii?"

"No. Farther south. Damned if I know what they call it today. I got hard up, mighty hard up, and sold my sextant. Pretty soon—or maybe quite a while—I could have passed for a native. I lived like one. It didn't seem to matter. But one day I caught a look at myself in a mirror." Lazarus sighed gustily. "I beat my way out of that place shipmates to a cargo of green hides, which may give you some idea how scared and desperate I was!"

Libby did not comment. "What do you do with your time, Lib?" Lazarus persisted.

"Me? Same as always. Think about mathematics. Try to figure out a dodge for a space drive like the one that got us here."

"Any luck on that?" Lazarus was suddenly alert.

"Not yet. Gimme time. Or I just watch the clouds integrate. There are amusing mathematical relationships everywhere if you are on the lookout for them. In the ripples on the water, or the shapes of busts—elegant fifth-order functions."

"Huh? You mean 'fourth order.' "

"Fifth order. You omitted the time variable. I like fifth-order equations," Libby said dreamily. "You find 'em in fish, too."

"Hummph!" said Lazarus, and stood up suddenly. "That may be all right for you, but it's not my pidgin."

"Going some place?"

"Goin' to take a walk."

Lazarus walked north. He walked the rest of that day, slept on the ground as usual that night, and was up and moving, still to the north, at dawn. The next day was followed by another like it, and still another. The going was easy, much like strolling in a park . . . too easy, in Lazarus' opinion. For the sight of a volcano, or a really worthwhile waterfall, he felt willing to pay four bits and throw in a jackknife.

The food plants were sometimes strange, but abundant and satisfactory. He occasionally met one or more of the Little People going about their mysterious affairs. They never bothered him nor asked why he was traveling but simply greeted him with the usual assumption of previous acquaintanceship. He began to long for one who would turn out to be a stranger; he felt watched.

Presently the nights grew colder, the days less balmy, and the Little People less numerous. When at last he had not seen one for an entire day, he camped for the night, remained there the next day—took out his soul and examined it.

He had to admit that he could find no reasonable fault with the planet nor its inhabitants. But just as definitely it was not to his taste. No philosophy that he had ever heard or read gave any reasonable purpose for man's existence, nor any rational clue to his proper conduct. Basking in the sunshine might be as good a thing to do with one's life as any other—but it was not for him and he knew it, even if he could not define how he knew it.

The hegira of the Families had been a mistake. It would have been a more human, a more mature and manly thing, to have stayed and fought for their rights, even if they had died insisting on them. Instead they had fled across half a universe (Lazarus was reckless about his magnitudes) looking for a place to light. They had found one, a good one—but already occupied by beings so superior as to make them intolerable for men . . . yet so supremely indifferent in their superiority to men that they had not even bothered to wipe them out, but had whisked them away to this—this overmanicured country club.

And that in itself was the unbearable humiliation. The *New Frontiers* was the culmination of five hundred years of human scientific research, the best that men could do—but it had been flicked across the deeps of space as casually as a man might restore a baby bird to its nest.

The Little People did not seem to want to kick them out but the Little People, in their own way, were as demoralizing to men as were the gods of the Jockaira. One at a time they might be morons but taken as groups each rapport group was a genius that threw the best minds that men could offer into the shade. Even Andy. Human beings could not hope to compete with that type of organization any more than a back-room shop could compete with an automated cybernated factory. Yet to form any such group identities, even if they could which he doubted, would be, Lazarus felt very sure, to give up whatever it was that made them *men*.

He admitted that he was prejudiced in favor of men. He *was* a man.

The uncounted days slid past while he argued with himself over the things that bothered him—problems that had made sad the soul of his breed since the first apeman had risen to self-awareness, questions never solved by full belly nor fine machinery. And the endless quiet days did no more to give him final answers than did all the soul searchings of his ancestors. Why? What shall it profit a man? No answer came back—save one: a firm unreasoned conviction that he was not intended for, or not ready for, this timeless snug harbor of ease.

His troubled reveries were interrupted by the appearance of one of the Little People. ". . . greetings, old friend . . . your wife King wishes you to return to your home . . . he has need of your advice . . ."

"What's the trouble?" Lazarus demanded.

But the little creature either could or would not tell him. Lazarus gave his belt a hitch and headed south. ". . . there is no need to go slowly . . ." a thought came after him.

Lazarus let himself be led to a clearing beyond a clump of trees. There he found an egg-shaped object about six feet long, featureless except for a door in the side. The native went in through the door, Lazarus squeezed his larger bulk in after him; the door closed.

It opened almost at once and Lazarus saw that they were on the beach just below the human settlement. He had to admit that it was a good trick.

Lazarus hurried to the ship's boat parked on the beach in which Captain King shared with Barstow a semblance of community headquarters. "You sent for me, Skipper. What's up?"

King's austere face was grave. "It's about Mary Sperling."

Lazarus felt a sudden cold tug at his heart. "Dead?"

"No. Not exactly. She's gone over to the Little People. 'Married' into one of their groups."

"*What?* But that's impossible!"

Lazarus was wrong. There was no faint possibility of interbreeding between Earthmen and natives but there was no barrier, if sympathy existed, to a human merging into one of their rapport groups, drowning his personality in the ego of the many.

Mary Sperling, moved by conviction of her own impending death, saw in the deathless group egos a way out. Faced with the eternal problem of life and death, she had escaped the problem by choosing neither . . . selflessness. She had found a group willing to receive her, she had crossed over.

"It raises a lot of new problems," concluded King. "Slayton and Zaccur and I all felt that you had better be here."

"Yes, yes, sure—but where is Mary?" Lazarus demanded and then ran out of the room without waiting for an answer. He charged through the settlement ignoring both greetings and attempts to stop him. A short distance outside the camp he ran across a native. He skidded to a stop. "Where is Mary Sperling?"

". . . I am Mary Sperling . . ."

"For the love of—— You *can't* be."

". . . I am Mary Sperling and Mary Sperling is myself . . . do you not know me, Lazarus? . . . I know you . . . "

Lazarus waved his hands. "No! I want to see Mary Sperling who looks like an Earthman—like me!"

The native hesitated. ". . . follow me, then . . ."

Lazarus found her a long way from the camp; it was obvious that she had been avoiding the other colonists. "Mary!"

She answered him mind to mind: ". . . I am sorry to see you troubled . . . Mary Sperling is gone except in that she is part of us . . ."

"Oh, come off it, Mary! Don't give me that stuff! Don't you know me?"

". . . of course I know you, Lazarus . . . it is you who do not know *me* . . . do not trouble your soul or grieve your heart with the sight of this body in front of you . . . I am not one of your kind . . . I am native to this planet . . ."

"Mary," he insisted, "you've got to undo this. You've got to come out of there!"

She shook her head, an oddly human gesture, for the face no longer held any trace of human expression; it was a mask of otherness. ". . . that is impossible . . . Mary Sperling is gone . . . the one who speaks with you is inextricably *myself* and not of your kind . . ." The creature who had been Mary Sperling turned and walked away.

"Mary!" he cried. His heart leapt across the span of centuries to the night his mother had died. He covered his face with his hands and wept the unconsolable grief of a child.

5 Lazarus found both King and Barstow waiting for him when he returned. King looked at his face. "I could have told you," he said soberly, "but you wouldn't wait."

"Forget it," Lazarus said harshly. "What now?"

"Lazarus, there is something else you have to see before we discuss anything," Zaccur Barstow answered.

"Okay. What?"

"Just come and see." They led him to a compartment in the ship's boat which was used as a headquarters. Contrary to Families' custom it was locked; King let them in. There was a woman inside, who, when she saw the three, quietly withdrew, locking the door again as she went out.

"Take a look at that," directed Barstow.

It was a living creature in an incubator—a child, but no such child as had ever been seen before. Lazarus stared at it, then said angrily, "What the devil is it?"

"See for yourself. Pick it up. You won't hurt it."

Lazarus did so, gingerly at first, then without shrinking from the contact as his curiosity increased. What it was, he could not say. It was not human; it was just as certainly not offspring of the Little People. Did this planet, like the last, contain some previously unsuspected race? It was manlike, yet certainly not a man child. It lacked even the button nose of a baby, nor were there evident external ears. There were organs in the usual locations of each but flush with the skull and protected with bony ridges. Its hands had too many fingers and there was an extra large one near each wrist which ended in a cluster of pink worms.

There was something odd about the torso of the infant which Lazarus could not define. But two other gross facts were evident: the legs ended not in human feet but in horny, toeless pediments—hoofs. And the creature was hermaphroditic—not in deformity but in healthy development, an androgyne.

"What is it?" he repeated, his mind filled with lively suspicion.

"That," said Zaccur, "is Marion Schmidt, born three weeks ago."

"Huh? What do you mean?"

"It means that the Little People are just as clever in manipulating us as they are in manipulating plants."

"What? But they agreed to leave us alone!"

"Don't blame them too quickly. We let ourselves in for it. The original idea was simply a few improvements."

" 'Improvements!' That thing's an obscenity."

"Yes and no. My stomach turns whenever I have to look at it . . . but actually—well, it's sort of a superman. Its body architecture has been redesigned for greater efficiency, our useless simian hangovers have been left out, and its organs have been rearranged in a more sensible fashion. You can't say it's not human, for it *is* . . . an improved model. Take that extra appendage at the wrist. That's another hand, a miniature one . . . backed up by a microscopic eye. You can see how useful that would be, once you get used to the idea." Barstow stared at it. "But it looks horrid, to me."

"It'd look horrid to anybody," Lazarus stated. "It may be an improvement, but damn it, I say it ain't human."

"In any case it creates a problem."

"I'll say it does!" Lazarus looked at it again. "You say it has a second set of eyes in those tiny hands? That doesn't seem possible."

Barstow shrugged. "I'm no biologist. But every cell in the body contains a full bundle of chromosomes. I suppose that you could grow eyes, or bones, or anything you liked

141

anywhere, if you knew how to manipulate the genes in the chromosomes. And they know."

"I don't want to be manipulated!"

"Neither do I."

Lazarus stood on the bank and stared out over the broad beach at a full meeting of the Families. "I am——" he started formally, then looked puzzled. "Come here a moment, Andy." He whispered to Libby; Libby looked pained and whispered back. Lazarus looked exasperated and whispered again. Finally he straightened up and started over.

"I am two hundred and forty-one years old—at least," he stated. Is there anyone here who is older?" It was empty formality; he knew that he was the eldest; he felt twice that old. "The meeting is opened," he went on, his big voice rumbling on down the beach assisted by speaker systems from the ship's boats. "Who is your chairman?"

"Get on with it," someone called from the crowd.

"Very well," said Lazarus. "Zaccur Barstow!"

Behind Lazarus a technician aimed a directional pickup at Barstow. "Zaccur Barstow," his voice boomed out, "speaking for myself. Some of us have come to believe that this planet, pleasant as it is, is not the place for us. You all know about Mary Sperling, you've seen stereos of Marion Schmidt; there have been other things and I won't elaborate. But emigrating again poses another question, the question of where? Lazarus Long proposes that we return to Earth. In such a ——" His words were drowned by noise from the crowd.

Lazarus shouted them down. "Nobody is going to be forced to leave. But if enough of us want to leave to justify taking the ship, then we can. I say go back to Earth. Some say look for another planet. That'll have to be decided. But first—how many of you think as I do about leaving here?"

"I do!" The shout was echoed by many others. Lazarus peered toward the first man to answer, tried to spot him, glanced over his shoulder at the tech, then pointed. "Go ahead, bud," he ruled. "The rest of you pipe down."

"Name of Oliver Schmidt. I've been waiting for months for somebody to suggest this. I thought I was the only sorehead in the Families. I haven't any real reason for leaving— I'm not scared out by the Mary Sperling matter, nor Marion Schmidt. Anybody who likes such things is welcome to them—live and let live. But I've got a deep-down urge to see Cincinnati again. I'm fed up with this place. I'm tired of being a lotus eater. Damn it, I want to *work* for my living! According to the Families' geneticists I ought to be good for another century at least. I can't see spending that much time lying in the sun and daydreaming."

142

When he shut up, at least a thousand more tried to get the floor. "Easy! Easy!" bellowed Lazarus. "If everybody wants to talk, I'm going to have to channel it through your Family representatives. But let's get a sample here and there." He picked out another man, told him to sound off.

"I won't take long," the new speaker said, "as I agree with Oliver Schmidt. I just wanted to mention my own reason. Do any of you miss the Moon? Back home I used to sit out on my balcony on warm summer nights and smoke and look at the Moon. I didn't know it was important to me, but it is. I want a planet with a moon."

The next speaker said only, "This case of Mary Sperling has given me a case of nerves. I get nightmares that I've gone over myself."

The arguments went on and on. Somebody pointed out that they had been chased off Earth; what made anybody think that they would be allowed to return? Lazarus answered that himself. "We learned a lot from the Jockaira and now we've learned a lot more from the Little People—things that put us way out ahead of anything scientists back on Earth had even dreamed of. We can go back to Earth loaded for bear. We'll be in shape to demand our rights, strong enough to defend them."

"Lazarus Long——" came another voice.

"Yes," acknowledged Lazarus. "You over there, go ahead."

"I am too old to make any more jumps from star to star and much too old to fight at the end of such a jump. Whatever the rest of you do, I'm staying."

"In that case," said Lazarus, "there is no need to discuss it, is there?"

"I am entitled to speak."

"All right, you've spoken. Now give someone else a chance."

The sun set and the stars came out and still the talk went on. Lazarus knew that it would never end unless he moved to end it. "All right," he shouted, ignoring the many who still wanted to speak. "Maybe we'll have to turn this back to the Family councils, but let's take a trial vote and see where we are. Everybody who wants to go back to Earth move way over to my right. Everybody who wants to stay here move down the beach to my left. Everybody who wants to go exploring for still another planet gather right here in front of me." He dropped back and said to the sound tech, "Give them some music to speed 'em up."

The tech nodded and the homesick strains of *Valse Triste* sighed over the beach. It was followed by *The Green Hills of Earth*. Zaccur Barstow turned toward Lazarus. "You picked that music."

143

"Me?" Lazarus answered with bland innocence. "You know I ain't musical, Zack."

Even with music the separation took a long time. The last movement of the immortal Fifth had died away long before they at last had sorted themselves into three crowds.

On the left about a tenth of the total number were gathered, showing thereby their intention of staying. They were mostly the old and the tired, whose sands had run low. With them were a few youngsters who had never seen Earth, plus a bare sprinkling of other ages.

In the center was a very small group, not over three hundred, mostly men and a few younger women, who voted thereby for still newer frontiers.

But the great mass was on Lazarus' right. He looked at them and saw new animation in their faces; it lifted his heart, for he had been bitterly afraid that he was almost alone in his wish to leave.

He looked back at the small group nearest him. "It looks like you're outvoted," he said to them alone, his voice unamplified. "But never mind, there always comes another day." He waited.

Slowly the group in the middle began to break up. By ones and twos and threes they moved away. A very few drifted over to join those who were staying; most of them merged with the group on the right.

When this secondary division was complete Lazarus spoke to the smaller group on his left. "All right," he said very gently, "You . . . you old folks might as well go back up to the meadows and get your sleep. The rest of us have plans to make."

Lazarus then gave Libby the floor and let him explain to the majority crowd that the trip home would not be the weary journey the flight from Earth had been, nor even the tedious second jump. Libby placed all of the credit where most of it belonged, with the Little People. They had straightened him out with his difficulties in dealing with the problem of speeds which appeared to exceed the speed of light. If the Little People knew what they were talking about—and Libby was sure that they did—there appeared to be no limits to what Libby chose to call "para-acceleration" —"para-" because, like Libby's own light-pressure drive, it acted on the whole mass uniformly and could no more be perceived by the senses than can gravitation, and "para-" also because the ship would not go "through" but rather around or "beside" normal space. "It is not so much a matter of driving the ship as it is a selection of appropriate potential level in an n-dimensional hyperplenum of n-plus-one possible——"

Lazarus firmly cut him off. "That's your department, son, and everybody trusts you in it. We ain't qualified to discuss the fine points."

"I was only going to add——"

"I know. But you were already out of the world when I stopped you."

Someone from the crowd shouted one more question. "When do we get there?"

"I don't know," Libby admitted, thinking of the question the way Nancy Weatheral had put it to him long ago. "I can't say what year it will be . . . but it will seem like about three weeks from now."

The preparations consumed days simply because many round trips of the ship's boats were necessary to embark them. There was a marked lack of ceremonious farewell because those remaining behind tended to avoid those who were leaving. Coolness had sprung up between the two groups; the division on the beach had split friendships, had even broken up contemporary marriages, had caused many hurt feelings, unresolvable bitterness. Perhaps the only desirable aspect of the division was that the parents of the mutant Marion Schmidt had elected to remain behind.

Lazarus was in charge of the last boat to leave. Shortly before he planned to boost he felt a touch at his elbow. "Excuse me," a young man said. "My name's Hubert Johnson. I want to go along but I've had to stay back with the other crowd to keep my mother from throwing fits. If I show up at the last minute, can I still go along?"

Lazarus looked him over. "You look old enough to decide without asking me."

"You don't understand. I'm an only child and my mother tags me around. I've got to sneak back before she misses me. How much longer——"

"I'm not holding this boat for anybody. And you'll never break away any younger. Get into the boat."

"But——"

"Git!" The young man did so, with one worried backward glance at the bank. There was a lot, thought Lazarus, to be said for ectogenesis.

Once inboard the *New Frontiers* Lazarus reported to Captain King in the control room. "All inboard?" asked King.

"Yeah. Some late deciders, pro and con, and one more passenger at the last possible split second—woman named Eleanor Johnson. Let's go!"

King turned to Libby. "Let's go, Mister."

The stars blinked out.

They flew blind, with only Libby's unique talent to guide them. If he had doubts as to his ability to lead them through the featureless blackness of other space he kept them to himself. On the twenty-third ship's day of the reach and the eleventh day of para-deceleration the stars reappeared, all in their old familiar ranges—the Big Dipper, giant Orion, lopsided Crux, the fairy Pleiades, and dead ahead of them, blazing against the frosty backdrop of the Milky Way, was a golden light that had to be the Sun.

Lazarus had tears in his eyes for the second time in a month.

They could not simply rendezvous with Earth, set a parking orbit, and disembark; they had to throw their hats in first. Besides that, they needed first to know what time it was.

Libby was able to establish quickly, through proper motions of nearest stars, that it was not later than about 3700 A.D.; without precise observatory instruments he refused to commit himself further. But once they were close enough to see the Solar planets he had another clock to read; the planets themselves make a clock with nine hands.

For any date there is a unique configuration of those "hands" since no planetary period is exactly commensurate with another. Pluto marks off an "hour" of a quarter of a millennium; Jupiter's clicks a cosmic minute of twelve years; Mercury whizzes a "second" of about ninety days. The other "hands" can refine these readings—Neptune's period is so cantankerously different from that of Pluto that the two fall into approximately repeated configuration only once in seven hundred and fifty-eight years. The great clock can be read with any desired degree of accuracy over any period —but it is not easy to read.

Libby started to read it as soon as any of the planets could be picked out. He muttered over the problem. "There's not a chance that we'll pick up Pluto," he complained to Lazarus, "and I doubt if we'll have Neptune. The inner planets give me an infinite series of approximations—you know as well as I do that "infinite" is a question-begging term. Annoying!"

"Aren't you looking at it the hard way, son? You can get a practical answer. Or move over and I'll get one."

"Of course I can get a practical answer," Libby said petulantly, "if you're satisfied with that. But——"

"But me no 'buts'—what year is it, man!"

"Eh? Let's put it this way. The time rate in the ship and duration on Earth have been unrelated three times. But now they are effectively synchronous again, such that slightly over seventy-four years have passed since we left."

Lazarus heaved a sigh. "Why didn't you say so?" He had been fretting that Earth might not be recognizable . . . they might have torn down New York or something like that. "Shucks, Andy, you shouldn't have scared me like that."

"Mmm . . ." said Libby. It was one of no further interest to him. There remained only the delicious problem of inventing a mathematics which would describe elegantly two apparently irreconcilable groups of facts: the Michelson-Morley experiments and the log of the *New Frontiers*. He set happily about it. Mmm . . . what was the least number of para-dimensions indispensably necessary to contain the augmented plenum using a sheaf of postulates affirming——

It kept him contented for a considerable time—subjective time, of course.

The ship was placed in a temporary orbit half a billion miles from the Sun with a radius vector normal to the plane of the ecliptic. Parked thus at right angles to and far outside the flat pancake of the Solar System they were safe from any long chance of being discovered. A ship's boat had been fitted with the neo-Libby drive during the jump and a negotiating party was sent down.

Lazarus wanted to go along; King refused to let him, which sent Lazarus into sulks. King had said curtly, "This isn't a raiding party, Lazarus; this is a diplomatic mission."

"Hell, man, I can be diplomatic when it pays!"

"No doubt. But we'll send a man who doesn't go armed to the 'fresher."

Ralph Schultz headed the party, since psychodynamic factors back on Earth were of first importance, but he was aided by legal, military, and technical specialists. If the Families were going to have to fight for living room it was necessary to know what sort of technology, what sort of weapons, they would have to meet—but it was even more necessary to find out whether or not a peaceful landing could be arranged. Schultz had been authorized by the elders to offer a plan under which the Families would colonize the thinly settled and retrograded European continent. But it was possible, even likely, that this had already been done in their absence, in view of the radioactive half-lifes involved. Schultz would probably have to improvise some other compromise, depending on the conditions he found.

Again there was nothing to do but wait.

Lazarus endured it in nail-chewing uncertainty. He had claimed publicly that the Families had such great scientific advantage that they could meet and defeat the best that Earth could offer. Privately, he knew that this was sophistry and so did any other Member competent to judge the matter. Knowledge alone did not win wars. The ignorant fanatics

147

of Europe's Middle Ages had defeated the incomparably higher Islamic culture; Archimedes had been struck down by a common soldier; barbarians had sacked Rome. Libby, or some one, might devise an unbeatable weapon from their mass of new knowledge—or might not. And who knew what strides military art had made on earth in three quarters of a century?

King, trained in military art, was worried by the same thing and still more worried by the personnel he would have to work with. The Families were anything but trained legions; the prospect of trying to whip those cranky individualists into some semblance of a disciplined fighting machine ruined his sleep.

These doubts and fears King and Lazarus did not mention even to each other; each was afraid that to mention such things would be to spread a poison of fear through the ship. But they were not alone in their worries; half of the ship's company realized the weaknesses of their position and kept silent only because a bitter resolve to go home, no matter what, made them willing to accept the dangers.

"Skipper," Lazarus said to King two weeks after Schultz's party had headed Earthside, "have you wondered how they're going to feel about the *New Frontiers* herself?"

"Eh? What do you mean?"

"Well, we hijacked her. Piracy."

King looked astounded. "Bless me, so we did! Do you know, it's been so long ago that it is hard for me to realize that she was ever anything but my ship . . . or to recall that I first came into her through an act of piracy." He looked thoughtful, then smiled grimly. "I wonder how conditions are in Coventry these days?"

"Pretty thin rations, I imagine," said Lazarus. "But we'll team up and make out. Never mind—they haven't caught us yet."

"Do you suppose that Slayton Ford will be connected with the matter? That would be hard lines after all he has gone through."

"There may not be any trouble about it at all," Lazarus answered soberly. "While the way we got this ship was kind of irregular, we *have* used it for the purpose for which it was built—to explore the stars. And we're returning it intact, long before they could have expected any results, and with a slick new space drive to boot. It's more for their money than they had any reason to expect—so they may just decide to forget it and trot out the fatted calf."

"I hope so," King answered doubtfully.

The scouting party was two days late. No signal was received from them until they emerged into normal space-time, just before rendezvous, as no method had yet been devised for signalling from para-space to ortho-space. While they were maneuvering to rendezvous, King received Ralph Schultz's face on the control-room screen. "Hello, Captain! We'll be boarding shortly to report."

"Give me a summary now!"

"I wouldn't know where to start. But it's all right—*we can go home!*"

"Huh? How's that? Repeat!"

"Everything's all right. We are restored to the Covenant. You see, there isn't any difference any more. *Everybody is a member of the Families now.*"

"What do you mean?" King demanded.

"They've got it."

"Got what?"

"Got the secret of longevity."

"Huh? Talk sense. There isn't any secret. There never was any secret."

"*We* didn't have any secret—but they thought we had. So they found it."

"Explain yourself," insisted Captain King.

"Captain, can't this wait until we get back into the ship?" Ralph Schultz protested. "I'm no biologist. We've brought along a government representative—you can quiz him, instead."

6 King received Terra's representative in his cabin. He had notified Zaccur Barstow and Justin Foote to be present for the Families and had invited Doctor Gordon Hardy because the nature of the startling news was the biologist's business. Libby was there as the ship's chief officer; Slayton Ford was invited because of his unique status, although he had held no public office in the Families since his breakdown in the temple of Kreel.

Lazarus was there because Lazarus wanted to be there, in his own strictly private capacity. He had not been invited, but even Captain King was somewhat diffident about interfering with the assumed prerogatives of the eldest Member.

Ralph Schultz introduced Earth's ambassador to the assembled company. "This is Captain King, our commanding officer—and this is Miles Rodney, representing the Federation Council—minister plenipotentiary and ambassador extraordinary, I guess you would call him."

"Hardly that," said Rodney, "although I can agree to the 'extraordinary' part. This situation is quite without precedent. It is an honor to know you, Captain."

"Glad to have you inboard, sir."

"And this is Zaccur Barstow, representing the trustees of the Howard Families, and Justin Foote, secretary to the trustees——"

"Service."

"Service to you, gentlemen."

"——Andrew Jackson Libby, chief astrogational officer, Doctor Gordon Hardy, biologist in charge of our research into the causes of old age and death."

"May I do you a service?" Hardy acknowledged formally.

"Service to you, sir. So you are the chief biologist—there was a time when you could have done a service to the whole human race. Think of it, sir—think how different things could have been. But, happily, the human race was able to worry out the secret of extending life without the aid of the Howard Families."

Hardy looked vexed. "What do you mean, sir? Do you mean to say that you are still laboring under the delusion that we had some miraculous secret to impart, if we chose?"

Rodney shrugged and spread his hands. "Really, now, there is no need to keep up the pretense, is there? Your results have been duplicated, independently."

Captain King cut in. "Just a moment—— Ralph Schultz, is the Federation still under the impression that there is some 'secret' to our long lives? Didn't you tell them?"

Schultz was looking bewildered. "Uh—this is ridiculous. The subject hardly came up. They themselves had achieved controlled longevity; they were no longer interested in us in that respect. It is true that there still existed a belief that our long lives derived from manipulation rather than from heredity, but I corrected that impression."

"Apparently not very thoroughly, from what Miles Rodney has just said."

"Apparently not. I did not spend much effort on it; it was beating a dead dog. The Howard Families and their long lives are no longer an issue on Earth. Interest, both public and official, is centered on the fact that we have accomplished a successful interstellar jump."

"I can confirm that," agreed Miles Rodney. "Every official, every news service, every citizen, every scientist in the system is waiting with utmost eagerness the arrival of the *New Frontiers*. It's the greatest, most sensational thing that has happened since the first trip to the Moon. You are famous, gentlemen—all of you."

Lazarus pulled Zaccur Barstow aside and whispered to him. Barstow looked perturbed, then nodded thoughtfully. "Captain——" Barstow said to King.

"Yes, Zack?"

"I suggest that we ask our guest to excuse us while we receive Ralph Schultz' report."

"Why?"

Barstow glanced at Rodney. "I think we will be better prepared to discuss matters if we are briefed by our own representative."

King turned to Rodney. "Will you excuse us, sir?"

Lazarus broke in. "Never mind, Skipper. Zack means well but he's too polite. Might as well let Comrade Rodney stick around and we'll lay it on the line. Tell me this, Miles; what proof have you got that you and your pals have figured out a way to live as long as we do?"

"Proof?" Rodney seemed dumbfounded. "Why do you ask —— Whom am I addressing? Who are you, sir?"

Ralph Schultz intervened. "Sorry—I didn't get a chance to finish the introductions. Miles Rodney, this is Lazarus Long, the Senior."

"Service. 'The Senior' what?"

"He just means 'The Senior,' period," answered Lazarus. "I'm the oldest Member. Otherwise I'm a private citizen."

"The oldest one of the Howard Families! Why—why, you must be the oldest man alive—think of that!"

"You think about it," retorted Lazarus. "I quit worrying about it a couple o' centuries ago. How about answering my question?"

"But I can't help being impressed. You make me feel like an infant—and I'm not a young man myself; I'll be a hundred and five this coming June."

"If you can prove that's your age, you can answer my question. I'd say you were about forty. How about it?"

"Well, dear me, I hardly expected to be interrogated on this point. Do you wish to see my identity card?"

"Are you kidding? I've had fifty-odd identity cards in my time, all with phony birth dates. What else can you offer?"

"Just a minute, Lazarus," put in Captain King. "What is the purpose of your question?"

Lazarus Long turned away from Rodney. "It's like this, Skipper—we hightailed it out of the Solar System to save our necks, because the rest of the yokels thought we had invented some way to live forever and proposed to squeeze it out of us if they had to kill every one of us. Now everything is sweetness and light—so they say. But it seems mighty funny that the bird they send up to smoke the pipe of peace with us should still be convinced that we have that so-called secret.

"It got me to wondering.

"Suppose they hadn't figured out a way to keep from dying from old age but were still clinging to the idea that we had?

151

What better way to keep us calmed down and unsuspicious than to tell us they had until they could get us where they wanted us in order to put the question to us again?"

Rodney snorted. "A preposterous idea! Captain, I don't think I'm called on to put up with this."

Lazarus stared coldly. "It was preposterous the first time, bub—but it happened. The burnt child is likely to be skittish."

"Just a moment, both of you," ordered King. "Ralph, how about it? Could you have been taken in by a put-up job?"

Schultz thought about it, painfully. "I don't think so." He paused. "It's rather difficult to say. I couldn't tell from appearance of course, any more than our own Members could be picked out from a crowd of normal persons."

"But you are a psychologist. Surely you could have detected indications of fraud, if there had been one."

"I may be a psychologist, but I'm not a miracle man and I'm not telepathic. I wasn't looking for fraud." He grinned sheepishly. "There was another factor. I was so excited over being home that I was not in the best emotional condition to note discrepancies, if there were any."

"Then you aren't sure?"

"No. I am emotionally convinced that Miles Rodney is telling the truth——"

"I am!"

"—and I believe that a few questions could clear the matter up. He claims to be one hundred and five years old. We can test that."

"I see," agreed King. "Hmm . . . you put the questions, Ralph?"

"Very well. You will permit, Miles Rodney?"

"Go ahead," Rodney answered stiffly.

"You must have been about thirty years old when we left Earth, since we have been gone nearly seventy-five years, Earth time. Do you remember the event?"

"Quite clearly. I was a clerk in Novak Tower at the time, in the offices of the Administrator."

Slayton Ford had remained in the background throughout the discussion, and had done nothing to call attention to himself. At Rodney's answer he sat up. "Just a moment, Captain——"

"Eh? Yes?"

"Perhaps I can cut this short. You'll pardon me, Ralph?" He turned to Terra's representative. "Who am I?"

Rodney looked at him in some puzzlement. His expression changed from one of simple surprise at the odd question to conplete and unbelieving bewilderment. "Why, you . . . *you* are *Administrator Ford!*"

7 "One at a time! One at a time," Captain King was saying. "Don't everybody try to talk at once. Go on, Slayton; you have the floor. You know this man?"

Ford looked Rodney over. "No, I can't say that I do."

"Then it *is* a frame up." King turned to Rodney. "I suppose you recognized Ford from historical stereos—is that right?"

Rodney seemed about to burst. "No! I recognized him. He's changed but I knew him. Mr. Administrator—look at me, please! Don't you know me? I *worked* for you!

"It seems fairly obvious that he doesn't," King said dryly.

Ford shook his head. "It doesn't prove anything, one way or the other, Captain. There were over two thousand civil service employes in my office. Rodney might have been one of them. His face looks vaguely familiar, but so do most faces."

"Captain——" Master Gordon Hardy was speaking. "If I can question Miles Rodney I might be able to give an opinion as to whether or not they actually have discovered anything new about the causes of old age and death."

Rodney shook his head. "I am not a biologist. You could trip me up in no time. Captain King, I ask you to arrange my return to Earth as quickly as possible. I'll not be subjected to any more of this. And let me add that I do not care a minim whether you and your—your pretty crew ever get back to civilization or not. I came here to help you, but I'm disgusted." He stood up.

Slayton Ford went toward him. "Easy, Miles Rodney, please! Be patient. Put yourself in their place. You would be just as cautious if you had been through what they have been through."

Rodney hesitated. "Mr. Administrator, what are *you* doing here?"

"It's a long and complicated story. I'll tell you later."

"You are a member of the Howard Families—you must be. That accounts for a lot of odd things."

Ford shook his head. "No, Miles Rodney, I am not. Later, please—I'll explain it. You worked for me once—when?"

"From 2109 until you, uh, disappeared."

"What was your job?"

"At the time of the crisis of 2113 I was an assistant correlation clerk in the Division of Economic Statistics, Control Section."

"Who was your section chief?"

"Leslie Waldron."

"Old Waldron, eh? What was the color of his hair?"

153

"His hair? The Walrus was bald as an egg."

Lazarus whispered to Zaccur Barstow, "Looks like I was off base, Zack."

"Wait a moment," Barstow whispered back. "It still could be thorough preparation—they may have known that Ford escaped with us."

Ford was continuing, "What was *The Sacred Cow?*"

"*The Sacred*——— Chief, you weren't even supposed to know that there was such a publication!"

"Give my intelligence staff credit for some activity, at least," Ford said dryly. "I got my copy every week."

"But what was it?" demanded Lazarus.

Rodney answered, "An office comic and gossip sheet that was passed from hand to hand."

"Devoted to ribbing the bosses," Ford added, "especially me." He put an arm around Rodney's shoulders. "Friends, there is no doubt about it. Miles and I were fellow workers."

"I still want to find out about the new rejuvenation process," insisted Master Hardy some time later.

"I think we all do," agreed King. He reached out and re-filled their guest's wine glass. "Will you tell us about it, sir?"

"I'll try." Miles Rodney answered, "though I must ask Master Hardy to bear with me. It's not one process, but several—one basic process and several dozen others, some of them purely cosmetic, especially for women. Nor is the basic process truly a rejuvenation process. You can arrest the progress of old age, but you can't reverse it to any significant degree—you can't turn a senile old man into a boy."

"Yes, yes," agreed Hardy. "Naturally—but what is the basic process?"

"It consists largely in replacing the entire blood tissue in an old person with new, young blood. Old age, so they tell me, is primarily a matter of the progressive accumulation of the waste poisons of metabolism. The blood is supposed to carry them away, but presently the blood gets so clogged with the poisons that the scavenging process doesn't take place properly. Is that right, Doctor Hardy?"

"That's an odd way of putting it, but——"

"I told you I was no biotechnician."

"—essentially correct. It's a matter of diffusion pressure deficit—the d.p.d. on the blood side of a cell wall must be such as to maintain a fairly sharp gradient or there will occur progressive autointoxication of the individual cells. But I must say that I feel somewhat disappointed, Miles Rodney. The basic idea of holding off death by insuring proper scavenging of waste products is not new—I have a

154

bit of chicken heart which has been alive for two and one half centuries through equivalent techniques. As to the use of young blood—yes, that will work. I've kept experimental animals alive by such blood donations to about twice their normal span." He stopped and looked troubled.

"Yes, Doctor Hardy?"

Hardy chewed his lip. "I gave up that line of research. I found it necessary to have several young donors in order to keep one beneficiary from growing any older. There was a small, but measurable, unfavorable effect on each of the donors. Racially it was self-defeating; there would never be enough donors to go around. Am I to understand, sir that this method is thereby limited to a small, select part of the population?"

"Oh, no! I did not make myself clear, Master Hardy. There are no donors."

"Huh?"

"New blood, enough for everybody, grown outside the body—the Public Health and Longevity Service can provide any amount of it, any type."

Hardy looked startled. "To think we came so close . . . so that's it." He paused, then went on. "We tried tissue culture of bone marrow *in vitro*. We should have persisted."

"Don't feel badly about it. Billions of credits and tens of thousands of technicians engaged in this project before there were any significant results. I'm told that the mass of accumulated art in this field represents more effort than even the techniques of atomic engineering." Rodney smiled. "You see, they *had* to get some results; it was politically necessary—so there was an all-out effort." Rodney turned to Ford. "When the news about the escape of the Howard Families reached the public, Chief, your precious successor had to be protected from the mobs."

Hardy persisted with questions about subsidiary techniques—tooth budding, growth inhibiting, hormone therapy, many others—until King came to Rodney's rescue by pointing out that the prime purpose of the visit was to arrange details of the return of the Families to Earth.

Rodney nodded. "I think we should get down to business. As I understand it, Captain, a large proportion of your people are now in reduced-temperature somnolence?"

("Why can't he say 'cold-rest'?" Lazarus said to Libby.)

"Yes, that is so."

"Then it would be no hardship on them to remain in that state for a time."

"Eh? Why do you say that, sir?"

Rodney spread his hands. "The administration finds itself in a somewhat embarrassing position. To put it bluntly, there

155

is a housing shortage. Absorbing one hundred and ten thousand displaced persons can't be done overnight."

Again King had to hush them. He then nodded to Zaccur Barstow, who addressed himself to Rodney. "I fail to see the problem, sir. What is the present population of the North American continent?"

"Around seven hundred million."

"And you can't find room to tuck away one-seventieth of one per cent of that number? It sounds preposterous."

"You don't understand, sir," Rodney protested. "Population pressure has become our major problem. Co-incident with it, the right to remain undisturbed in the enjoyment of one's own homestead, or one's apartment, has become the most jealously guarded of all civil rights. Before we can find you adequate living room we must make over some stretch of desert, or make other major arrangements."

"I get it," said Lazarus. "Politics. You don't dast disturb anybody for fear they will squawk."

"That's hardly an adequate statement of the case."

"It's not, eh? could be you've got a general election coming up, maybe?"

"As a matter of fact we have, but that has nothing to do with the case."

Lazarus snorted.

Justin Foote spoke up. "It seems to me that the administration has looked at this problem in the most superficial light. It is not as if we were homeless immigrants. Most of the Members own their own homes. As you doubtless know, the Families were well-to-do, even wealthy, and for obvious reasons we built our homes to endure. I feel sure that most of those structures are still standing."

"No doubt," Rodney conceded, "but you will find them occupied."

Justin Foote shrugged. "What has that to do with us? That is a problem for the government to settle with the persons it has allowed illegally to occupy our homes. As for myself, I shall land as soon as possible, obtain an eviction order from the nearest court, and repossess my home."

"It's not that easy. You can make omelet from eggs, but not eggs from omelet. You have been legally dead for many years; the present occupant of your house holds a good title."

Justin Foote stood up and glared at the Federation's envoy, looking, as Lazarus thought, "like a cornered mouse." "Legally dead! By whose act, sir, by whose act? Mine? I was a respected solicitor, quietly and honorably pursuing my profession, harming no one, when I was arrested without cause and forced to flee for my life. Now I am blandly told that my property is confiscated and my very legal existence

156

as a person and as a citizen has been taken from me because of that sequence of events. What manner of justice is this? Does the Covenant still stand?"

"You misunderstand me. I——"

"I misunderstood nothing. If justice is measured out only when it is convenient, then the Covenant is not worth the parchment it is written on. I shall make of myself a test case, sir, a test case for every Member of the Families. Unless my property is returned to me in full and at once I shall bring personal suit against every obstructing official. I will make of it a *cause celebre.* For many years I have suffered inconvenience and indignity and peril; I shall not be put off with words. I will shout it from the housetops." He paused for breath.

"He's right, Miles," Slayton Ford put in quietly. "The government had better find some adequate way to handle this—and quickly."

Lazarus caught Libby's eye and silently motioned toward the door. The two slipped outside. "Justin'll keep 'em busy for the next hour," he said. "Let's slide down to the Club and grab some calories."

"Do you really think we ought to leave?"

"Relax. If the skipper wants us, he can holler."

8 Lazarus tucked away three sandwiches, a double order of ice cream, and some cookies while Libby contented himself with somewhat less. Lazarus would have eaten more but he was forced to respond to a barrage of questions from the other habitués of the Club.

"The commissary department ain't really back on its feet," he complained, as he poured his third cup of coffee. "The Little People made life too easy for them. Andy, do you like chili con carne?"

"It's all right."

Lazarus wiped his mouth. "There used to be a restaurant in Tijuana that served the best chili I ever tasted. I wonder if it's still there?"

"Where's Tijuana?" demanded Margaret Weatheral.

"You don't remember Earth, do you, Peggy? Well, darling, it's in Lower California. You know where that is?"

"Don't you think I studied geography? It's in Los Angeles."

"Near enough. Maybe you're right—by now." The ship's announcing system blared out:

"Chief Astrogator—report to the Captain in the Control Room!"

"That's me!" said Libby, and hurriedly got up.

The call was repeated, then was followed by, "All hands

—prepare for acceleration! All hands—prepare for acceleration!"

"Here we go again, kids." Lazarus stood up, brushed off his kilt, and followed Libby, whistling as he went:

> *"California, here I come,*
> *Right back where I started from——"*

The ship was underway, the stars had faded out. Captain King had left the control room, taking with him his guest, the Earth's envoy. Miles Rodney had been much impressed; it seemed likely that he would need a drink.

Lazarus and Libby remained in the control room. There was nothing to do; for approximately four hours, ship's time, the ship would remain in para-space, before returning to normal space near Earth.

Lazarus struck a cigaret. "What d'you plan to do when you get back, Andy?"

"Hadn't thought about it."

"Better start thinking. Been some changes."

"I'll probably head back home for a while. I can't imagine the Ozarks having changed very much."

"The hills will look the same, I imagine. You may find the people changed."

"How?"

"You remember I told you that I had gotten fed up with the Families and had kinda lost touch with them for a century? By and large, they had gotten so smug and sot in their ways that I couldn't stand them. I'm afraid we'll find most everybody that way, now that they expect to live forever. Long term investments, be sure to wear your rubbers when it rains . . . that sort of thing."

"It didn't affect you that way."

"My approach is different. I never did have any real reason to last forever—after all, as Gordon Hardy has pointed out, I'm only a third generation result of the Howard plan. I just did my living as I went along and didn't worry my head about it. But that's not the usual attitude. Take Miles Rodney—scared to death to tackle a new situation with both hands for fear of upsetting precedent and stepping on established privileges."

"I was glad to see Justin stand up to him." Libby chuckled. "I didn't think Justin had it in him."

"Ever see a little dog tell a big dog to get the hell out of the little dog's yard?"

"Do you think Justin will win his point?"

"Sure he will, with your help."

"Mine?"

"Who knows anything about the para-drive, aside from what you've taught me?"

"I've dictated full notes into the records."

"But you haven't turned those records over to Miles Rodney. Earth *needs* your starship drive, Andy. You heard what Rodney said about population pressure. Ralph was telling me you have to get a government permit now before you can have a baby."

"The hell you say!"

"Fact. You can count on it that there would be tremendous emigration if there were just some decent planets to emigrate to. And that's where your drive comes in. With it, spreading out to the stars becomes really practical. They'll have to dicker."

"It's not really my drive, of course. The Little People worked it out."

"Don't be so modest. You've got it. And you want to back up Justin, don't you?"

"Oh, sure."

"Then we'll use it to bargain with. Maybe I'll do the bargaining, personally. But that's beside the point. Somebody is going to have to do a little exploring before any large-scale emigration starts. Let's go into the real estate business, Andy. We'll stake out this corner of the Galaxy and see what it has to offer."

Libby scratched his nose and thought about it. "Sounds all right, I guess—after I pay a visit home."

"There's no rush. I'll find a nice, clean little yacht, about ten thousand tons and we'll refit with your drive."

"What'll we use for money?"

"We'll have money. I'll set up a parent corporation, while I'm about it, with a loose enough charter to let us do anything we want to do. There will be daughter corporations for various purposes and we'll unload the minor interest in each. Then——"

"You make it sound like work, Lazarus. I thought it was going to be fun."

"Shucks, we won't fuss with that stuff. I'll collar somebody to run the home office and worry about the books and the legal end—somebody about like Justin. Maybe Justin himself."

"Well, all right then."

"You and I will rampage around and see what there is to be seen. It'll be fun, all right."

They were both silent for a long time, with no need to talk. Presently Lazarus said, "Andy——"

159

"Yeah?"

"Are you going to look into this new-blood-for-old caper?"

"I suppose so, eventually."

"I've been thinking about it. Between ourselves, I'm not as fast with my fists as I was a century back. Maybe my natural span is wearing out. I do know this: I didn't start planning our real estate venture till I heard about this new process. It gave me a new perspective. I find myself thinking about thousands of years—and I never used to worry about anything further ahead than a week from next Wednesday."

Libby chuckled again. "Looks like you're growing up."

"Some would say it was about time. Seriously, Andy, I think that's just what I have been doing. The last two and a half centuries have just been my adolescence, so to speak. Long as I've hung around, I don't know any more about the *important* answers, the *important* answers, than Peggy Weatheral does. Men—*our* kind of men—Earth men—never have had enough time to tackle the important questions. Lots of capacity and not time enough to use it properly. When it came to the important questions we might as well have still been monkeys."

"How do you propose to tackle the important questions?"

"How should I know? Ask me again in about five hundred years."

"You think that will make a difference?"

"I do. Anyhow it'll give me time to poke around and pick up some interesting facts. Take those Jockaira gods——"

"They weren't gods, Lazarus. You shouldn't call them that."

"Of course they weren't—I think. My guess is that they are creatures who have had time enough to do a little hard thinking. Someday, about a thousand years from now, I intend to march straight into the temple of Kreel, look him in the eye, and say, 'Howdy, bub—what do *you* know that *I* don't know?' "

"It might not be healthy."

"We'll have a showdown, anyway. I've never been satisfied with the outcome there. There ought not to be anything in the whole universe that man can't poke his nose into—that's the way we're built and I assume that there's some reason for it."

"Maybe there aren't any reasons."

"Yes, maybe it's just one colossal big joke, with no point to it." Lazarus stood up and stretched and scratched his ribs. "But I can tell you this, Andy, whatever the answers are, here's one monkey that's going to keep on climbing, and looking around him to see what he can see, as long as the tree holds out."